The Lost Children of the Undead . . .

"A starship intended to carry fifteen thousand colonists and all the supplies they'd need to start a colony was missing," Lavelle continued. "There were more than forty-seven thousand missing children.

"We think the dying alien somehow took possession of Yag Chan before its own body died. We think it stole the children and escaped in the starship.

"We've been searching for those children for three thousand years."

"Here?" Dorjii asked. "Us?"

Books by Scott Baker

Dhampire
Nightchild

Published by TIMESCAPE BOOKS

Most Timescape Books are available at special quantity discounts for bulk purchases for sales promotions, premiums or fund raising. Special books or book excerpts can also be created to fit specific needs.

For details write the office of the Vice President of Special Markets, Pocket Books, 1230 Avenue of the Americas, New York, New York 10020.

NIGHTCHILD

Scott Baker

A TIMESCAPE BOOK
PUBLISHED BY POCKET BOOKS NEW YORK

A different version of this book was originally published by Berkley Publishing Corporation in 1979.

 A Timescape Book published by
POCKET BOOKS, a division of Simon & Schuster, Inc.
1230 Avenue of the Americas, New York, N.Y. 10020

ISBN: 0-671-46931-2

First Timescape Books printing November, 1983

10 9 8 7 6 5 4 3 2 1

First, Nosferatu:

The planet seemed perfect for human colonization. It was colder than Terra but a little warmer than Mig Mar, and with allergy treatments men could eat a few of the native plants. There were no land animals to compete with the settlers; the most highly developed life form the Hegemonic Survey was able to discover was a small shell-less mollusk that lived in one of the tiny equatorial seas.

As soon as the Survey declared the planet provisionally open, colonists began to arrive. The soil proved fertile, the days pleasant if uneventful; since there were more Terrans than MigMartians among the colonists, a Terran, and not a Tibetan, name was chosen for the planet. The colonists called it Shovak's New Rural Siberia, after the last expanse of agricultural land on Terra to be domed.

The Hegemony had a ten-year ban on childbearing on all newly opened worlds. By the end of the fifth year—their crops flourishing and they themselves in perfect health—most of the colonists thought the wait unreasonable.

In the sixth year the research team that had accompanied the colonists found the first evidence that Shovak's New Rural Siberia had once housed a full spectrum of highly developed life forms. By the seventh year they had discovered proof that one of those life forms had been a technologically sophisticated city dweller.

5

All higher life on the planet had died out three million years earlier. There was no evidence of atomic war, no other obvious explanation.

More researchers arrived.

The probationary period passed uneventfully, and it was judged safe for the colonists to reproduce.

Three children were born; there were a number of miscarriages. In every case the birth was fatal to the mother. The fathers of the three living infants had also died, their deaths roughly coinciding with the times their children had to have been conceived.

No explanation for the deaths was found, but their fact was evidence enough; the colony was abandoned. The researchers remained.

The children—Yag Chan, Chordeyean and Dawa Tsong, all three of MigMartian ancestry—seemed perfectly normal and quite healthy; none of the tests to which they were subjected linked them in any way with the deaths of their parents. They were adopted by the research community and grew up reasonably well liked. Eventually all three were sent to Mig Mar for adept training.

Soon after they left a new geological scanning technique revealed a huge cube, kilometers on a side, buried hundreds of kilometers beneath the planet's surface. It took two years to reach the cube, another year to force a way in through one of the walls to the thousand-leveled vault inside.

Yag Chan, who had returned to the planet of his birth as a second-degree adept, was a member of the first research team to enter the vault.

Some time after the research team returned to the surface the planet was renamed Nosferatu, after an ancient Terran legend.

The legend of the Vampire.

After Nosferatu, Nal-K'am:
Sixteen years before Nal-K'am was rediscovered by the Terran Hegemony, a three-thousand-year-old conditioning machine malfunctioned and failed to implant

all the proper directives in a newly initiated priest of Night.

The priest was assigned to help in the relocation of refugees from a series of flash floods and mud slides that had devastated a small village far from Temple City. The village was too small to have its own Shrine, so for the first time since his Naming Day the priest was forced to spend a night outside the sealed buildings in which his kind customarily slept.

Knowing that he had only to obey the commands of the Goddess within him and all would be well, the priest retired to the private room that was his right when among the laity. There he saw nothing wrong in the removal not only of his boots and Nightmask, but of his stockings, undermask and gloves, as well. Wriggling his toes, extending and stretching his fingers, he spent a few instants enjoying the unaccustomed pleasure of free air on his skin, then placed his mask upright against the wall, to which it clung, and made his devotions to Her in whose image it was fashioned: the Goddess Night, in the Aspect of the Preserver. He waited until he saw Her other two Aspects superimposed on the features of his mask, then lay down and repeated his sleep-syllable.

He slept as he had in the orphanage in the days before his election, with the window open. The warm breeze played over his unprotected skin and he was repeatedly bitten by vasanas—small blood-sucking insects especially common in the lowlands.

His fifth morning in the village he was needed early. A priest with the red circle of the administrator on the forehead of his mask opened the door to the room in which the young priest was sleeping and discovered him there, still asleep, with his skin exposed to the air.

The newly initiated priest was returned to the Temple. The malfunctioning conditioner was replaced.

The vasanas remained.

One of the many vasanas that had bitten the priest later bit Ugyen Dochen, then aged eleven.

Another, a gravid female, deposited a clutch of

7

seventy eggs in a nearby swamp. One of the many vasanas hatched from her eggs later bit the village civil administrator's daughter.

Six years later Ugyen Dochen married the administrator's daughter. A son was conceived the second night of their marriage; Ugyen Dochen died two days later. His wife died in childbirth; she was never recognized as a victim of the new plague that had taken her husband.

The boy was sent to an orphanage.

Chapter One

THE TEMPLE OF NIGHT WAS A JAGGED black wedge gouged out of the late-afternoon sun.

The Sun. Ts'a-ba, the Hell of Burning Heat. Within it, Rab-tu T'sa-wa, the Hell of Great Burning Heat, where the fires of torment were ten times as painful as those of Ts'a-ba. Within Rab-tu T'sa-wa, at the core of the Sun, Mnar-med, the Hell of Endless Torment, where suffering was a thousand times more intense than in Rab-Tu T'sa-wa, from within which the sinners looked out upon the inhabitants of Nal-K'am with the envy that the damned of Nak-K'am felt when they thought of the Gods, the Lha, in the highest of the Lha Heavens.

The Temple. Had it been graceful it would have soared; as it was, its tremendous height was only an excuse for its breadth. The city at its feet did not stretch half the length of one wall; the starport outside that city could have been fitted a hundredfold onto the Temple's smallest terrace.

The Temple's shadow had spread to engulf Agad Orphanage's outer wall by the time Lozan returned from the port tea shop. It had been a long walk, and as he ducked into the shadow he was grateful for the relief it gave him from the still-considerable heat of the setting sun.

He was not supposed to be out, so he made his way cautiously, making sure he was unobserved even well before he was close enough to see the gate and its leering tutelary demons of black stone. A Hegemonic starship slipped by overhead—a broad, softly glowing silver disk heading for the port he'd just left. Involuntarily he glanced back over the barley fields he'd just crossed, but there was no sign of Dorjii or anyone else who might have followed him from the tea shop.

When the starship was gone he looked around one more time to be sure there was no one to see what he was doing, then climbed nimbly over loose stone and crumbled masonry, following a route through the wall used by generations of orphans before him.

Act dead, he reminded himself, letting his shoulders slump. *Don't let them see you know you're alive.*

Nal-K'am. The Hell That Was Five Lesser Hells. Yan-sos, the Hell of Repetition. T'ig-nag, the Hell of Black Lines. Bsdus'joms, the Hell of Concentrated Oppression. Nu-bod, the Hell of Screaming. Nu-bod Ch'en-po, the Hell of Great Screaming, where the heretics suffered.

Lozan was a heretic: he did not believe he was damned and in Hell.

The courtyard was deserted, so Lozan had no trouble circling around its edge and joining the orphans in Dusum's work party just before they entered the eating hall. He pushed his way into line just in front of Ranchun, jostling him a little more than necessary; the look on Ranchun's face told Lozan that the other would have loved to report him to the orphanmaster, but Lozan knew he'd never have the courage. Not only would Dusum always cover for Lozan, leaving whoever'd reported Lozan looking like a liar, but Lozan would find out who'd reported him—no one in the orphanage could lie to Lozan and get away with it—and then either Lozan or Dorjii would make the one responsible regret what he'd done.

Dusum saw Lozan, fell back a step. At a gesture from Lozan the orphans surrounding them moved away so that they could talk without being overheard.

"Where's Dorjii?" asked Dusum.

"Still out."

"I can't protect him if Sren sees he's not with us. Did he get it?"

"I've got it. Here." Lozan took a small block of Dakkini wood from his tunic pocket. It vanished beneath Dusum's tunic.

"It's too small."

"They wanted more money this time." Actually, Dorjii had cut a piece off one end, as he always did. "I couldn't get you as much."

"Is it good?"

"Better than last time. Dorjii tried it."

"I still can't do anything for him."

"Not if Sren's watching. But if he isn't—. It's important this time."

"I'll try."

Once inside the eating hall they left their shoes on the racks by the door and separated, each taking his assigned place in the Bhakti formation. Lozan was in the second rank, only a few meters away from Tsong, who stood waiting stiffly, supporting his scrawny, trembling body in its black and gray robes on his two canes; Lozan prostrated himself, waited in silence for the other orphans to take up position behind him.

Sren and the other monitors were all in front, constrained to face the Bhakti-monitor, who for the duration of the devotions would be the supreme authority at Agad. Dorjii's place was in the back and Tsong was half-blind—he'd refused the glasses his position gave him the right to wear so that his sacrifice could buy eyes for one of the damned in one of the lower Hells, just as he always refused most of the food served him so that the starving in the lower Hells could know a moment's freedom from hunger—all of which meant that Dorjii could almost always sneak into formation late without being caught at it.

When at last everybody in the hall had prostrated himself, Tsong began his praise of the Goddess Night in Her three Aspects: Night the Mother, Night the Preserver, and Night the Dakkini of the Just Wrath. His voice a thin, angry mumble, Tsong reminded them

11

all that they were dead and damned sinners whose time in the lower Hells had earned them Pret'yaka, this bubble of seeming mortal existence suspended precariously over the other Hells, from which they could accede to mortality in this or later lives by proving themselves worthy of the Goddess and serving in Her priesthood.

Tsong's discourse went on and on as he detailed the tortures the Preserver kept them from, the possibilities for direct rebirth as mortals or in the Lha Heavens that the Mother in Her compassion had granted them.

When the devotions were finally over, Lozan joined the others in the food line, listening to them speculate about Naming Day and the Testing beginning tomorrow, without participating. Dorjii still hadn't returned. As Lozan picked up the greasy, all-purpose utensil and watched the assistant ladle flesh stew into his bowl—with very little flesh in it despite the emphasis Tsong always put on the fact that as Agad orphans they were the only orphans on all Nal-K'am given meat to eat, and so had to prove themselves worthy of the gift granted them—he saw that Sren had stationed himself where he could survey most of the hall.

There was a faint smirk on the orphanmaster's puffy face—the look he always got when he'd just caught somebody at something. (And the same look, Lozan realized, glancing from Sren to Ranchun and then back again, that Ranchun was trying to assume, as though he thought imitating the orphanmaster's grimaces would help assure his selection as a monitor come Naming Day.) All the monitors were on watch; Sren had stationed them where they'd be sure to see anyone trying to sneak in or out of the hall. It was hot and muggy inside; sweat was running down the orphanmaster's forehead and into his eyes. Sren wiped his face with a gray sleeve, then noticed Lozan watching him. Catching his eye, Lozan gave him an innocent smile. The orphanmaster's smirk vanished.

Lozan slid into his customary place behind one of the pillars, sat down on his cushion across from Tad,

12

who glanced up at him, then went back to sucking at his stew. There was old stew caked around the rim of Tad's bowl but he ignored it, as Lozan did the caked stew on his own bowl. The only times Lozan had ever eaten from a truly clean bowl had been in the port tea shop.

Nidra came to the table, hoping to catch Lozan before he started on his stew. Nidra was probably the reason behind Sren's smirk: Lozan had heard he'd been caught stealing food from the kitchen a few nights back, which meant that he'd have already spent two days locked up without food or water in a darkened contemplation cell and that now he'd have to spend the next week without the right to speak to anyone, eating only whatever was put in his bowl by the other orphans.

Lozan had had a meatroll at the tea shop, so he gave Nidra most of his stew and half his bread. Tad took Nidra's bowl and added a spoonful—the recommended amount for one wishing to be generous—from his own stew before passing it on. The boy he passed it to pursed his lips to spit in it but saw Lozan's head-shake in time and contented himself with adding the proper amount of stew before passing the bowl to the next boy. Nidra was Lozan's friend—as much Lozan's friend as anyone at Agad but Dorjii had ever been—and, though Lozan was small, none of the other orphans wanted to risk a fight with him.

Lozan looked back at Sren. The orphanmaster was watching him . . . or watching the empty place next to him, more likely, waiting to catch Dorjii trying to sneak into it. Lozan was already safe, but Lozan never got caught at anything anymore. It was as though there were unsuspected holes in the orphanage's strict discipline and routine—holes that had begun opening for Lozan, and Lozan alone, just before his twelfth birthday and that always closed immediately behind him, leaving a furious orphanmaster, an envious Dorjii, and sometimes even a puzzled Lozan wondering just how he'd managed to escape.

Lozan stiffened, lowered his face to his bowl to hide his expression until he could get it back under his control: two priests had just entered the eating hall, moving with quick grace, as though the heat had no effect on them despite their heavy black robes, cowls, gloves, boots and masks.

Sren didn't see them at first, his attention riveted on an insect biting his left forearm—a chug—which he was cautiously stalking with his right hand. When he realized the priests were there he swiped quickly at the insect, missing it, then bowed low, moving with surprising grace for one so fat.

The priests' black backs were to Lozan. Between them he could see the gray-robed orphanmaster gesticulating, his heat-reddened face shining. Lozan tried to catch his words, but the noise in the hall was deafening and he could hear nothing.

The orphanmaster pointed in Lozan's direction. Lozan pretended to be fascinated by his stew. Could they have already caught Dorjii, perhaps have had a watch on Lavelle and the tea shop the whole time?

Across from Lozan, Tad had noticed the priests and Sren's pointing finger. He gave Lozan a pitying smile, then sat up straighter, his eyes modestly lowered, a meek smile on his face. Lozan could tell he thought he was about to be singled out for praise.

The priests had turned to face them. Lozan knew they were looking at him, not at Tad, though with their expressionless masks and concealed eyes he didn't know how he knew. Through a momentary lull in the noise the orphanmaster's voice came through with sudden clarity. Tad almost choked, but Lozan found himself relaxing: there'd been none of the gloating triumph he was sure he would have heard in the orphanmaster's voice if he were being taken away for punishment, only the familiar sanctimonious concern and frustrated anger.

Lozan finished his stew, began tearing off dry mouthfuls of bread. Sren's head was swiveling back and forth on his thick neck. He could still be looking

14

only for Dorjii—and that meant that whatever the two priests might have told him, it wasn't that they'd apprehended Dorjii with Lavelle or coming back from the port.

Two more priests, one a red-circle administrator, entered. They all had to be there for something to do with the next day's Testing.

Every few minutes Sren glanced around the eating hall. Typical luck for Dorjii—he'd make it back safely, then be caught trying to sneak into the eating hall with the priests looking on. At best he'd get a whipping with the knotted cords that Sren used on Dorjii more than on all the other orphans in Agad together; at worst, if the priests took an interest in him and found out what he and Lozan had been doing. . . .

It had been a few months before Lozan first met Dorjii, when he'd been ten, that all the Agad orphans had been taken to one of Temple City's lesser squares to watch criminals being punished. The priests had marched the prisoners to the gallows in a long line— there had been more than sixty of them—thin, ragged men with ulcerous sores on their faces and heavy chains on their wrists and ankles, their eyes long dead.

All except one man—a Nagyspa, to judge from the multicolored rags he wore, an animal trainer and hill sorcerer as Dorjii would later tell Lozan Dorjii's own father had been—though at first he'd seemed no different from his companions. But when one of the priests grew careless and came too close to the prisoner, the man's face had come suddenly alive with hatred and he'd struck the careless priest a killing blow on the back of his head with the chains wrapped around his wrists, and then a second blow before the others pulled him off.

The priest had died almost instantly, the rebellious Nagyspa very slowly, burned and stretched and broken on the heretic's rack—as Dorjii's father had undoubtedly died, as Dorjii and Lozan might well die if Dorjii gave them away.

And even if he didn't, even if no one ever found out

about their involvement with Lavelle, the Offworlder. . . . They were sixteen now and it was almost summer: Naming Day was less than a month away. Lozan had done well in his courses, had demonstrated his mechanical aptitude and avoided being caught for anything major now for over two years; he might still have a chance for the railroads or something else that would give him an approximation of the kind of life he'd once thought he wanted to live. But Dorjii would be lucky to get the sewers. He'd probably end up in the mines, or being eaten away from within working in one of the power plants.

So perhaps the chance that Dorjii was taking, that Lozan had refused, was worth it. That Lozan had had to refuse, though it was everything he wanted, everything he'd hoped for since that first meeting with Lavelle.

They'd been twelve then. Dorjii had been at Agad less than a year; violent, sullen and solitary, he was already well on the way to amassing what Sren now claimed was the worst disciplinary record in Agad's history. For most of that year they'd been each other's only friends. They'd started out by sneaking away to watch the trains together, fascinated with them since they both knew that their only real chance of escaping the lives of regimentation and stifling hierarchy that lay ahead for most of the Agad orphans was to be assigned to the trains on Naming Day, . . . and had kept on going a little farther from the orphanage each time, until at last they'd ended up defying not only the law and the orphanage's rules but their own fear of the wasting plague to visit the port.

Tsong had told them that the Offworlders were mortals so evil that they'd been condemned to visit Nal-K'am in their living flesh, so evil that their presence brought disease to the dead, and their lies the death that to the damned in the Hell That Was Five Hells brought no relief, but only rebirth in another, worse Hell.

So Tsong had said, and Lozan even then had been

16

able to tell that the Bhakti-monitor believed his own words. But Dorjii had mocked Lozan for his fears as he hung back on the last hill before the port, had reminded him that he was alive, not dead and damned; and there had been as much truth in Dorjii's voice as Lozan had sensed in Tsong's, so Lozan had accompanied his larger and braver friend down into the streets of the port. If anyone had cared to examine them they could have been identified as orphans by the cut of their brown tunics and by their short-cropped hair, but no one noticed them, then or ever.

Sitting slouched at a table outside a tea shop, a cracked tslin-wood Go board with more lines on it than they were used to in front of him, the Offworlder had looked at first glance like almost any other old man sitting in the sun. Only his pale skin and rounded ears revealed him for what he was, but to Lozan and Dorjii he'd been the most fascinating thing they'd ever seen.

They'd stood in the shadows on the other side of the street, staring at him, trying to be inconspicuous, until at last he'd become aware of them and asked them to join him at his table. This time Dorjii'd been the one who'd hung back, Lozan the one who taunted his friend on.

When they'd taken their places on the cushions around the Offworlder's low table, the man told them his name was Lavelle and asked them if they played Go. Since everyone at Agad was taught the game—though they played it on a board with only twenty-one ranks and files—Lozan said that he did. Lavelle asked him if he'd like to play a game, and when Lozan had once again said yes the Offworlder had ordered meatrolls and buttered tea for both boys.

The meatrolls were better than anything Lozan could remember ever having eaten, the tea stronger and the butter in it fresh instead of rancid. Lozan had been too nervous to do much except concentrate on the infinite complexities of Go played on the larger board, but Lavelle seemed to accept his nervousness as only natural. Before the game was over Lozan

17

found himself beginning to relax, so that when he relinquished his place to Dorjii he found the courage to begin asking the Offworlder a few timid questions, and finally to try talking with him as he would have talked to anyone else.

It was only that evening, as he lay in his dormitory bed pretending to be asleep while he went over the day again in his mind, that Lozan first asked himself what it could have been about the two of them that had interested the Offworlder.

Perhaps he'd just needed someone—anyone—to talk with. Lozan had noticed how the tea shop's proprietor had treated the man with a strange mixture of abject servility and angry contempt, how the shop's terrace had been otherwise empty of customers though every other tea shop they'd passed had been full of men talking and disputing, playing Go and card games, even risking the Fire-Insect Hell by drinking intoxicants.

Perhaps, he decided that night, it had been the fascination with which they'd first regarded him, and with which they'd later greeted almost everything he'd told them—the way they'd drunk in the stories he'd recounted them over the Go board of all the strange worlds he'd visited.

Whatever it had been, they'd come back the next day, hoping to find him there, terrified that if they did he'd have lost interest in them; but he was sitting there in the sun again, and he'd greeted them like old friends, ordered rolls and tea for them, set up Lozan's handicap stones without asking. Only this time, while he talked, he pulled things from a shoulder bag to show them—holophotos startling in their vivid, three-dimensional reality, in the way they showed worlds with red skies and blue skies and dark purple or black skies through which thousands of stars shone, worlds with orange forests and yellow plants and no plants at all . . . world after world, and none of them Nal-K'am.

When they had to leave, Lavelle gave them each a tiny metal sculpture made of some dull black metal,

18

like the bracelet he wore on his left wrist and which weighed more that Lozan had ever imagined anything that small could weigh. Lozan got a small sextapod with open jaws and sharp fangs, and Dorjii what the Offworlder said was a falcon, a bird now extinct on his homeworld but surviving elsewhere.

They didn't dare take them all the way back to the orphanage, of course, where Sren or Tsong might have found them, so they'd hidden them among the jumbled rocks in the grove where Dorjii went to be alone with his birds. A few days later they'd returned to find them gone; but though they were especially circumspect for the next few weeks, nothing was ever mentioned about the animals at the orphanage, and they finally decided that they'd been stolen by some random passerby who'd happened upon them.

They returned to the tea shop whenever they could sneak away from the orphanage. After a while the proprietor started serving them their meatrolls and tea even when Lavelle wasn't there, treating them with the same mechanical politeness he now showed the Offworlder, never demanding any money from them.

After the years of hard work and punishment, of lectures on self-renunciation and the necessity to understand the hidden, festering sins of their past lives in order to escape from Hell, to avoid falling through Ts'a-ba and Rab-tu T'sa-wa to an eternity of torment in Mnar-med, they found his tales of the many strange worlds he'd seen—and on dozens of which, if his stories could be believed, he'd played some sort of heroic role—endlessly fascinating. Though perhaps the real source of the pleasure they found in his company was the knowledge that he was a mortal who recognized them as fellow mortals, and not as the damned souls that Agad and all Nal-K'am taught them they were.

Lavelle's stories. Lozan was sure there was some truth in all of them, though he was just as sure that Lavelle had not played the leading role he claimed for himself in more than a very few of them. Yet there was something disturbing about the stories, just as there was something disturbing about Lavelle himself, something that nagged at Lozan like the feeling he used to get in his teeth before the real toothaches developed—that sort of half-pleasurable soreness he'd never been able to keep himself from probing with his tongue. But until about a year ago Lozan had always told himself it was only the Offworlder's foreignness—that and the way his very existence denied everything Lozan had always been taught was true.

So ever since that first chance meeting Lozan and Dorjii had frequented the tea shop, playing Go with Lavelle, listening to his endless stories, running small errands for him in Temple City, where Offworlders were forbidden to go. They could almost always find him there, sitting at his table in the late-afternoon sun, sometimes toying absentmindedly with the black bracelet on his left wrist, the skin that had been so pale when first they'd met him now a red brown darker than their own.

He told them he was a minor administrator, stranded on Nal-K'am by a bureaucratic error that could take years to correct, with nothing to do but draw his pay for sitting in the sun until the day came when he was recalled. They told him what they knew of Nal-K'am, what they'd seen for themselves and what they'd been taught of the Eight Hells, what they knew was true and what they were sure had to be false; and Lavelle listened attentively, respectfully, asking them questions that sometimes made them realize they knew things they hadn't been aware of knowing, more often showed them unsuspected gaps in their knowledge and understanding. Yet Dorjii in particular knew things that Lozan would never have guessed; his memories of the distant mountain village in which he'd lived his first ten years with his parents were vivid and precise, and Lavelle's questioning brought out whole sides of Lozan's friend that Dorjii had kept hidden at Agad and that Lozan had never even suspected existed.

It sometimes frightened him to realize how well Lavelle knew the two of them. But that was less frightening, finally, than it was important to have somebody willing to listen, someone who cared about what they thought and felt, about who they really were.

As their fascination with the limited freedom a life aboard the trains would have offered faded, they found themselves dreaming of the Offworlders' silent silver starships, of the worlds of the Terran Hegemony where Night was unknown and men knew themselves to be alive. And though Lozan told himself repeatedly that it was no use dreaming of things he'd never see, he listened as eagerly as Dorjii whenever Lavelle told them about the worlds he'd seen, and most especially when he spoke of his homeworld, Terra, from which he claimed all mankind had originally come.

"Terra is the Mother World of all mankind, of every inhabited world," he told them. "Or Grandmother, really, in your case, because your ears and the language you speak prove that you're of MigMartian descent."

"MigMartian?" Lozan asked, reaching up involuntarily to touch one of his large, mobile ears. He snatched his hand away as soon as he realized that Lavelle was watching him.

"Of course." Mig Mar, Lavelle explained, had been the only other potentially habitable planet in man's original stellar system, though it had had to be made over—terraformed—before men could live on it. But even terraformed, Mig Mar had been cold and inhospitable, so uninviting that only the Tibetans—a group of Terran humans driven in the earliest days of interplanetary flight first from their own harsh mountainous homeland, and later from the countries in which they'd then found refuge—had ever truly established themselves there. Though afterward, of course, Mig Mar had become the jumping-off point for all further human expansion into space. . . .

There'd been something in Lavelle's voice when he

spoke of the MigMartians, something that reminded Lozan of the utter contempt with which the Off-worlder always spoke of the nonhuman races man had met, and which made Lozan ask him, "But MigMartians are human? As human as Terrans?"

"Yes. Of course."

"As good as Terrans?"

"Some think better. They lead the race in the mental arts and sciences, and MigMartian adepts—or MigMartian-trained adepts, which comes to the same thing—are the only ones competent enough to be trusted with interstellar navigation and first contact with potentially dangerous aliens. They're a proud people, which is why they manipulated their germ plasm to give themselves ears like yours—a badge of distinction, as it were, to proclaim their MigMartian identity when they're among other humans. But even so, they're as human as you or I am, as human as everyone else on this planet is. Though the priests of Night—no one's ever seen a priest unmasked, have they? Perhaps not your priests—."

"Of course they're human," Dorjii said. "They took fourteen of us from Agad for the priesthood last Naming Day. They might even take Lozan, or me."

"You?" Lozan demanded. "They'll find out in Testing that your sin was killing without regret, and there you'll be in the sewers, crawling through hot excrement. For your own sake, of course, to teach you proper repentance so you can win your way back to life as a human. Not just because they need somebody to keep the sewers clean."

"No," Dorjii said. "You haven't been watching what they really do, the way I have. They choose people you'd never suspect—the ones who are smart but rebellious, not just the pious, p'rin-las-hungry ones like Tad. They took Tsains last year when we all thought he'd get the mines."

"They won't choose you," Lozan said.

"They took Tsains because he was a blasphemer. You and I both knew he was; just because he never got

22

caught and punished doesn't mean Tsong and Sren didn't know about it, too. Maybe they just said they were taking him for the priesthood so nobody would ask questions about what happened to him, but they took him."

"And you think they'll take you?" Lavelle asked.

"Maybe. Because of what I know." Dorjii paused, looked around, hesitating. The terrace was deserted. "My parents—the priests told me they died in a train wreck, but that they'd built up such a favorable store of p'rin-las in their existences here in Nal-K'am that I was to be granted the chance to come here, to Agad. They thought I was too young to know better and I pretended to believe them. But my father always told me that if they ever caught him he'd die on the heretic's rack."

"Caught him for what?" Lavelle asked softly. "You never told me anything about your father except that he was . . . an animal trainer, wasn't he?"

"A Nagyspa, yes, but *his* grandfather was an adept—. Do you know what the Vajrayana is?"

"A MigMartian discipline," Lavelle said. "I studied with a Vajrayana adept once."

"Anyway," Dorjii continued, "he taught father some of what he knew before the priests took him. That's why father was so good with his animals. . . . He could look at something and know what it really was, or listen to somebody and know what they really meant, even if they were trying to keep it secret and saying something else. Father started teaching me, too. Not much, just enough so I knew the priests were lying when they told me about the train wreck, the same way I know I can trust the two of you."

He fell silent. Lozan said, "Dorjii can charm the birds from the trees. I've seen him do it."

They were all silent a while, Lozan remembering the first time he'd watched Dorjii with his birds. It had been three months after that other Nagyspa had killed the priest in Temple City, perhaps ten days after Dorjii had been brought to Agad. But though Dorjii had been new and without friends, he'd made no attempt to get to know the other orphans. Instead, he slipped away by himself whenever he got the chance. Curious, Lozan had followed him one day to a grove of frond trees a kilometer from Agad. There Dorjii had stood perfectly still, his left arm outstretched, singing softly in a high, quavering voice. Soon a tiny black bird with red wings had glided down from the purplish green fronds to perch on Dorjii's forearm. It stayed there, perched, while Dorjii talked to it and ruffled its feathers.

Lozan had always loved birds, envied them their freedom. From the moment he first saw Dorjii with the bird on his arm he'd been determined to become the taller boy's friend and learn his secret for himself.

Gaining Dorjii's trust and respect had proved unexpectedly easy. Dorjii had spotted him sneaking away from the grove—though Lozan had thought he'd slipped away without being seen—and when Dorjii arrived back at the orphanage, he'd been just in time to witness Lozan's public punishment: Sren had caught him sneaking back into the orphanage. But Lozan had refused to tell Sren where he'd been or what he'd been doing, even when Sren used the knotted cords on him, and that had been enough to win Dorjii's admiration and prepare the way for their later friendship.

Though Dorjii had never taught Lozan to call birds to him, he'd given him something far more important, the secret that had come down to him through his father and grandfather, for which they'd both been killed: that they were all of them on Nal-K'am alive, not dead and damned, so that anything else the priests told them was a lie.

And then, though Dorjii had never offered to teach Lozan the special way of listening that sometimes told him what a person speaking to him really meant, Lozan seemed to have learned it somehow on his own from his association with Dorjii, so that now he could read more in people's voices than Dorjii himself had ever been able to. That was the one secret he kept from his friend: Dorjii was so proud of his ability, was always trying so hard, risking so much, to prove himself, that Lozan had never dared tell him that even in this, as in so many other things, he'd now surpassed the boy whose example had taught him how to be himself.

Lavelle finally broke the silence. There was something tentative, probing, about the way he asked Dorjii, "What do you know about the Vajrayana Way?"

Dorjii shook his head, "I don't even know what it is. Just a word. Maybe that's all it was for my great-grandfather, even though they killed him for it."

"But you'd like to learn more about it someday if you could?" Lavelle had asked with what seemed only casual curiosity, and Dorjii had sighed, totally oblivious to the undertones that told Lozan that Lavelle's surface casualness concealed an almost frightening intensity of purpose, and said that of course he would. . . .

That conversation had taken place two years ago. A year later the Offworlder had asked them, "What do you know about how men came to Nal-K'am?"

"Just what the priests say," Lozan said. "How we sinned in our former lives and were condemned to Hell until we repented our sins."

"Dorjii? Did your father teach you any different?"

"Just that this isn't Hell and that we're alive. He never said we came from anywhere else."

"Why?" Lozan asked.

"We found the remains of an abandoned ship in the south. A colony ship, sent out by one of Mig Mar's own colonies. I just wondered if your people had any memory of the voyage. . . ."

Lozan had felt Lavelle's concealed purpose again, as he'd felt it so many times in the previous year, while the Offworlder ordered more sweetrolls and talked about other things, felt the tension that finally peaked when he told them, "On Terra we have the legend of the Pied Piper of Hamelin. Have I ever told you the story?"

"No," Dorjii said.

"Back when all mankind lived on Terra," Lavelle said, settling back on his cushion, "there was a town named Hamelin which, so the legend goes, was infested with rats. Rats are small, vicious creatures which multiply rapidly and eat human food. You're lucky you don't have anything like them here.

"Anyway, there were so many rats in Hamelin that they ate all the food and left the townspeople starving. So that when a man came along and offered to get rid of the rats if the town paid him a great sum of money, the people were glad to agree.

"The man had a magic flute. When he played it all the rats in the town fell under its spell, so that when the piper walked out of Hamelin still playing his flute, the rats followed him, never to return.

"Yet when the piper returned for his pay, the townspeople were greedy and refused to pay him. So he played his flute again, only this time it was the children of the town who fell under its spell and who followed him away, never to return."

"So?" Dorjii had asked when Lavelle finished.

"You don't have any similar stories here?"

"No. Why?"

"It's a very well known story on Mig Mar. I was just curious about how much of your original culture your people retained. . . ."

Lozan had sensed the lie, the hidden significance of what seemed to be just another story, and sillier than most; but though he'd questioned Lavelle further the Offworlder had turned his questions aside, laughing and calling out for more tea and another tray of sweets. Yet that day Lozan felt that for the first time he'd seen through clearly to the garrulous storyteller's hidden core, that for the first time he'd truly felt the fanatical strength of purpose which he'd vaguely sensed before beneath Lavelle's avuncular mask and which had so disturbed him whenever he felt it.

In the year that had followed he'd sensed that buried fanaticism more and more often. There'd been nothing he could tell Dorjii about, nothing he could be sure of himself, except that for all the sincerity of the Off-worlder's liking and concern for the two of them, he was lying to them, was using that very liking and concern to manipulate them. So Lozan had waited, watching and listening, keeping his feelings to himself, for the day when he'd see the pattern clearly, when he'd understand.

And that day had been today. They'd met Lavelle at the tea shop in the early morning. He'd asked them to be there then, and that was something new, for he'd never asked them to meet him at any specific time before.

"Can you keep a secret?" he'd asked.

"Of course," Dorjii said.

"From the priests?" And the grimness of purpose that Lozan had been sensing for so long was there, out in the open, in his face and eyes, making him look a brother to Tsong.

"Yes."

"Even if they question you? Even during your Testing? They know how to make people tell them their secrets."

"So?" Dorjii asked.

"I've had some training, on Mig Mar as well as elsewhere. I can help you keep a secret, if you'll let me."

"Yes," Dorjii said.

"Lozan?"

Lozan hesitated, finally said, "Yes."

"All right. You remember that story I told you, about the Pied Piper of Hamelin? That was just a story, a made-up tale. But three thousand years ago there was a real man we call the Pied Piper of Mig Mar. His name was Yag Chan and he was born on a planet called Nosferatu.

"Since his parents were MigMartian and he showed psychic potential, he was sent back to Mig Mar for adept training. While he was undergoing his training a huge vault was found far beneath the surface of Nosferatu. It was opened the year he returned to Nosferatu as an adept, and he was a member of the first party to enter it.

"Inside the vault they found millions of tubes, each containing a different kind of alien monster preserved in an orange gas. One tube had what seemed to be a human being in it, and for reasons we've never really understood the party took it to the surface and opened it.

"As soon as the tube was opened, the alien in it began to revive and the humans around it died—all but Yag Chan. When the party was discovered some hours later—they'd somehow managed to get to the surface and open the tube without being detected, though there were people all around the area—the alien was dead and Yag Chan was unconscious. When he was revived he was unable to account for anything that had happened after they'd entered the vault.

"When the being from the tube was dissected, it proved totally nonhuman. The scientists and adepts examining it were unable to explain how it could ever have been alive, much less how it had died.

"Yag Chan was taken back to Mig Mar for further examination. His experience seemed to have had no effect whatsoever on him, except that he'd totally lost all memory of everything that had happened after his party had entered the vault. But he was kept on Mig Mar while further tests were devised, and spent the time completing his adept's training at Gompa, the capital city.

"A year after his return to Mig Mar an epidemic of unconsciousness struck the people of Gompa. When it lifted eighteen hours later, all the children of the city old enough to walk were gone, and for the next few days children continued to pour into Gompa from the outlying towns. The children were dazed; none of them were able to explain what had happened to them.

"Yag Chan and two other men were missing—two men who proved to be the only other children ever born on Nosferatu. Everyone else in the dormitory where the three had shared a room was dead, as were thousands of other adults scattered across Gompa, and in their room two small objects, similar in some ways to the internal structure of the alien from the vault, were found.

"A starship intended to carry fifteen thousand colonists and all the supplies they'd need to start a colony was missing. There were more than forty-seven thousand missing children.

"We think the dying alien somehow took possession of Yag Chan before its own body died. We think it stole the children and escaped in the starship.

"We've been searching for those children for three thousand years."

"Here?" Dorjii asked. "Us?"

"Probably not. That starship we found in the south would seem to indicate that your people originated on Ne-chung, a MigMartian splinter colony. It could be— Ne-chung attempted to found a number of colonies and some of their ships were lost, including one carrying the members of a sect that could have been ancestor to your worship of Night."

"But you don't believe that," Lozan said.

"I'm suspicious of that Temple, and those priests. The Temple's too big. Inhuman."

"Human beings couldn't make a temple that big?" Dorjii demanded.

"Of course we could, with a big enough mountain to start with. But human beings would never want a temple that big.

"Listen. Naming Day is coming soon for both of you, and you won't be put to sweeping the streets or working the mines or sewers—you're too smart for that, smart even for Agad, and the priests don't waste intelligence. But with your orphanmaster tipping the scales against you, you won't get anything you'd like . . . the power plants possibly, or the priesthood. I'd guess the priesthood.

"If I were you, I'd want to get somewhere the priests couldn't follow me, somewhere off Nal-K'am altogether, to one of the Hegemony's worlds. That's what I'm offering—but there's a price. We need to know what it's like in that Temple, what happens in there—."

Dorjii's face hardened; Lozan felt an unfamiliar twisting inside.

The Offworlder looked at their faces, said, "Don't object. Neither of you is stupid enough to escape the priesthood. You're not afraid of the Goddess, are you?"

Lozan had not believed in the Goddess since that day when Lavelle had reproduced the miracles of Eclipse Day for him in miniature on the top of the table they were sitting around, and he was not afraid of Her now. But there was something about the priests and the Temple—something he'd always felt that he did not understand but that frightened him.

"You said—the priests aren't human? That they've been taken over by things like the one that took over Yag Chan?" But he would have known if they weren't human, if they'd been something different from other men, just as he always knew when people were lying to him—.

Lavelle's lying to us now, he realized. *Not lying, exactly, but—something. I can't trust him.*

"They're probably human. I hope they are."

"And if they're not? Can you protect us?"

"Like this." Lavelle's hands went to his shoulder bag lying open beside him on his cushion, did something inside it. Lozan felt his will seized, twisted, released. His head hurt. A strange series of bland images—drinking soup in the eating hall, listening to Sren lecture them on Eclipse Day, the way he'd once pictured life on the trains—kept repeating itself over and over somewhere in the back of his consciousness.

"I asked you earlier if you'd let me help you keep our secret from the priests and you agreed. Remember? That's what I just did: the secret is safe now; the priests can never force you to reveal it. And I can protect you in the same way."

30

"No." The decision was suddenly there, unpremeditated, irrevocable. "You can protect yourself, not us. No."

"Yes," Dorjii said. Lavelle's eyes were hard, Dorjii's scornful. "Even if they're not human. I'm not afraid—."

And now, in the eating hall, looking at the dull, familiar forms of the priests talking to Sren, Lozan couldn't understand why he'd run from the tea shop in such panic, why he'd disgraced himself in front of Dorjii.

The lies in Lavelle's voice. And the way the Offworlder had so, so casually seized Lozan's will, twisted it—. No.

Dusum walked up to Sren, asked him a question. As Sren turned to answer, Dorji slipped into his place next to Lozan and began eating rapidly. For once he'd made it past Sren and the others without getting caught. All the other monitors were watching Sren and the priests.

Dorjii ate ravenously, gulping his stew and tearing at his bread without pausing to speak. Finally he looked up, a small, sure smile on his face.

"Wish me luck, Lozan. I'll need it if—." He paused, looked lost and confused an instant, regained his poise. "I may need it."

"Dorjii, did you—?" But he couldn't ask it; his will was caught, trapped, while memories of Sren lecturing them on Eclipse Day invaded his mind again.

"Good luck," he told Dorjii softly when he could think normally again.

They were assigned to different dormitories, so they separated after the meal. Lozan had trouble getting to sleep and when he finally dozed off he was plagued with dreams. Dorjii laughed while a body with Lavelle's face but covered with crawling worms chased Lozan. The Offworlder's face became the mask of a priest and the flesh rotted from the body until it was nothing but white bone and writhing black worms. Lozan was running but the skeleton was faster. It caught him and held him, trying to kiss him with the dead Nightlips of its mask while worms dripped from the bones of its hands onto his flesh and began burrowing their way into him. They crawled over and through him, stripped the flesh from his bones as the other skeleton placed a Nightmask over his face. The Nightmask's lenses were black. He was blind, and in the darkness be became a worm, gnawing on the flesh of a priest who he realized was Dorjii. Dorjii began screaming, and Lozan awakened to realize the scream had been his own. The second moon was shining pinkly through the window and the other orphans in the dormitory were awake watching him. He stared back at them until they turned away. He did not go to sleep again that night.

Chapter Two

DURING THE NIGHT IT BEGAN TO RAIN. THE rain was still streaming down when morning came, a heavy, unseasonal rain, ceaseless, unvarying. The rains of Lozan's previous experience had all been winter or spring storms, short, cold, and violent, torrents of freezing rain torn by thunder, lit by lightning, all over in a few hours. But the thick monotony of the rain on the roofing stones, the heavy, moist air that made breathing more difficult, both were new and drove the night thoughts from his mind.

It was just after dawn. Through a window cut into the dormitory's eastern wall he could see a blue-white glare beginning to force its way through the mass of low gray clouds. No clouds, no matter how thick, could ever fully mask the Sun.

Lozan was the only one awake. His eyes were bleary from lack of sleep. The damp clothes were slimy to his touch and he shrank slightly from the feel of his clinging tunic and trousers. He dressed quickly, then went to the door and opened it.

Outside, the courtyard was a quagmire of red mud from which isolated paving stones jutted ineffectually. Fog hid the countryside beyond the gate in vagueness, sent drifting tendrils into the courtyard. Out there swamps would be forming.

A priest with a red circle on the forehead of his mask stepped through the gateway, not bothering to avoid puddles and mud holes. He climbed the steps to the eating hall and flung open its doors. In the brilliant light streaming out through the open door, Lozan could see that none of the red mud had clung to his boots and cloak.

The priest turned back to the gate, raised his right arm. Blue light flashed. A gleaming cylinder of white metal twice the length of a man floated in through the gate, came to rest hovering over the steps. The priest backed into the hall and the cylinder followed him. A second priest in an unmarked mask shut the doors.

There'd been nothing unhuman about the priests, nothing except the power so casually displayed and their anonymity to distinguish them from other men. And yet they still frightened Lozan, as they'd always frightened him.

He remained on the threshold, standing just inside the open door and looking out over the submerged courtyard. The eastern sky had become too hot to look at. Rain and puddles sparkled, steamed; silver mist softened the harsh outlines of the orphanage's stone walls. A yellow garuda flew by overhead and was lost again in the mist. In his imagination Lozan followed it on its flight, wishing that he too could soar over the walls on feathered wings. He felt what remained of the night's tension slipping away from him.

A bell sounded and he heard the orphans in the room behind him beginning to stir. He ignored the noise, watching the misty courtyard until the second bell, when boys began shoving past him to sprint across the courtyard. After Nidra collided with him full-on, Lozan followed the others, slowly picking his way between the deeper mud holes, ignoring the soaking he was getting.

The cylinder was gone and the eating hall's glow bulbs had dimmed to normal. Eyes swollen from lack of sleep, Sren himself guarded the threshold, picking the sixteen-year-olds out of the meal line and sending them to stand with their backs against the right wall. Everyone could see the cordoned-off area where the two priests Lozan had observed earlier were assembling complex equipment from gleaming black subassemblies.

Red-circle moved with a jerky, darting rhythm that Lozan found somehow disturbing. His assistant had a slower, more fluid way of moving, yet the two managed to coordinate their actions without conversation or delay.

As if they were pretending to be part of the same machine. Are they going to try to make me like that? Perhaps it was not too late; he could sneak out tonight, find Lavelle and—.

No. Never again, that twisting in his mind.

Red-circle and his assistant finished their work at the same time. The assistant beckoned to Sren, handed the orphanmaster a small box just as Dorjii joined the line of sixteen-year-olds. Sren carried the box over to the line of testees. He took a narrow, hinged bracelet of lustrous white metal from the box and held it up so that everyone could see it.

"Come by here and get one of these," he told the sixteen-year-olds. "When you've got one on your wrist, get something to eat—fast—then ask the priest with the red circle what he wants you to do next.

"Good luck, all of you."

The bracelet he snapped around Lozan's wrist was flat, almost as wide as Lozan's thumb and about half as thick. Once on his wrist, it looked as though it could never have been anything but an unbroken band. It was immensely heavy, too heavy for him to pretend it wasn't there, and chill, like a band of metallic ice glowing softly there against his darker skin.

In the meal line he tugged at it with his left hand but succeeded only in chafing the skin of his wrist. His fingernail could not scratch it and he had nothing with which to try to pry it off.

He sat in his usual place, saw that Dorjii was sitting

halfway across the hall, with some of the fifteen-year-olds. They were among the last to be seated; the monitors were already beginning to herd the younger boys out and Ranchun had presented himself for examination before Lozan had finished his first spoonful of barley mush. Some of the machines now glowed with a steady opalescence and there were occasional flashes of much brighter light.

Lozan dawdled over his meal until everyone else had finished. Dorjii had already presented himself, was being tested with the others. Lozan waited, watching Sren, until he was sure that the orphanmaster was ready to come get him, then stood up and walked very slowly to the counter. He scraped his dish as slowly as he could into the trash can, handed the plate to the dishwasher and walked over to the waiting priest.

The whole act was childish, even dangerously foolish, but it made him feel better anyway.

"Your will, Reverence?" he asked, his eyes lowered in modest imitation of Sren.

"The will of the Goddess, my son," the priest said. "Walk down this aisle. Whenever you see something like this"—he indicated the glowing, opalescent boss on the first machine—"touch your bracelet to it and you will be told what to do next."

Unwillingly Lozan stepped forward and pressed his bracelet to the machine. The bracelet began to glow. A low mechanical voice said, "Put your eyes to this slit." A light winked on for an instant to indicate the proper slit.

There was a momentary flash of intolerable light when he put his eyes to the slit. Then the neutral voice said, "Touch your bracelet to the machine once more and go on to the next test."

He shuffled from machine to machine. Every time he touched his bracelet to a boss there was a tingling sensation in his wrist and the cold white light with which the bracelet shone intensified. After encountering two dozen machines, some of which merely wanted to look at him while others wanted to touch him, sample his skin, taste his blood and inject him with things, his wrist blazed with light.

He felt a shock when he touched the bracelet to the final boss. All the tingling stopped and the bracelet faded to a dull black.

The same black as the bracelet Lavelle wore, that he played with absently from time to time. The priests must have fitted him with one the same way they had just done with Lozan.

The machine's soft voice said, "You have finished. Go join the others in your group."

The other sixteen-year-olds were already assembled against the wall. Lozan took a place in line. The bracelet was tight around his wrist. He put his hand behind him and rubbed the bracelet as hard as he could against the rough stone of the wall. When he examined it he saw that the metal was unscratched.

Red-circle's assistant was already beginning to disassemble the machines. Red-circle walked up to the testees, stopped in front of them. He spoke softly but with great clarity, his voice almost like that of one of his machines:

"Through the intercession of the Goddess, we of Her priesthood now know you as She knows you. We know your strengths and your sins, your pasts and your present.

"Know this: You are being judged. Yama, the Great Judge, weighs the black stones of your sins against the white stones of your repentances, and only the Mother's mercy holds you here, in Pret'yaka Naraka, this bubble on the surface of Nal-K'am. Beneath you are Yan-sos and T'ig-nag, Bsdus'joms, Nu-bod and Nu-bod Ch'en-po; in the sky T'sa-ba blazes. Let the Mother withdraw Her mercy and you fall—fall through all the Hells, fall for two thousand years, only to spend an eternity in Mnar-med.

"This bracelet you wear is the outward mark of Night upon you, the sign that She is interceding for you with Yama. Whatever your sins in your past lives, whatever vocations we discover for you, know you that so long as you remain here on the surface of Nal-K'am, in the fragile bubble which is Pret'yaka Naraka, for so long has Night's strength upheld you.

"Here at Agad it is a mark of distinction to wear Night's bracelet, and for the period of your examination it is the Goddess's will that you remain within Agad's walls. Should you attempt to leave, in express violation of the Goddess's will, She will let you taste of Yan-sos—only taste—until that taste has convinced you to return. Such is Her mercy.

"In Her mercy She gives you now this taste." The priest did nothing that Lozan could see, but suddenly Lozan's right wrist felt as though it were encircled by molten metal. He screamed. All the testees were screaming.

Except Tad. By some freak, Lozan's eyes came to rest on Tad. He was silent, standing with clenched jaw and eyes squeezed shut, his pride overshadowing the agony he could not hide feeling. Lozan could not admit that there was something Tad could endure that Lozan could not, so after that first involuntary scream he kept his teeth clenched and tried to keep the scream he felt from forcing its way out. The pain engulfed his hand and crept up his arm until he was sure he could bear it no longer.

And then it was over. Lozan looked at his hand, flexed his fingers. The pain was a fading memory. He forced himself to grin at Tad, then looked expressionlessly out at the priest.

"Tad, Lozan. For the two of you, a word of advice. Pride and strength are not the way out of Nal-K'am, not the way to achieve life as a mortal. Pride is the way of the Lha-ma-yin, and after their long lives of fruitless war are over they each and every one find themselves condemned to endless tortures in Mnar-Med."

He believes what he's saying, Lozan realized. *He really is trying to help us.* For some reason that was more frightening than the torture had been—that the priest would believe what he was saying.

"Lozan, Tad. You have endured a taste, an instant's taste, of Yan-sos. But Yan-sos is a great Hell and in it there are sixteen minor Hells, in each of which your suffering would be greater than in the one above it; and you have tasted only the least of these. Your pride is Moha, stupidity. If you cling to it you will fall, fall through the sixteen Hells of Yan-sos, fall and fall for two thousand years until you end up in Mnar-med. You must repent your pride, you must let it fall from you, if you are ever to achieve life as mortal men.

"Now, all of you, sit at these tables, taking every other chair. In Her mercy, the Goddess Night has seen fit to let you taste of Yan-sos. Now She grants you a taste of the Lha Heavens. Wait quietly. Soon you will taste Her Compassion."

Lozan stared fixedly at the table, determined to keep his rage and frustration hidden. It was not the time. Later he'd find a way to deal with the bracelet. Later.

The priest had believed what he said.

But wasn't it better to believe people? To be so truthful the world showed you nothing but truth?

Without warning Lozan was overwhelmed by a caressing tide of peace and reassurance while a silent explosion of sweet froth came swirling through his mind, a froth in which each iridescent bubble burst to release a delicious concept: *I will always tell the truth; Night and Her priesthood uphold and protect me; I will always do my best, without thought of personal reward, to help all those around me find rebirth as mortals. . . .* All the maxims and teaching tales the sleepspeakers in the nursery walls had whispered to him every night when he'd first come to Agad, mingled and confused with his thoughts and memories.

A thousand betrayals.

Somewhere he was aware of himself answering questions, but he was lost in rejoicing, dancing with the bubbles far above the plane where his voice responded to his interrogator, oblivious to the lower depths where he was a small animal, trapped and rigid, screaming with fear and fury, screaming . . . .

He was shuffling forward in the evening meal line by the time the bubbles became infrequent enough for his subterranean fury to break through and reunite itself with his conscious mind. All at once he was shaken by such self-loathing he could barely hang on to his tray. He was himself again—or almost himself again—and he hated that part of his mind which melted in ecstasy with every bursting bubble. But far more than he hated himself he hated the priests who had done this to him.

Dorjii was sitting alone in his usual place, a quiet smile on his face. Everything was still a little unreal for Lozan as he sat down by his friend; he could not feel the chair in which he was sitting and there was still a languid swirl of bursting bubbles weaving back and forth in his head.

This—this must have been what he had feared, this loss of himself, this sickly-sweet stranger in his skull. This would be how they'd make a priest out of him. He had to go back to the port, find Lavelle. Now, before it was too late.

If he could. If it wasn't already too late.

Lavelle commanded powers; otherwise he'd never have been able to do what he'd done with the priests' bracelet on his wrist. There was no other hope, no way Lozan could lose himself on Nal-K'am. Maybe Lavelle could save him, help him before he betrayed himself altogether and became just another Red-circle. Maybe.

Dorjii just sat there, a vacant smile on his face. Lozan kicked him under the table. Dorjii said, "Lozan," and smiled.

"Dorjii, what did you and—." He could not say Lavelle's name; the twist the Offworlder had put in his mind prevented him from it. One slavery or another.

But at least I can still think his name. At least I still know who I am.

40

"Dorjii, can you tell . . . tell. . . ." A dizzying confusion of bubbles and memories. "Dorjii, what happened last night?"

"I'm so happy, Lozan. So happy, even if this isn't real."

Lozan kicked him again, hard, without effect. All the other testees seemed in even worse shape than Dorjii, sunken into themselves, their unfocused eyes half-closed and blissful smiles on their faces. More than one slept, and the boy next to Ranchun seemed unaware that he was drooling.

Whatever the Offworlder had done for Dorjii, it hadn't been enough to enable him to resist the bubbles completely. But that didn't mean it wouldn't be enough for Lozan: Lozan was stronger, was already fighting his way free of the bubbles without outside help. He could do better than Dorjii.

Could he make it to the tea shop despite the bracelet? He had to try. Tonight. Now.

Trust the truthful, the bubbles sang.

He made sure that at least two monitors saw him enter his dormitory, then went out the window. It was a long drop—more than four meters—but he'd made it before and he didn't feel it this time.

Let your sins go, let them pass, rejoice!

He hugged the courtyard wall, grateful for the concealment the rain lent him. He reached the hole in the outer wall without incident. Climbing the jumbled blocks of broken stone was difficult. It was dark, neither moon showing through the clouds, and the rain made his footing treacherous. He slipped twice and scraped an elbow on one fall but was otherwise unharmed. He was following a route he knew as well by night as by day.

Once past the wall, he circled around to avoid the gate and made off to the right, heading for the monorail track. It was usually shorter to go in a straight line, but the lowlands would all be flooded now, slowing him up, and he didn't trust his way in the dark, not with so little feeling in his body and limbs. He could be trapped in deep mud without realizing it until it was too late.

The bracelet grew warm. Without the after-effects of whatever they'd done to him, he'd probably be in agony. As it was he felt only a prickling sensation; it was a good thing he'd left immediately.

But he was coming to himself. The walking seemed to clear his head. With each step the stinging in his wrist increased, the bubble flow within grew stiller. By the time he climbed the embankment and began following the track, there was a thin band of utter pain around his wrist.

At first, as he followed the track the pain diminished: the track must have been curving back towards Agad. But soon the pain began to increase again until it was worse than before.

Lozan looked at his wrist. The band was glowing with smoky red light. He touched it with his other hand to see if it was truly on fire. There was no sensation until his fingers actually touched the band; then the agony was in both hands. He snatched his left hand back.

When he let his right hand fall back to his side, the bracelet brushed his flank. The touched muscles flared with pain, though his tunic had insulated them from direct contact with the bracelet. Lozan had to hold the arm slightly away from him from then on.

He began to run clumsily on his still-unfeeling legs. Running, he forgot time, distance; existence was the rain, the track, the pain.

Once, when the pain had taken his arm almost to the elbow, he fell and rolled completely off the embankment to lie in the sticky mud. His arm was pinned under him, and the pain had locked his muscles and prisoned the bracelet in the pit of his stomach.

With the other hand Lozan pushed his right arm out from under him, whimpering as the band traveled slowly across his side. Then his body was again free of pain, though the agony in his right arm reached up past the elbow. The band was flaming.

He would not give in. Defiance brought weary anger, and with anger came strength. Dragging his useless arm, he crawled back up the embankment. Then he was running again, the mud sucking at his feet.

After a while the pain in his arm began to lessen. He ran faster, gladly, until he realized that he must be running the wrong way. Stifling a sob, then sobbing, he turned around and began to run back the way he'd come. The mud pulled at him. Sensation was beginning to creep back into his legs and every step brought shooting pains and a new weariness. His breath rasped between his teeth. He had to stop as a spasm of coughing hit him. The rain continued to fall. He ran.

Suddenly the lights of the port were close. He had been running with his head down, seeing only the track in front of him. He stopped, panting. He had to think.

If only he hadn't refused Lavelle's offer.

The pain had taken his entire arm. It stood out stiff and useless from his side, the effort of keeping it away from his body no longer conscious, the burning agony beginning to creep into the lesser pain of his abused shoulder muscles. The bracelet danced red on his wrist, burning with unclean fire.

That way. He stumbled from the embankment. He'd never taken this way before and it was hard to think, hard to concentrate on anything but the agony that was his arm.

There. He saw the lighted window off to the right. He forced his arm in closer to his body, hiding his blazing wrist in his pocket. The loose tunic pulled away from his side, but it was no longer far enough. His side was burning.

He opened the door with his left hand and walked in. His walk was stiff, jerky, and his teeth were clenched in a rictus of pain.

Lavelle was gone. There was only the proprietor, looking at him blankly, without a spark of recognition in his eyes. It had all been for nothing.

"Where is he?" Lozan managed to force out.

"Who?" The man seemed genuinely puzzled by his question.

"You know who. Lavelle." But as Lozan spoke his hand lifted from his pocket. He tried to keep it hidden, could not force his muscles to obey him, could not keep his arm from extending rigidly out in front of him. The proprietor saw the blazing bracelet.

"There's nobody here! Get out! Now!" The man picked up a short, stout piece of wood and began advancing on Lozan with it.

"Out!"

Lozan lurched back into the night. To the left. He saw the embankment and headed for it. He reached the track and tried to run, but his legs would not obey him. He walked and crawled. There was nothing but the pain.

The pain was a narrow band around his wrist when he again saw the distant lights of Temple City. He continued on, feeling the pain increase slowly until he was back where he remembered he'd climbed up onto the embankment. By luck alone he kept his balance as he stumbled down it. From there he walked and waded back to the orphanage, almost losing himself in the unlighted succession of unfamiliar pools.

The pain in his wrist gave way to the lesser pain of his bruised and strained muscles. He had to crawl with only one usable arm up the rubble and through the wall. He staggered across the courtyard into his dormitory, too tired to care whether or not he was seen. He slept.

When he awakened, there was a bloated swamp spider clinging with its mandibles and hollow legs buried in his right side, just below his armpit. He ripped it out of his flesh with his good hand and crushed it underfoot, but it left a huge purplish swelling on his side.

There was no way to disguise his condition. His legs were so stiff and pain-filled he could barely walk; his right arm hung dead at his side. With contemptuous charity, he was plucked from the morning meal line by one of the red-circle priest's assistants. His shoulder and arm were treated with a salve, which cut the pain a little, and the swamp spider's bite was treated with a disinfectant. Nothing was said, no questions asked or accusations voiced. He hated them for their smug confidence.

Still, this time he made no protest, attempted no resistance, when the bubble-stream swept him away from his pain.

Chapter Three

A FEW TIMES DURING THE NEXT FEW weeks, Lozan made some token attempt at resistance—tried to get Dorjii to tell him how to get in touch with Lavelle, or attempted to hold on to himself against the bubble flow or pull himself out of the residual flow in the evening—but each day he surrendered himself with more abandon, each day he made less attempt to find any purchase on reality in the evening. He woke and slept to the iridescent flow.

Then, late in the Testing, he found the bubbles dulling, the flow slowing, the soundless explosions no longer irresistible. The insects that had fed on him unhindered the last few weeks began to irritate him once more. He was torn between clinging to himself and clinging to the oblivion the bubbles offered. Neither could claim him. He would take shelter in the bubble-stream only to be brought up short by self-loathing or hold hard to his thoughts only to find himself thinking, *Lovely, lovely,* when he confronted Sren. He slept each night with the sick knowledge that he would give way again the next morning, yet never escape his accusing self.

The week before Naming Day his nightmares resumed.

Naming Day morning, the sixteen-year-olds were awakened before dawn. A priest was waiting to take them to the central orphanage in Temple City.

They left Agad at first light, without having eaten.

The priest kept on high ground, so it took them most of the morning to get to the monorail line. Sren kept pace about two meters behind the priest, careful not to trample his shadow.

Behind the orphanmaster came the orphans, led by Dorjii and Lozan. Dorjii was in an excellent mood, taking care to trample Sren's shadow whenever possible and do anything else he could to demonstrate his insolence in ways that wouldn't give the orphanmaster grounds to punish him. Lozan kept pace with Dorjii but felt none of his friend's exuberance, though he attempted to keep up the pretense that he was having an equally good time.

That morning, just before they'd left the orphanage, he'd made a final attempt to get Dorjii to put him into contact with Lavelle. Dorjii had pretended not to know what he was talking about.

A train was waiting for them on the embankment. The orphans had the first car, where they were all crushed together in a space meant for perhaps a third of their number. The windows were sealed closed and the air inside was hot and sticky. They were already covered with mud and, most of them, with scabs. As they rubbed against each other, the mud, kept liquid by the moist air and their sweat, gradually covered their entire bodies and faces with a thin film. The car stank. Ever present, vasanas and dbee flitted among them. The orphans were too tired to kill more than a few of them.

Lozan was near the center of the car, with three boys on either side of him, so he saw little of the city through which they were passing. A glimpse of low stone buildings, purplish when they weren't gray, a brief view of sodden streets full of trudging people.

He could see more whenever the train made one of its frequent stops, though the doors to their car were never opened. At each stop, small cloth stalls crowded the station-yard walls and thin-faced children hawked sweetrolls through the open windows to the passengers in the other cars. The children would look through the sealed windows of Lozan's car at the packed orphans within, then turn incuriously away.

Though few people got on or off at any given stop, each station yard was crowded with petty officials, vendors, fortune-tellers, beggars, and relatives of the travelers, plus a few people just watching the trains. The beggars all had their left ears cropped—the traditional license of their profession—and each of them had the number of the station where he or she was allowed to beg tattooed in purple just below the right eye.

A fortune-teller standing just outside Lozan's window invited passersby to learn the future his trained birds would select for them out of a deck of Miso cards. Lozan wondered, not for the first time, if that was what Dorjii's father had really done.

There was a loud retching sound somewhere in back as the train accelerated. Lozan looked back. Tad had vomited and those in front of him, too closely packed to have been able to move away, were now yelling at him and beating him as best they could in the cramped space. Lozan grinned. This train ride was the kind of thing he could endure without effort, the kind of thing that would never get to him. It reassured him, made him feel less impotent, less helpless, despite the immense black bulk of the Temple looming ahead.

Finally, at the largest station they'd yet seen, Sren and the priest unlocked the door and the orphans stumbled out. The priest let them catch their breath and stretch for a moment, then led them out of the station yard and down a long deserted street leading toward the Temple. At the far end of the street Lozan could see the warning statue of a tutelary demon, gray against the black stone of the Temple behind it. But, distant though they really were, they were still so close to the Temple that only the face of the lowest level could be seen through the mist and rain—a looming wall of smooth black featureless stone, rising until it was lost in the distance overhead.

The priest led them down the right side of the street

along the edge of a wide gutter brimming with foul-smelling water. One of the orphans at the head of the line slipped on a slimy spot where the gutter had overflowed and fell into the water. Moments later, Lozan heard another splash. He glanced back, saw Tad being held under water by four grim-faced orphans.

The street was still empty, except for an old female beggar sleeping in the shade of an archway on the far side. The priest led them past a shrine—an intricately carved cube of black stone two hundred meters on a side and surmounted by a tapering golden dome—and on to a gateway in a long wall of smooth gray stone. In the arch above the gate the words "All is transitory, painful, and unreal" were carved.

At the gate Sren and the priest surrendered them to a balding monitor, who told them his name was Randal. He checked their names off on a list, led them through the gate and across a wide open space into a large building, then down a flight of narrow stairs to a wide, low-ceilinged room with three great tubs set into its floor. Here he had them strip and bathe, two at a time in each tub. Lozan and Dorjii were the first in; the water in the tubs at Agad was never changed, and if you didn't get in early you might as well not get in at all. Dorjii and Lozan had both been notorious at Agad for their fastidiousness—the result of a chance remark by Lavelle early in their association with him that had made them associate the disregard for cleanliness with which they'd been raised with Nal-K'am's primitive civilization.

Emerging from the tub, Lozan was handed fresh clothing by a boy Randal had impressed as an assistant. The clothing was identical with that he'd worn all his life, except that the tunic was black instead of brown. The new clothes fit no worse than his old ones had.

When all the Agad orphans had bathed, Randal took them to the eating hall. It was huge—at least ten times as big as the one at Agad—and filled. In a corner, away from the other tables, Lozan could see a party of about two hundred girls, their hair cropped as short as his, presumably from Tara Orphanage. Some of the Agad orphans were pointing at them and discussing them in loud voices.

Lozan dismissed them from his thoughts and ate hungrily, though the food was far worse than that he'd learned to despise at Agad. The easily resisted discomfort of the journey had revived his spirits. It had been part of the familiar world—the world that had never posed him a problem he couldn't solve or evade. As long as there was nothing to turn him traitor to himself, nothing like what Lavelle had done to him, or the bubble stream. And why should there be? They'd learned too much to ever risk putting him in a position of trust.

Unless they could catch and twist his will the way Lavelle had, could make him into someone else.

Unless Lavelle was right. But the priests were human, as human as he or the Offworlder was.

Three years ago they'd taken Tsains the blasphemer for the priesthood, and the year after that Sung and Michel, the two sneak thieves who'd almost been caught trying to steal from Sren himself, though nothing had ever been proved against them.

The meal over, they scraped their dishes and followed Randal through a doorway into another hall. High above them on the far wall an unsupported stone slab jutted out. They were crowded in close to the slab's shadow. Behind them the other orphans pushed and shoved, attempting to get to the front.

Everywhere except above the slab the glow bulbs dimmed and went out. A white-circle priest came to the edge of the slab and silently surveyed the upraised faces.

Almost directly below, Lozan and Dorjii craned their necks, looking up at him.

"Old," Dorjii said. Lozan could see that the dark figure was racked with tremors which cloak, cowl and mask could not quite conceal. The priest's stance was unbending, only the trembling of his cloak revealing his state, and that only to those close enough to him to see it.

When he spoke, his voice was steady and powerful, though thin with age.

"Praise Be to Night.

"Praise Be to the Mother. Praise Be to the Preserver. Praise Be to the Dakkini of the Just Wrath.

"Praise Be to the Mother, Who alone intercedes for us in Nal-K'am with Yama the Stern, the Unmerciful Judge. Praise Be to the Mother, Whose compassionate love outweighs the black pebbles of our sins on Yama's scales. Praise Be to the Mother, Who has given up the Bliss of Abiding with the Empty One that we may be reborn mortal, and alive.

"All Praise Be to Night the Mother.

"Praise Be to the Preserver, Whose mercy alone keeps us suspended here in Pret'yaka Naraka, here on the outer skin of the Hell That Is Five Hells, here where our suffering is so much less than we merit.

"Her mercy alone keeps those among us who have killed without desire to repent from Yan-sos, where the S'in-je would cut and tear us to pieces again and again.

"Her mercy alone keeps those among us who have killed without desire to repent and who have stolen that which we were not worthy to possess, who have taken the food and bedding and medicine of the sick for our own use, from the Hell of T'ig-nag, where the S'in-je would nail us to a floor of burning iron and draw sixteen black lines upon our body to guide them in cutting us asunder with their saws of burning iron.

"Her mercy alone keeps those among us who have killed and stolen without desire to repent and who have indulged their thirst for improper love without desire to repent from Bsdus'joms. In Bsdus'joms, the S'in-je lead us into forests of trees whose leaves are sword blades. In these forests are women so irresistibly desirable that the sinner pursues them up and down the trees though the bladed leaves slice and hack his body, shredding flesh, muscle, and bone.

"Her mercy alone keeps those of us who have killed and stolen and indulged in improper love without desire to repent and who have wrongly engaged in the use of intoxicants from falling to Nu-bod, where the S'in-je pry open our mouths and pour molten copper down our throats before they deliver us to the Fire-Insect Hell, where one hundred and one wind diseases, one hundred and one yellow diseases, one hundred and one cold diseases, and one hundred and one other maladies scour our flesh while the insects pierce and devour our flesh.

"All Praise Be to Night the Preserver.

"Praise Be to the Dakkini of the Just Wrath, Who casts down those among us who lie and slander Her name, Who takes those among us who would condemn the rest of us to further damnation by their lying blasphemies and foul persuasions, and casts them down into Nu-bod Ch'en-po, where She watches with compassion as the S'in-je boil them in iron kettles and cause the lies they have uttered to become snakes that come to life within them and eat out their entrails.

"Praise Be to the Dakkini of the Just Wrath, Who in Her compassion torments us to enable us to escape those infinitely greater torments we merit.

"All Praise Be to Night, the Dakkini of the Just Wrath, Who even when She casts us into Nu-bod Ch'en-po, yet saves us from Ts'a-ba, from Rab-tu T'sa-wa, and from the endless torments of Mnar-med.

"You, Orphans—you are those who would have passed your existences here in Pret'yaka Naraka, suspended over the torments of the Hell That Is Five Hells, in greater hunger, in greater thirst, than the Tantalized Ghosts, were Her mercy not infinite. She has clothed you, She has fed you, She has caused you to be sheltered, while many of those outside these walls, rejecting Her favor, have been given Yama's justice and starve, naked and unprotected. Be thankful. Praise Her.

"Praise Her, thank Her yet again, for from you alone in all Nal-K'am does She choose those whom it pleases Her to elevate to Her priesthood and sisterhood—and only to those who have become priests and sisters does she grant the hierosgamos that leads to mortal incarnation.

"Be loyal to Her, for Her hand and Her hand alone holds you here in Pret'yaka Naraka, and She alone can grant you living incarnation in the next life.

"Be worshipful, for She alone is worthy of your worship.

"Praise Her, for She alone withholds Yama's torments and keeps you here, in Pret'yaka Naraka, and this from mercy alone.

"Obey Her, for She alone is your true Mistress and in Her service alone does Righteousness lie.

"And fear Her, fear Her always, for none can stand against Her wrath."

The priest paused, then continued in a harsher voice:

"Abase yourselves! Kneel and hold your foreheads to the floor. Remain thus, thanking Her for Her mercy, until you are led from here."

The glow bulbs above the slab went out and Lozan could see that the priest was surrounded by a corona of blue flame. Then that too was gone and the hall was in darkness.

The floor was cold against his forehead.

Gently, so smoothly that he was not aware just when it had begun, a languid upwelling of silver-gleaming bubbles invaded him. This was not the violent explosion that had torn him from himself during Testing but a subtler chorus: *Praise Her, Be Thankful, Trust.* . . . Around him he heard sighs of pleasure as his companions abandoned themselves to it. Only Lozan resisted.

A priest was standing beside him, his robes glowing

with a deep-purple luminescence. The priest tapped Dorjii on the shoulder. Dorjii looked up at him.

"Follow me."

"The Temple?"

"Follow me."

Dorjii left. Lozan remained kneeling until he too felt a tap on his shoulder. Gingerly, afraid of losing the profound concentration that enabled him to keep hold of his sense of identity, he rose to his feet.

"Follow me," the priest's soft voice said, and Lozan followed as his guide unerringly picked his way through the crowd of kneeling figures. They stepped through a doorway and it was suddenly light, though no light had shone through the open door.

The light came from beneath the surface of a pool of slow-swirling water. The sweet, heavy perfume of djaka blossoms pervaded the air. On the wall behind the pool a great mask of the Mother hung.

"Bathe," the priest said. He waited until Lozan had entered the pool, then left, taking Lozan's clothes with him. The water was warm and more than warm, with a deep-seated heat that seeped through the skin and soothed the muscles underneath. The water tasted sweet on Lozan's lips. There was no danger here and Lozan allowed himself to relax.

"Come with me." The priest was back, a new set of clothes in his arms. As Lozan stepped from the pool, he noticed a cloud of short, black hairs floating on its surface. Startled, he put his hand to his head. He was bald. Even his eyebrows were gone.

He took the clothes the priest held out to him—green trousers and a tight-fitting shirt the color of blood, with shiny red metallic threads woven into the material. Red and green: the colors of Yama, God of Judgment.

"Yama?" he asked, hesitating. "Am I to be judged?"

The priest shook his head impatiently. "Night has not abandoned you. Dress."

Lozan dressed and followed the priest through the

door by which he'd entered, but instead of finding himself back among the kneeling orphans, he was in a small, dimly lit room. A priest wearing blood-red robes and a dark green mask sat on a massive chair of rough red stone; the priest's whole body blazed with shifting purple fires. Through the flames Lozan could see the white circle on the forehead of the green mask. The body shook and quivered beneath its cloak and the flames wavered around it, yet the mask hung steady and unmoving, its black lenses fixed on Lozan's face.

"Kneel," the guide whispered. "Kneel and kiss his left foot! Quickly!" he snapped when Lozan made no move to obey.

Lozan knelt, conscious of the black bracelet's weight on his wrist. The flames withdrew from the priest's left leg and Lozan kissed the smooth surface of his boot.

The flame-wrapped priest raised his hand and stretched his fingers toward the kneeling orphan. The room exploded with unseen light. Everything was transfigured. The priest radiated holiness, authority and strength, as though Yama Himself animated his frail frame. When he spoke his voice was more than human.

"Lozan, Yama relinquishes you to Night, and the Goddess takes you for Her own. You are not Lozan now but another, nameless, Her servant and nothing more."

Lozan looked up at the priest. The priesthood? But he was wearing Yama's colors—.

The priest shriveled; he was dying, rotting, his robes filthy rags through which Lozan could see his flesh being eaten by long, black worms. Yet throughout he remained a figure of majesty.

"I give myself to Yama in your place," the priest told him. "For you I endure the Burning Hell of String-Like Worms in Rab-tu T'sa-wa."

Horror gave Lozan the strength to say, "Reverence, I am unworthy."

"Silence." The priest gestured with a skeletal arm

and the horror receded. His robes were whole again, brimming with light, and an expression of godlike pity gave life to the features of his mask. "The Goddess uplifts whom She wills. Do you think She is unaware of your petty transgressions? She ignores them! It is not for such as us to question Her mercy. Stand!" His voice filled the tiny room.

Lozan stood while a red cloak was placed over his shoulders and a green mask was set upon his face, where it adhered like a second skin.

"You think yourself Yama's still," the old priest said, "but soon you will know yourself reborn to Night."

Lozan's guide took him by the arm, led him from the room. They went down a long flight of stairs, along a narrow corridor. The corridor ended in a wall.

The priest's black-gloved hand traced a pattern in the air and the wall swung away. They stepped into a huge cubical chamber of blazing white stone. The light was fierce, constant but with a strange subliminal rippling. The air itself seemed luminous.

A platform of red metal in the center of the room was ringed with concentric circles of the same metal. The outer circle was low, only a few centimeters high, but each ring in was a little higher than the one surrounding it. On the platform stood three dark figures. The strange light made it impossible to tell how big or how far away they were.

Lozan looked back. The wall behind him was an unbroken expanse of blazing white. The priest was continuing toward the platform at the center of the pattern, stepping over the raised metal circles as though afraid to touch them.

Lozan followed, imitating his caution, though it was increasingly difficult to keep his unfamiliar cloak from brushing against the red metal. Once, when he'd reached a circle that rose a little higher than his knee, a corner of the cloak escaped his grasp and touched the metal, but nothing happened. When Lozan looked up he saw the priest climbing the four steps leading up to the platform.

The three figures on the platform were huge, fashioned from some shiny black substance that could have been stone or metal or neither. They stood with their backs to Lozan, but even so he felt he should know them, though he did not. From beyond the figure closest to him came a faint blue glow that the room's pervading luminosity had earlier masked.

The priest disappeared behind the figure, which stood three times his height. As Lozan ascended the stairs, recognition came: the Dakkini of the Just Wrath. How could he have failed to recognize Her before? The other two could only be the Mother and the Preserver.

Now that Lozan had reached the platform he could see that the blue glow was coming from a fourth statue lying crumpled on its side—a fallen figure that Lozan recognized as Sin Vanquished, though Sin's body was more youthful and sensually androgynous than in any representation Lozan had seen before. Behind the twisted figure, the priest stood watching Lozan.

"Stand there," he commanded, indicating a black disk set into the platform at the point where the gazes of all four figures met. Lozan did as he'd been told.

There was something disturbing about all the figures. Each was—wrong. It was not just that Sin was youthful and healthy, His face alive with intelligence when He should have been stretched skin over diseased, crumbling bone, and His expression that of a rapacious idiot. Why was there a definite hint of deformity beneath the Preserver's cloak, and why did it seem that one of Her shoulders was higher than the other? The Mother's face had never worn that look of cow-like stupidity, and Her body was too slim, too sensual, not matronly enough. The Dakkini of the Just Wrath—that was harder. Only a hint of cruelty in Her mouth, a look of calculation in Her eyes, a total lack of compassion in Her face and attitude—yet it was the

Dakkini of the Just Wrath who was the most disturbing.

Is that how the priests picture Night? Lozan asked himself, unsure why the figures disturbed him as profoundly as they did.

"Place your left arm at your side and extend your right in front of you. Gaze into the Preserver's eyes." The priest's voice came from behind him.

The room's luminosity seemed to increase. Pinpoints of swirling fire covered the Three Aspects, and Lozan could feel a swelling vibration through his feet. There was an instant of total pain and the bracelet fell from his wrist.

The world shattered into slow-drifting fragments.

The drift coalesced into a new world. Everything was veiled by an ever-thickening orange mist. Lozan was in some sort of transparent cylinder and around him stretched endless vistas of similar cylinders with nude bodies floating in them. He tried to move his head and could not. He could not feel his body.

Tubes stretching away to infinity, as in the vault on Nosferatu. Lavelle had been right.

A priest in multicolored robes came walking slowly up the corridor between the rows of tubes. Lozan was sure the man was coming for him. The priest's movements became slower and slower until he froze, balanced in midstep.

Chapter Four

LOZAN'S GAZE WAS FIXED ON THE FROZEN figure of the approaching priest. Was the priest paralyzed, too? But then, why didn't his unbalanced body fall forward?

Nowhere in the great hall was there any motion. None of the bodies in the tubes bobbed or drifted. The orange cast of everything remained constant. It was as if time had stopped.

It's me, Lozan realized. *They did something to me, stopped me so completely I keep seeing what I saw when they did it.*

A strange, passionless fear was growing in him. He pictured black worms making slow tunnels through his unresisting flesh. Would he even feel them?

Yet his anxiety was disembodied, abstract, of the mind only.

As much as he wanted anything, he wanted to shut out the image of the approaching priest, but there was nothing he could do. When he tried to close his eyes there was no sense of resistance, but his will was dissipated, lost in the nothingness where his body had been. How could you command the fading memory of an eyelid to close?

Would he even feel it if they killed him?

He examined the bodies in the frozen field of his peripheral vision. They were both male and female, about his own age, hairless like himself. Undoubtedly other orphans who'd been entombed on their Naming Days.

At least they all looked healthy. There were too many bodies for them all to have been entombed when he'd been, and if they were being eaten away from within, they showed no signs of it.

How long had he been here? Where was he? How had he gotten here? There was no way of knowing, no way of finding out.

No way of knowing: the final end to all his questions. He went over what had happened again and again, found only more questions without answers.

Growing bored with fruitless reexamination of the same limited facts, he tried to lose himself in fantasies of escape and revenge. But, devoid of emotional content, his fantasies soon irritated him and he gave them up.

At least he supposed it was soon. His mind never tired; he'd thought his way over the same courses so many times he'd lost count. He grew as detached from his thoughts as he already was from his emotions. The rows of encapsulated bodies were inescapable but he ceased to regard them; the questions and fantasies still passed through his mind but he'd lost all interest in them. They persisted mechanically, as though happening somewhere outside of him.

Gradually he became aware of a darkness, a way of seeing somehow below or behind the unchanging images to a restful dimness, a soft comfortable space that was strangely familiar, though he'd never before been aware of it. He allowed himself to slip down into it.

Lozan floated in darkness. The cycle of fears, plans and memories had been left behind with the image of the hall. So gradually that his first awareness was of having been seeing them for a long time, the darkness came alive with stars of every imaginable color. He was floating in a thick fog of softly blazing lights. They were all around him, filling all space. He felt a pleasant sense of anticipation.

In the distance a star began to move. It grew to a ball

of golden light arching towards him. It struck, defining his chest where before there had been only void, sank through him: a softly spreading pool of tingling warmth and awareness. As the tingling spread, he began to feel his body with a clarity which was more like vision than touch but which had the intimacy of touch.

An emerald star came curving in from the right. It sank gently into the face that materialized when it struck. Lozan was lost in a universe of soft green radiance. Warmth and awareness spread from his head down into his body. The emerald wavefront met the pulsations spreading from his chest and reinforced them. He felt his bodily awareness attain a clarity and precision transcending anything he had ever before experienced.

Stars of every color were coming at him from all directions. With each gentle impact came greater detail, further precision; with each impact he perceived the individual stars in the cloud surrounding him with greater clarity.

Each muscle fiber was limned, distinct and clear . . . he was gliding through the living bone, touching the marrow with invisible fingertips . . . then following the blood cells born there out into the bloodstream, aware of the path each corpuscle would have followed had his heart been beating. And within each cell, each organ, he could feel the ghosts of other possibilities clustered like golden shadows.

His awareness of one of those shadows grew until he found himself in a second body, experiencing its unfamiliar muscles, altered tensions, the unaccustomed ways his new facial muscles attached themselves to a different skull. He encompassed the different cellular structure, the unique energy configurations . . . and then, with an almost imperceptible shift, he became aware of a new body, a new set of configurations.

He drifted from shadow to golden shadow, exulting in the altering flesh, the shifting bone. Some were male, others female: he drifted through all with an equal, fascinated interest that was not curiosity but was content to rejoice in what it found.

And it was real, no illusion, with a rightness and an evidence that could only mean that this was the truth that had always lain within and behind the world whose appearances he had taken for real.

His own body built itself up again around him, its familiar contours charged with ecstatic energy. From the six directions, multicolored rivers of light came rushing in dancing turbulence, meeting and merging within him until he was nothing but light, each atom of his being a sphere of lambent joy. The golden shadows radiated out from the core of his self until they merged with the most distant stars. This went on forever.

And then he was wrenched from eternity, falling, collapsing back into a body of dull flesh. The rivers flickered, dimmed, went out. The stars, the spiraling shadows were gone. There was a sudden, twisting moment of vertigo, then the sharp pain of something striking his forehead. He was lying sprawled and twisted on some cold, smooth, unyielding surface. He felt nauseated, dizzy. The chill ate into him and he tried to draw himself up into a tight ball for protection. He couldn't move.

His head throbbed and he could feel a warm, sticky pool—blood—forming beneath his right cheek. He must've fallen. His thoughts were unbearably sluggish.

I'm not in the tube anymore. It was dark. He couldn't tell if his eyes were open or closed, if he was sighted or blind. Panic lapped at him; his mind skittered from impossible hope to impossible fear, doing anything to avoid confronting his real helplessness, the dull inescapability of the cold floor beneath him.

They had to be ready to use him for whatever they'd kept him in storage in the tube for. And he was helpless, paralyzed, perhaps blind, as defenseless as he'd been in the tube itself.

Could he escape to the void, to the bodies he'd had

there, so much more alive than his own had ever been?
If the void was real, and not just another illusion, a
priestly seduction like the bubble-stream . . . .

No. He was certain, though unable to account for
his certainty: whatever the void had been—an illusion
or the reality he'd been sure it was when he'd been in
it—he'd gotten there on his own. And he could sense it
all around him, waiting beneath the surface of the
reality his senses reported to him.

He tried to move again, failed.

Even if the void was only an illusion and all he'd be
doing would be hiding from the knowledge of what was
really happening to him, it was worth it. Anything was
better than lying helpless and blind on this cold floor.

He tried to disengage himself from his thoughts and
feelings, tried to slip behind them to the void's welcoming dimness. But the void eluded him; he could not
escape the stubborn reality of the floor beneath him or
the pain in his twisted legs. Perhaps being able to feel
his body cut him off from the void. But he had no
choice: he concentrated harder, willing his mind to
complete stillness.

Voices. They seemed to come beating in on him
from the void—soft, shimmering whispers he could
almost see, almost hear, almost feel. Then the whispers were blazing, burning incomprehensibly into his
mind, each image/word/sensation so powerful, so resonant, that it refused to link up with the others in any
pattern he could understand.

He concentrated harder, tried to open himself totally to the voices. He saw:

*Lozan lies naked on a shadow-draped altar of intri-
cately carved white stone. A figure approaches, crimson, indistinct. The Lozan on the altar looks up at it
with love and trust, offers himself to it. . . .*

*And THE BLADE flashes, gold and glittering, the
Lozan on the altar watching it descend, watching his
blood spurting, watching himself die, all with that
same passive trust and adoration—.*

63

No! He thrust the images from him, refused them.

Silence/blindness/the feel of the floor beneath him and the pain in his legs. The voices were gone. In Lozan's mind, half-glimpsed fragments of alien meanings still floated—a confused mass of glimmering strands winding in and out of darkness.

The blade posed over his chest, descending, ripping him open—.

They're going to kill me. Sacrifice me to the Goddess.

He felt sweat tracing its way over his shuttered eyelids, knew an instant's relief that his eyes were closed, not open and unseeing.

The Lozan on the altar had seen the knife descending. Seen it and welcomed it and done nothing to escape it or stop it.

No. A slow rage was building within him, driving out all fear. He remembered the Nagyspa he'd seen kill the priest. *No.*

He tried to open his eyes. His eyelids twitched, as if at the feel of insects walking over them; but he could not force his eyes to open.

He tried again, putting all the strength of his will into the effort. He was swimming in chill sweat before he was rewarded with a blurred glimpse of black floor; then he was blind again.

He'd seen himself naked and unbound on the altar, a willing victim. They had to be expecting his cooperation—else why all the preparations, why the confrontation with the old priest before they'd put him in the tube? He might be able to grab the knife, use it on the one planning to kill him with it.

Unless they knew he knew. He realized then that he was certain that they—who?—didn't know, that the certainty was as much part of what he'd sensed as his knowledge of what was being planned for him. But he couldn't risk trying to eavesdrop on them again: if he did anything to let them know what he'd learned, he'd have lost the only chance he had.

Who were they, to talk among themselves in blazing whispers? Lavelle's aliens? But why would aliens keep up the pretense among themselves and actually sacrifice him to their invented Goddess?

He tried to open his eyes again, succeeded. But it took a great effort to keep them open and he allowed them to close a moment later.

A few meters in front of him a low arc of red metal rose from the smooth black floor. Just beyond the ridge, the black surface ended in a curving wall that glowed red, as though with dull flame. The color of the wall reminded him of something, but he couldn't bring it to mind.

He opened his eyes again, managed to keep them open . . . drew his arms in under him and pushed himself upright, his muscles responding smoothly but without strength. He was having trouble keeping his eyes open.

How much time did he have left?

The arc was part of a circle, with himself as a center. The red wall was actually a glowing hemisphere arching over Lozan, enclosing him completely.

He pushed himself to a sitting position, caught his breath, then got shakily to his feet. His legs were wobbly. But the throbbing in his head was gone, and when he touched an exploratory hand to his forehead he found the shallow gash in it had already closed. Absentmindedly, he scraped dried blood from his cheek.

He pivoted, examining the hemisphere above him. It was featureless and gave off no heat he could feel, though it looked hot. He was reaching out to touch it when things came together in his mind and he realized what it reminded him of: the way the bracelet had burned on his wrist when he'd tried to reach Lavelle. He snatched his hand back, crouched down in the center of the circle again.

If he could only get in touch with Lavelle! He must've learned enough to buy his way off planet. The hall he'd been in, the tubes like those Lavelle had described—that was all the proof the Terran needed. If he could find his way to Lavelle—.

Unless Dorjii had already done so and Lavelle had left Nal-K'am with him. Lavelle had promised Dorjii a way to get in touch with him; if Dorjii was still here, Lozan would have to find him, escape with him—.

No. It was too complicated, impossible. There was no shelter he could count on anywhere on Nal-K'am, no one he could count on for help. Better to do as much damage as he could. Like the Nagyspa with his chained wrists.

I'm not afraid, he realized. *Not afraid of dying.*

His weakness was gone. Strength was flowing into him now—strength such as he had never imagined. In a way it was like bathing again in the rivers of the void. Perhaps he still retained some connection with it after all. He felt alive with an insane confidence that ignored the odds against him.

Careful, he told himself. *You don't know enough to be confident. All they have to do is paralyze you again, or use the bubbles—.*

But he felt strong enough to resist the bubble-stream. And they wouldn't paralyze him; he'd already decided they expected some sort of cooperation from him. What he had to do was concentrate all of his energies on staying alert and ready for his chance, on not giving himself away. They'd be coming for him soon. He had to be ready.

Though he was waiting in a tense half-crouch, without moving or relaxing, he did not tire. The energy flooding him showed no sign of peaking, was still building as the hemisphere dimmed to a smoky red bubble and flickered out of existence.

He was alone in a huge, cylindrical arena of smooth black stone. The walls must have been thousands of meters high.

The Temple. This could be nowhere else.

At the center of the arena was a block of white alabaster the shape of a man's coffin. It rested on another, similar block that looked as though it had been extruded from the black floor beneath. On the far side of the blocks Lozan could see a ring of red metal that looked exactly like the one in which he was standing.

Statues of the Three Aspects of Night as he'd seen them in the Temple City orphanage jutted from the left wall, their united gazes falling on the white stone. Above Lozan and to his right, half-hidden in a sparkling crystalline haze, were three tiers of what he finally realized were seats fashioned from intricate rococo filigrees of glistening red metal.

The seats were empty.

Lozan walked warily towards the center stone, looking for something he could use as a weapon. But the stone hid nothing, though now that he was close he could see the intricate pattern of grooves carved into its upper surface, all of them coming together in a small hole.

A ways below the hole, a cylindrical cavity twice the size of his hand was cut into the white stone. It was empty, but there was a tiny point of light on its floor from the hole in its roof. The smooth alabaster surface was clean, but a faint odor Lozan could not identify still lingered about it.

Looking up, he found himself staring into the stone eyes of the Dakkini of the Just Wrath. The center stone was located where Sin Vanquished had been lying in the tableau at the Temple City orphanage, and the carvings on the smooth white stone—.

When he'd seen them earlier, whisper-imaged, they'd been running with his blood.

They're going to kill me here. He had to get away from the center.

He backed away, turned to run, realized he might be being watched, and forced himself to walk calmly back in the direction from which he'd come.

He didn't stop until he had his back pressed against the black, chill stone of the arena wall.

Strength and energy were still flooding into him. He

knew he didn't dare trust the assurance that accompanied the energy, yet he still found himself relaxing a little. So far, at least, he was still free to run or attack; though he was weaponless, he was still unchained, and there was no bracelet on his wrist to compel his obedience.

A sound just over the threshold of audibility penetrated to him. Low wailing notes and muffled drumbeats. The sound penetrated him, sinking into his thoughts and merging with him until it was the beating of his heart, the rhythm of his breathing.

And then a voice—a voice that seemed to come from everywhere in the vast arena:

"Nameless One, you are here to receive the Mother's mercy. Your time of purification is past and you have been washed free of sin through the Mother's intercession. Surrender your will to Her, lay down your past and all your memories, for you are to be granted that most precious of gifts: the hierosgamos, the sacred marriage which leads to life itself, the life of a mortal free to perfect himself further until he attains rebirth in the Lha Heavens.

"Know that you are to be observed by S'in-je set here for their own punishment, that they may watch you and envy the perfection of the reward granted you and denied them. Know this and be not afraid, but await the Mother with glad heart.

"For you are to be granted not only mortal life but that most precious of gifts, mortal love."

The haze over the tiers of seats thickened, hiding them from view. It solidified, becoming for an instant a single billion-faceted crystal. Then it faded to a thin mist and was gone.

Chapter Five

GIANT MEN AND WOMEN WERE STANDING
in front of the seats of the highest of the three tiers.
They seemed at least three meters tall, their heavily
muscled bodies covered with intricate serpentine patterns—patterns that covered their arms and legs as
well and rose to flower on their faces and bald skulls.
No two patterns were similar except in the dissonance
of their colors, and Lozan was somehow sure that
what he was seeing was neither paint nor costume but
flesh. Each giant was dressed in a black kilt and,
except for the jewels scattered seemingly at random
over their heads and bodies, was otherwise nude.

Lavelle's aliens.

Lozan glanced quickly back at the arena. He was
still alone. The giants looked powerful but they might
be too massive to move quickly—.

The giants stood like rigid statues of bright oiled
metal. Around them the haze was reforming, thickening and brightening until it was once again a single
gigantic crystal. When it was gone again, there was a
second tier of motionless beings beneath the first. It
was hard to make out the details; the new arrivals
sparkled and glittered as though encased in layers of
diamond, but even so it was plain to see there was no
uniformity among them. Some were larger than the
giants above them, others smaller than Lozan. Many
were totally inhuman—one had antlers, a second a
ring-shaped head through which the seat behind it

showed clearly. Beneath the glittering surfaces, colors writhed and flowed in fascinating, almost intelligible sequences.

Once again the haze appeared, solidified and vanished. Five figures sat in the bottom tier. The outside two were masked and cloaked like priests, except that their robes and masks glittered with prismatic fires. But if those two were almost familiar, the other three were so contrary to reason that Lozan thought they had to be illusions like those the priests created for Eclipse Day. He could see them with unnatural clarity, with no blurring or loss of detail despite the distance, and this too made him doubt their reality.

The one on the right looked human, except for its great size and the two gnarled growths protruding from its skull where a man's ears would have been. The growths curved gently upward until they stood upright like the weathered trunks of trees; and, indeed, they seemed to be topped with thick foliage. They were miniature trees with curved trunks, and though the air of the arena was still, their boughs whipped back and forth as though tossed by a strong wind.

When Lozan first glimpsed the being, both trees were green and lush; but almost immediately the tree on the left began to change color, its leaves fading to a sickly yellow, then darkening through reds and purples to a dull brown. The dead leaves withered and fell to the figure's bare shoulder, where they vanished. For a moment the wind-whipped branches were bare; then buds appeared and the cycle began to repeat itself.

The being on the left was by far the largest creature present. Shifting patterns of blue flame flickered across its gray skin. Its head was a huge, puffy globe, featureless except for a ring of eye sockets around its equator. A single red eye seemed to swim beneath its skin, surfacing in turn in each eye socket. Its arms ended in red-lipped mouths with gleaming white teeth.

But bizarre though the others were, it was the central figure that finally caught and held Lozan's eye. Its iron black body was human-seeming except for the many-fingered hands at the ends of its overlong arms, but it had no head. Instead, directly above its shoulders the neck flared out into a wide, flat pedestal on which two figures—one male, one female—were in constant motion: leaping, dancing, touching and making love as though they were independent entities. As Lozan stared, the two tiny figures reached down to the pedestal and each picked up an eye which it held cradled in its arms so as to train it on the arena. The standing figures seated themselves. All motion ceased.

Something was standing in the other set of rings.

Lozan could not force his eyes to focus on it. The thing was a blur, a vague multiple image—size, shape and color all uncertain. But he knew what it had to be.

It was becoming visible, drawing in on itself, flickering in and out of a constantly sharpening focus. The figure seemed smaller than he had feared it would be, though with the flickering distortion it was still impossible to be sure.

He tensed himself to run forward, take the knife away before the other realized what he was doing . . . stopped himself just in time. He couldn't trust that overwhelming feeling of strength and confidence he was feeling; it might be part of the way they expected to lead him, willing, to his sacrifice.

But there was no giant or monster, no knife to seize—only a slender girl, as lovely as the creatures watching them were grotesque. She was dressed in a long red cloak made of some sheer, nearly transparent material through which the amber skin of her body glowed with a soft warmth that made Lozan feel he had never before seen true skin. Her hair was long and strange, a deep red that was sometimes black and that swirled around her when she moved like a cloud of dark flame. Her small, finely boned face framed eyes of lambent jade, cool in the warmth of her skin and hair, yet glowing with their own light. She seemed a creature of light—light made flesh—and yet there was nothing insubstantial or unreal about her.

Lozan's hands were clammy and the sweat of his

excitement was rank in his nostrils. He felt a Dakkini-sliver tautness in his groin. His stomach knotted and he was briefly conscious of his nakedness.

The voice spoke again, repeating for the girl what it had already told Lozan, but adding, "Together you two shall be united in Her name and substance. Together you shall receive your reward."

The girl shivered in the cold air and wrapped her thin cloak more tightly about her. She looked uneasily about, poised as if to run, perhaps trying to locate the voice's source. She was slender and her movements were full of nervous grace, but there was no exaggerated frailty to her; every angle of her face, every line of her high-breasted body expressed a flamelike vitality, a burning aliveness so pure and forceful that Lozan was bewildered by it.

Her eyes had found the watchers and she was staring up at them in frozen shock or fear, yet even so she seemed in motion. What if she wasn't the one who was going to kill him? What if she was another victim like himself, and he'd been meant to overhear that whisper-imaged conversation so that he'd make her *his* victim? Who knew what amused those things watching them?

Where was her knife? If she was going to kill him, where was her knife?

She looked away from the immobile watchers and her gaze came to rest on Lozan. A tentative smile lit her face. Lozan felt a surge of tenderness and concern wash over him. He wanted to go to her, comfort her. But he could only watch her, his back to the cold wall.

As he studied her he felt her presence engulfing him, warm, velvet soft . . . ; the green glow of her eyes was plunging him into gentleness, lassitude . . . ; everything but her green eyes was fading, gone . . . ; her eyes, expressing something Lozan could never have named but which drew him in, soothed him and yet simultaneously awakened new longings within him which he knew instinctively only she could satisfy.

The world was green mist. From it the voice sounded: "The Goddess commands you to come to Her to receive your reward. Come to the center, come to your sacred marriage and mortal lives."

The voice was the voice of the world.

The girl. . . . He took a step forward, into the mist, then another, quicker step, ignoring the voice within him that was only now beginning to protest. There was no floor beneath his feet; his steps carried him forward through soft silky emerald clouds toward a crimson sunrise—.

And somehow that part of him that had been screaming at him to stop made contact with the alien energy fountaining inside him and turned it to its own use, made it its own strength.

He could feel the floor, cold and smooth beneath his feet again. Lozan halted, shielded his eyes behind his hand.

He could still see the girl, the green mist, through the flesh of his hand.

She wasn't real. Not real, only in his mind. His leg muscles were straining against one another with contradictory commands as his will fought hers for control of his body; he could feel his lips stretched tight in a mindless grin. How could he strike back when his opponent was inside himself? When it would be so easy to take just one step, feel the ecstatic play of muscles fulfilled as he abandoned himself to the joy of running toward her—.

No! He caught hold of himself, thrust the image of the waiting knife, the spurting blood, between himself and the compulsion. Only the certainty that obedience meant death gave him the will to resist, only the alien vitality filling him gave him the strength.

But she doesn't have a knife. She doesn't have a knife.

The girl was walking toward him, moving as lightly as though gravity had no hold on her, the blazing darkness of her hair swirling about her as she came. There was a shyness, a timid determination beneath

73

her grace that stirred Lozan's sympathy despite all his will to resist.

She knelt a moment behind the stone, then stood and faced him, her hands held open before her in supplication or reassurance.

He had seen her through the flesh of his hand. She wasn't real.

The voice spoke again: "Nameless One, you displease the Goddess. Yet still will the Mother grant you Her mercy if only you go to the center stone and there abase yourself to Her image. Only submit your will to Hers and She will yet grant you your hierosgamos and escape from Nal-K'am."

Lozan fought to keep the image of the waiting knife before him; though there was no knife he concentrated on it until he could almost see its curving length. He told himself her hair was the color of dried blood, but he knew it for a lie—her hair was a cloud of flaming crystal filaments and it floated in his mind as it floated in the light.

No.

The arena was changing. A dank wind blew from walls wet and glistening—stone no longer but fleshy stretched membranes through which nightmare creatures struggled to force their way into the arena. Impossible arrays of teeth and suckered tentacles, clutching fingers and talons threatened to erupt into the arena; holes like hungry mouths appeared unexpectedly in the floor, closed with wet smacking sounds. Only a narrow corridor leading to the calm center where the girl waited remained free of menace.

She was on her knees, praying in a voice so beautiful and truthful it made him forget where he was. A prayer he'd been taught in his first years at Agad. The floor beneath him was heaving, slick and slippery like the inside of a mouth. He fell, made it back to his feet, fell again.

There was a feather touch on his shoulder. He whirled, almost losing his balance, to confront a wall transformed, through which questing cilia reached out for him. The surface was translucent and from the depths lidless eyes followed his movements.

The cilia were lengthening, thickening into tentacles. He jumped back, onto the slack, blubbery lip of a huge mouth that had opened in the floor behind him, and leaped free just before it closed. The wall bulged outward and its substance began to ooze from it, flowing like some thick pulpy liquid across the heaving floor. Half-formed limbs were visible in the churning depths. There was a smell like that of rotting meat.

Lozan ran, skirting a second mouth's quivering lips. As soon as he passed the second mouth the floor beneath his feet was solid again, but he continued to run until he was once again in the red rings.

Around the still-calm center where the girl knelt, the radiance was slowly being leached from the air. The shapes animating the arena's periphery now moved half-shrouded in the deepening twilight, but an aureole of pure light still lingered around the girl. The radiance intensified her loveliness, purged it of any hint of menace, said that only with her would he find safety and refuge.

No. Whatever she really was, she was waiting there to kill him. If nothing else, he could cheat them of their willing victim. He turned his back on the center and its illusion of sanctuary, stood his ground as the sluggish mass oozed across the arena floor toward him.

At the last moment his nerve broke but it was too late; he was held fast by suckered tentacles that burned where they touched him, that tightened on him as they dragged him closer to the multiple arrays of needle teeth which gaped open, began to close on him, piercing his skin and—.

Were gone. He lay sprawled once again on the cold floor. His skin felt as though it had been splashed with acid and he was bleeding from hundreds of tiny, shallow puncture wounds. But the arena around him was solid stone again.

He got back to his feet. The spectators were once again hidden in the crystalline haze. He stared at the girl, refusing the image she offered him, willing himself to see her as she really was.

She seemed to waver, as though he were looking at her through a curtain of moving water. Her image shifted, altered, became something different; she grew, elongating and swelling like an infant exploding into adulthood in a fraction of a second.

A slumped giantess confronted him, her splotchy red body covered with lifeless jewels. In her right hand she held a great golden cup, while with her left she grasped a long knife of the same metal. Her hands shook as though she could barely maintain her grip on them. Her eyes were fixed on the floor.

An intricate pattern of blue gems winked from the curved blade; from the pommel of the knife a great blue gem protruded, catching the light and shattering it into a million fragments. The cup was fashioned like a flower with four overlapping petals, and each petal was the face of a skull. In the eye sockets, red gems gleamed.

Behind the giantess the fading light died. Something was forming, as though the darkness itself were taking on substance. But Lozan's attention had been caught and held by the knife. It fascinated him, not just because it was a weapon he could use against the giantess, not just because it had almost been the instrument of his own death, but because he recognized it as somehow almost a part of himself, a manifestation of his will as the girl had been a manifestation of his desires.

He advanced on the giantess, his eyes fixed on the precious blade.

He never had a chance to take it from her. By the time he registered the dark form taking on solidity behind her, it had reached out to cloak her exhausted form in its own substance. Then it curled back from the rejuvenated giantess, now a vivid crimson, and drew in on itself, curdling until it seemed its darkness hid a deeper darkness, its shapelessness some ultimate form. Lozan could feel its multiple awarenesses focused on him, and before its irresistible command reached him and took him over he recognized it for what it was—no priest-generated sham, but Night Herself.

Helpless, his muscles no longer under his own control, he made his way forward to meet the Goddess.

The giantess stepped to one side. Lozan felt himself kneel and prostrate himself to the darkness, heard his voice say, "To you, Goddess, I relinquish my life." The crimson giantess silently handed him the knife. He kissed its blade, then drew it across the inside of his right arm and offered the bloodied blade to the shadow form. The giantess took the knife from him and handed him the cup. He kissed it as he had the knife and allowed a drop of his blood to fall into it before offering it to the Goddess. The giantess took the cup from him.

He felt himself stand, watched numbly as his body climbed onto the center stone and lay loosely on its back in the center of the carved pattern. He could feel the stone ridges digging into his back and buttocks but he was not uncomfortable. He felt relaxed, at peace for the first time since he'd found himself in the arena.

He didn't know how long the giantess had been standing over him. The curved blade glinted. She was all crimson: skin, eyes, nails, the crimson lips drawn back from sharp, delicate crimson teeth. He knew she was beautiful, with a beauty strangely akin to that of the illusion she had created for him, and that that was all that mattered: her beauty.

The Goddess had withdrawn from him but he felt no desire to struggle, not even when the giantess raised her knife and began to cut. She was too beautiful, too terrible, like a living flame.

She made a shallow incision in his throat, working the blade slowly back and forth so the blood would flow freely. The knife cut through the veins on the inside of his forearms, made deep incisions in his inner thighs, his belly, chest, and again in his neck. The crimson hand cut deliberately, methodically, and he could feel the blood running out of him and flowing through the channels beneath him, feel it streaming through the hole in the stone into the waiting chalice as distinctly and intimately as though it were still pulsing through his veins. The knife's jeweled blade and pommel burned steadily brighter. Lozan felt only a soft lassitude, a sort of wonder.

His hands rose from his sides, took the knife from the giantess, held it poised over his heart. He could see his knuckles white with tension, the blade shaking almost imperceptibly, could feel, somewhere very far away, his rigid, straining muscles protesting. But his trivial pains were lost in the onrush of her need as she came flooding into him, a torrent of avid feather-touches and hungry, burning caresses.

The past came alive again, faces long forgotten, memories long buried swirling up in him like sediment from the bottom of a disturbed pond. He was sick with the intolerable, cloying, butter-richness of himself, everything he'd ever been and felt all churning together in one interminable, inescapable moment; his will was paralyzed, lost in memories, drowned in fat, drifting confused through changes taking place in a body that might have been either his/hers or the one he/she was feeding on.

He shared her hunger; her greed to complete her transformation was mirrored in the relief he felt whenever she freed him from a part of himself and he felt it burn, giving up its existence in an explosion of clean ecstasy that left him feeling purged and purified. He wanted to be clean and clear and cold, as empty as the wind; he shared her frustration with the fact that despite everything he could do to aid her his disintegration was proceeding so slowly. She had isolated the center of his being, licked at it with the flames of her hunger, but it resisted her, refused to be consumed.

He tried to help her, to open and offer himself to her as she bent all her efforts to his destruction, frantic now with the need for energy her metamorphosing body imposed on her. She concentrated herself around

78

the seat of his selfhood, striving with all her being to absorb it.

And was riven, shattered, swallowed up and herself consumed as the nightmare shapes of the arena came surging out of the inner darkness where they'd lain hidden all his life, rending, ripping, burning. He reached out, grasped the flame-like vitality that animated her, tore it from her and devoured her as she had tried to devour him, leaving only a burnt-out husk behind.

The battle lasted forever and was over in a fraction of a second. His nightmare projections melted into quicksilver pools and retreated back to his unconscious. Out of a confusion of memories alien and familiar, yet all become strange, his identity coalesced again and he was himself once more, but a self transformed, reborn a creature of living fire. He pulsed with energy; he was the stone on which he lay, the chill air around him, everything and nothing burning in an illimitable now. It was as though he had been straining for color in the blacks and grays of an eternal twilight when suddenly he saw the dawn glowing with its thousand colors, as though his eyes had been being blasted unmercifully by the killing light of Nal-K'am's unshielded sun when suddenly he found himself perched beneath cool starlight at the edge of a silvered waterfall.

He could hear—see? feel? taste? touch?—the aliens all around him, a confusion of voices like ringing crystals, images and incomprehensible sensations.

RILG? . . . floating cold and naked in darkness, clutching someone to him as a voice like a steel needle in his brain whispered a message he refused to understand . . . VOTRASSANDRA! . . . the agony crawling from mind to mind, the jeweled cities shattered as time shattered into twisted fragments and the present was lost in the infinite reverberation of echo and anticipation, their minds flaring and burning out with the overload . . . NO, HUMAN, BUT—.

Lozan shoved the voices and images to the back of

his mind. Fronds of alien memory waved in the crystal landscape of his thoughts, showing him abilities he'd never known he possessed. He healed his wounds and only when he was whole again did he realize how weak he really was. He had lost a lot of blood.

He could feel the cloud of darkness extending into his mind, warm and resonant—a part of him, yet separate from him. He opened himself to it as his memories told him to, and then he knew what he had to do.

He lifted the paralysis which held him and allowed feeling to flow back into his body, got shakily to his feet. The giantess lay on the floor, her heart still beating faintly in her misshapen body, her melted features vacant. Lozan lifted her and put her in his place on the altar. Her skin had faded to a pinkish gray broken by purple splotches. Nothing remained of her former beauty.

Taking the skull-flower from its cavity, he emptied it of all but a little blood, then put it back in place. He picked up the knife and made the proper incisions in the huge body and neck, noting that the blood flowed sluggishly, as though it had already begun to congeal. When the cup was full he placed the knife in the giantess's huge hand, gently bending her fingers around it. It was more than he could do unaided to control her dying muscles, and he had to ask Night's help. He felt no new influx of energy from her when the knife plunged home in her heart. She had already been dead in all but name.

The cup was full. Slowly he lifted it to his lips and drank, almost gagging at first on the thick, sweet, salty taste. When he'd drained the cup he placed it on the altar by one of the dead hands. He pulled the knife from her chest and placed it beside the cup. Then he collapsed against the white stone, so weak he could not stand.

He offered them no resistance when they came for him. They were he as he was them; there was no one for him to fear.

Chapter Six

A FLOATING CONFUSION FILLED JANESHA'S mind. Thoughts kept drifting away from her or melting into a meaningless flow of random pleasure and mind-less peace, and she could not remember what had happened.

She was unable to order her perceptions of the space around her, but from scattered flashes of clear percep-tion she had deduced that she was lying on her back with her eyes closed somewhere in the Hall of the Crimson Cloud. Her hall. But its familiar geography was vague in her mind, and in the disordered impres-sions she received she seemed to sense some mon-strous change. . . .

She concentrated, and in time enough new informa-tion seeped through her confusion to enable her to pinpoint some of the changes. The rose pillars had been filled and there was a skull, her first, in her Place of Remembrance. Relieved, she realized that the chaos which enveloped her must be some sort of side effect to her transformation, though she'd experienced nothing like it in the Key Memories. She'd have to consult Chordeyean—.

Her fingers groped for the new circle of bone on the necklace around her neck. But they moved stiffly, clumsily, and the bone disk felt oddly repellent, not at all as she'd imagined it. And there was something about the skull in her Place of Remembrance that frightened her, something that kept her from attempting to visualize it more clearly.

She couldn't visualize his death, couldn't remember it. She remembered him lying on the altar, still and waiting, but the Ritual itself, the ceremony in which she'd killed her ties to ancestral humanity and became fully Lha—that was gone, hidden from her, confused with a fantasy in which she saw her own body lying slack and flaccid on the altar. Yet she remembered the salt taste of his blood, warm and thick as she drank it.

She should have been conscious of her body's functioning on every level from the intracellular up, but now her internal perceptions seemed distorted or altogether absent. She was no longer mistress of her own body and it felt strange and cramped to her in ways she could not define.

For the first time she felt fear. This was no proper transformation effect, nor even any of the dangers against which she'd been warned. She forced her eyes open and laboriously lifted one hand up to where she could see it. It was small, too small, brown where it should have been crimson; and it was the wrong shape.

She stared at the too-long fingers, the too-narrow palm, and began to understand. It was no confused picture of her own body she was sensing but a true picture of another body, a male body, the body of a boy, the body of the boy who remembered looking down at her DEAD face as she consumed her mind—.

Music penentrated Lozan's sleep, pulled him from the dream in which the crimson giantess had been telling him so much. As consciousness returned, he felt the measured beating of a drum join the quiet droning which had first roused him. Each drumbeat reverberated in him as though he were inside the drum itself, yet at the same time the sound remained muted and distant.

He heard a gong struck sharply, then held. In the ensuing silence Lozan could hear the blood moving in his veins. The gong was struck again and the air was full of its frenzied clanging. Shell and thigh-bone trumpets of the types sacred to Night began to weave a rapid pattern around drum and gong, while in the background the quiet drone continued unchanged.

Lozan felt no urge to open his eyes, though he was thoroughly awake. Beneath him he could feel a warm surface, unyielding yet comfortable, and he was content for the moment to lie on it while the music skirled around him.

My lotus throne, he thought. *I am Lha, this is my lotus throne, and I am in the Hall of the Crimson Cloud. My hall.*

The knowledge was just there, unquestioned, no more surprising than the knowledge that he had five fingers or only one nose. Below the surface of his thoughts, the ecstasy he had felt at the completion of the Ritual still simmered and he could feel it stir in response to the music—a slow surge of fire.

He thought of the giantess he had killed, and her face was as clear to him as it would have been had he been looking directly at her. Despite his underlying joy he felt uneasy, though he had no fear that the other Lha would blame him for her death. Any true fear was far away, and he still felt some of that ecstatic certainty he had known as he drank from the skull-flower.

Remembering Night's soothing presence in his mind, he knew that certainty had not been his alone. The knowledge pleased him.

But Night had withdrawn from him and the slack face of the dead giantess would not leave his thoughts, its image tinged with a strange sense of loss, almost of mourning.

As though I'd lost someone I loved. Why?

Abruptly the music rose to an intricate and sustained crescendo, then ceased, abruptly complete. In the sudden silence, Lozan found his disinclination to move gone. He opened his eyes and sat up. Something flapped against his chest and a flash of unformed anxiety made him look down at himself.

His body was whole and unscarred, betraying no

83

signs of the treatment it had received in the Place of the Ritual. He was wearing a black kilt like those the watching giants and monsters had worn—further proof that he had been given a place among them.

Not giants, monsters. Lha. Like I am. Lha. One of the Gods.

Around his neck hung a necklace of thumb-sized pieces of turquoise on which a white disk was so strung that its sharp edge pressed against his chest. He'd felt it flap against him when he moved. The disk was ringed with alternate bands of tiny, faceted green and white gems. Lozan held it up to his face to examine it more closely.

It's different, seeing and remembering. Remembering? But this was all new to him.

No. I remember it.

As Lozan's fingers held the disk, he knew it for a circle of bone from the forehead of the dead giantess. Janesha. Her name had been Janesha. He continued to examine the disk, and all his remaining anxiety seemed to flow out of him into it, leaving him through his fingertips. When he finally let the necklace drop back to his chest, he was at peace with himself. He looked around.

It's different, seeing and remembering.

He was in a world of vivid color, sitting in the center of a huge golden-yellow flower whose marbled surface was shot through with twisting pink and green veins. The flower had at least a thousand petals radiating from its center in thick, overlapping rings. It floated on the surface of an emerald-bottomed lake, though it seemed to be polished stone.

Overhead hung a shimmering crimson mist, covering the sky without coming within a dozen meters of the ground. Through it filtered an abundance of impossible amber light, in whose rays the flower glowed. And though the air was cool, the stone surface was warm to the touch.

The Crimson Cloud.

He was thirsty. He leaned over, cupped water from

the lake, brought it to his lips and drank it. It had a faintly sweet taste.

A slender silver bridge spanned the distance to the Lake's white shore. At regular intervals along the shore were slender pillars of rose-colored crystal. Twined around each pillar was a complex lattice of interwoven vines of some scarlet-red metal. The vine's heart-shaped leaves hugged the pillars' smooth crystal surfaces.

Between the pillars, thick jungle showed—a dense mass of brown and red tree trunks, black roots, green fronds and leaves, all laced with a multitude of brightly flowering vines. But Lozan could see that it was not truly a jungle: the dense vegetation was neither choked nor tangled, but ordered and spaced in tightly patterned configurations whose final effect was of great formality.

In the trees brightly colored birds sang. The whole scene was exotic and exhilarating, yet profoundly restful. Lozan loved it.

I've got to do something with the vines. They're too passive, too boring. Memory again. But this time, he found he disagreed; he could see nothing wrong with the vines.

A path of pink quartz led from the water into the trees. Lozan decided to follow it, his awakening anticipation tinged with a vague uneasiness.

The silver bridge swayed beneath him as he crossed. In the water below tiny opalescent fish were darting.

When he reached the far shore the air was suddenly rich with the jungle's heavy scent, as though in crossing the bridge Lozan had crossed some invisible barrier holding back the forest's influence. He reached for an explanation, found none. But the explanation could come later; it was the pleasure he took in the exotic tapestry of scents that counted.

Amid the trees the air was even richer, velvet and intoxicating. A perfumed current seemed to sweep along the smooth quartz path, and Lozan allowed himself to be caught up by it. He began to run, moving as lightly as in a dream. Thick foliage closed him in on both sides. The path was a ribbon of living light winding through fertile shadow. Ahead of him he heard a bird's shrill cry. He ran.

The path curved sharply to the right, led into a small clearing. Waiting for Lozan at its center was the Lha with the two trees growing from the sides of his head.

Seeing him, Lozan knew him: Yag ta Mishraunal. The Eldest.

Chapter Seven

STANDING, YAG TA MISHRAUNAL conveyed an impression of limitless strength, of indomitable force in repose. The leaves gleamed on the branches of the two tree-like growths that grew from his head; light seemed to shine through his alabaster skin and from his large golden eyes. Though the boughs of the trees whipped back and forth in response to winds which only they felt, Yag ta Mishraunal's face was serene.

From him radiated a sense of welcome so powerful Lozan could feel it as he would have felt a breeze, or sun on his face. It warmed, enfolded him; he felt himself cherished.

Perched on the Lha's right forearm was a huge crimson hawk. The raptor's eyes were bright and fierce, but when Lozan met their gaze he knew that the hawk, too, was welcoming him in its way, with a welcome granted to him and him alone. For an instant his sight blurred and he was looking through the hawk's eyes, seeing a world divided into two separate visual fields, in one of which Lozan stood out in sharper definition than would have been possible had he been observing himself through merely human eyes. Then his vision blurred and was normal again.

The hawk lifted its head and screamed. Almost of its own accord—was this too memory?—Lozan's arm came up, caught the hawk on his wrist when it flew to him and perched, gripping him carefully with its powerful talons. He was surprised at how light it was.

"You recognize me," the Lha said.

"Yag ta Mishraunal. The Eldest. But—."

"You remember nothing else?"

"Some things, but . . . nothing about you."

"The rest of it will come back to you in time. Until then, I will serve as your teacher. Because I, too, once thought that I was a human being. Your Terran has told me about you: I was born on Nosferatu, where I was Yag Chan."

"The Pied Piper of Mig Mar." Lozan found himself unsurprised.

"Yes. Follow me, please. The hawk will accompany us."

He led the way out of the clearing and down a new path, the hawk flying above them.

I know this path. Yet every turn brought him face to face with something unexpected, something which an instant later seemed as though he'd known it all his life. He found himself nodding when the jungle abruptly ended and they emerged onto a black and green checkerboard plain, which seemed to stretch away for kilometers beneath the crimson mist. In the distance he could see statues, fountains, pools and pavilions, all of them new and surprising, all of them familiar after the first shock of recognition passed.

Yag ta Mishraunal led Lozan across the plain to a circular structure of smooth green stone surmounted by an alabaster dome in which thousands of green and white gems scintillated. A complex pattern of inlaid lines of scarlet metal swirled around the building, came together in a large, slightly concave disk of red metal which projected slightly from the green stone.

The foliate Lha stepped through the disk's seemingly solid surface. The hawk swooped low and followed him through.

After a moment's hesitation, Lozan followed. He met with no resistance, but when he reached back to feel the disk from the other side his hand encountered cool, unyielding metal.

The walls inside were covered with screens of black silk, on which purple and blue demons had been painted in glowing colors. With their fanged mouths, many arms and multiple heads they resembled the stone figures which stood guard around the Temple and Shrines.

Yag ta Mishraunal directed Lozan to a mat, seated himself facing him. Lozan sat in conscious imitation of the other's posture, cross-legged with his right ankle resting on his left thigh.

Everything was at the same time totally familiar and totally strange. It was like a dream, where you could be anyone, do anything, endure anything, because none of it was real.

The hawk drowsed on a perch beside a large crystal globe held cupped in the concave center of a circular table of twisted strands of red, gold and white wire. Within the globe a tiny landscape shone. In the foreground, a tree fashioned of jade like flowing water rose from a field of jeweled grain, its sinuous twisted branches and tiny pointed leaves all carved from a single stone. The tree was simultaneously flowering and in bud, yet hung with tiny globes of opalescent white fruit. Beneath its branches a tiny deer-like animal stood staring out over the field with eyes of amber, and each stalk of grain was composed of tiny gems—amethysts, sapphires, topazes and other, less familiar stones.

A surabha, Lozan thought. It was very beautiful. "Janesha made that?" he asked, almost remembering.

"Like everything here. How much do you really remember?"

"Remember?" He shook his head. "Things seem familiar; words pop into my mind for things I've never seen before; I catch myself thinking things I don't understand—."

"I know. It was the same way for me." The alabaster giant made a quick twisting gesture with the fingers of his right hand. Two cups of tea materialized on the table's twisted-wire rim.

Lozan found himself nodding again. That was what a surabha was for.

Yag ta Mishraunal picked up one cup, motioned for Lozan to take the other. Lozan sipped cautiously at the thick buttered tea.

"Everything I have to tell you you already know, but the knowledge may not be available to you or may not make sense to you at first. So pardon me if I make things too simple, too obvious. If anything is unclear, ask me about it. I am here to teach you, not to hear myself talk.

"You are—all of us here are—the product of a partnership between a human being and an artificial entity, a symbiote, created on the planet Nosferatu—or Rildan, as it is properly called. We call ourselves the Lha—not because we are under any delusion that we are really gods or any other sort of supernatural beings, but because it amuses us to do so—and we live here in the Refuge, which you know as the Temple."

"But I'm not like you," Lozan said, feeling a vague disquiet, an unformed dissatisfaction stir within him. "I look—like anyone else. Like everyone else."

"As we all do, before we learn to take control of our physical forms. I once looked as human as you do now; Janesha looked much like the illusory form she produced for you."

The denial was a certainty within him. He felt he had no choice but to say, "But I'm not one of you. Not a Lha. I'm a human being. Just a human being."

"No. You are no more human than I am. I examined your mind while you slept and confirmed the fact. You could not have absorbed Janesha otherwise."

"Are you examining my mind now?" He was suddenly terrified.

"No. Until you have learned to . . . safeguard yourself, any contact with one of us could be dangerous to you. For the present we will have to limit ourselves to the spoken word.''

Lozan nodded, relieved.

"We are beings who can merge their individual selves into a single greater self, which it amuses us to call the Goddess Night, as it amuses us to call ourselves the Lha. Do you understand?''

"No. . . . It sounds like I've heard it before, but that's all.''

"Do you remember—in the Place of the Ritual, the being who helped first Janesha and then you at the end?''

"That was . . . all of you together?''

"Yes. Through our partners, our symbiotes, we can merge—give up a part of our separate identities and become something greater than any one of us. Think back. Remember. Remember Night.''

The warmth. Being within, part of the—all-around-ness. The cherishing. Not lonely, not different, not afraid. . . . My own kind at last.

No. "Night helped Janesha try to kill me. I remember, I was winning, then Night came and took control of me for her. That—thing's not part of me, not the same as—.''

I don't understand. It doesn't feel right, I shouldn't be saying these things to him—but I've got to tell him that I'm not—.

Not Lha. But I am.

"Night never attempted to kill you. She lent Janesha some of her force, but it was Janesha and Janesha alone who used that force against you.''

"But that doesn't make sense! If I'm—a Lha, why'd you leave me out there for sixteen years? And then put me there so Janesha could kill me?''

"Because we were unaware of your existence . . . that someone like you even could exist outside the Refuge. At your age and your stage of development you appear human, and you yourself had no idea that you were anything else.''

91

"But if I'm part of Night—."

I don't—why am I fighting him like this? Why?

"You have the potential to merge with Night, but you are not yet part of Her. Just as Janesha had only a very limited participation in the Goddess's being at her stage of development.

"You appear human because you were born to human host-parents. No Lha can bear children, for a Lha must kill and absorb its parents to achieve birth.

"I told you you were the product of the symbiosis between a human being and an entity created on the planet Rildan. No human being can survive such a partnership unless he is born into it—and then the symbiosis modifies him so that he is no longer human.

"The entity which makes you Lha—you might think of it as a virus with a nonmaterial extension—can be transmitted like a disease. A little over sixteen years ago an error was committed which allowed the entity to spread beyond the Refuge. You know it as the Wasting Plague."

"My parents died of the Wasting Plague?" It was the first information he'd ever received about them.

"No. You killed them, as every Lha has to kill its parents to obtain the life-force it needs to survive.

"Inside the Refuge we inoculate members of the priesthood and sisterhood with the entity to ensure our own reproduction, though only very rarely do such priests and sisters survive to conceive a child, and only more rarely does the child itself survive long enough to be born. So when our records showed no children born to victims of the Wasting Plague we assumed there were none. But we are very few and children are rare among us; you will find yourself valued and cherished here."

The truth was there, still there, unmistakable in the other's voice.

But I could hear the truth in her voice when she was praying . . . and she was trying to kill me!

"Had we known you for who you are, you would never have been forced to confront Janesha in the

92

Ritual. But raised as you were by human beings, believing as you did that you were a human being, you seemed human to Janesha when she examined you. She was at a stage of her development when it was dangerous for her to have too much contact with Night; she alone examined you and she was too inexperienced to recognize you for what you are."

"I don't understand why—how she died. What I did that killed her." He found himself picturing Janesha as she'd first appeared—a slim girl with amber skin and red-black hair and eyes of melting green. He felt a strange weakness, a longing for what she had pretended to be.

"You absorbed her, as she was attempting to absorb you. The first law of our kind is that we are one self, that we cannot prey off each other. We are predators, dependent on the life-force of other sentient beings for our survival, but any Lha trying to consume another Lha is himself consumed, himself destroyed.

"Thus, trying to absorb you in violation of her Lha nature, Janesha was herself absorbed. And, though we mourn even the loss of one such as her, she alone bears the final responsibility for her fate. Though I could not take the risk of endangering you by a too prolonged or too profound contact, I examined enough of her memories in you while you slept to be sure that she suspected your true nature at the end. Yet in her need she was unable to free herself of her human selfishness and egotism, unable to accept her Lha nature, and so destroyed herself. Understand: you killed her by reflex, by instinct, by the mere fact that you were what you were. As I, at one time, killed Mishraunal—which is another reason I chose to become your teacher for a while."

"Mishraunal? Another Lha?"

"A Rilg. From Rildan. You know part of the story; Lavelle told you how we found him in the vault and brought him to the surface. He tried to absorb my mind and was himself absorbed."

Of course, I already knew that.

"So I am Lha. One of you. What does that mean?"

"To live among us you need to develop your innate powers to the point where you can control your environment—things like the surabha, for example—and participate safely in the mind of Night. Once you can do that you are free to do whatever you wish to do, as long as you do nothing to hinder or endanger any other Lha. We are all free here, free to choose our bodies, our minds, our lives."

"Free to leave?"

"Eventually, if you wish, with proper precautions to keep your presence outside the Refuge from endangering us."

"But until then I have to stay here. What else?"

"You are free to do anything you are able to do. Until you have learned to teleport yourself from hall to hall you will have to remain here, in the Hall of the Crimson Cloud—though you are, of course, free to visit my Hall if you would like—but I think you will find the room ample."

"All this?" Lozan whispered, the extent of the plain, the jungle, the emerald-bottomed lake he'd been taking for granted suddenly registering. "All this?"

"It was Janesha's. It's yours now."

Lozan had never before owned so much as the cup from which he drank his tea; the bed in which he slept had been his only by virtue of some administrative whim. Now he was being given an area far greater than all Agad, and the reality of it stunned him.

Yet—he must not allow himself to be distracted. He was still trapped here, still dependent on Yag ta Mishraunal for everything he knew about his situation . . . and something within him denied the Lha with desperate strength.

"When can I leave this Hall?"

"When your training has progressed far enough to enable you to do so."

It was as though he were once again seeing the slender girl Janesha had pretended to be, but now the girl was dead, her face slack and lifeless, her dull eyes staring, her hacked-open body black with dried blood.

"Which means what? When I've killed some other defenseless orphan for you?"

The hostility in his voice surprised him, but Yag ta Mishraunal ignored it. "No. You can leave as soon as you know how to tap Night's knowledge safely so you can use the teleportation matrices which are the only connection between the various parts of the Refuge." He paused, added, "If it's important to you I can arrange to show you the other Halls before you're ready to reach them on your own."

"You said it wouldn't be safe for me to tap Night's knowledge. Why not?"

"Because your individuality has as yet no defenses, and you would lose yourself in Night if you attempted to merge with Her. Do you remember the two Lha dressed like priests, but in colored robes, from the Place of the Ritual?"

Lozan nodded.

"They attempted to merge with Night before they were ready. They are gone now; Night alone looks out of their eyes. It was to prevent something similar happening to Janesha that we kept her from too-intimate contact with Night."

"And what do I have to do to defend myself? Learn to kill other orphans like she tried to kill me?"

"You do not understand. We must kill to survive, but we are not cruel. The Ritual is kind."

"No."

"It is kind. Have you ever seen cattle being slaughtered?"

"No."

"The more terrified a cow is before it dies, the more the hormones in its blood improve the flavor of the meat. So each cow being slaughtered is forced to witness the death of the preceding cow, and when its turn comes it is killed slowly to enhance the quality of its meat."

"You said the Ritual is kind."

"Yes. Understand, we Lha are not like human beings, choosing to eat meat when we could remain healthy on a diet of vegetables. We need the—there is no word for it, but you can think of it as the life-force of sentient creatures. The universe is itself a living thing and there is in every thinking, feeling creature something—an energy, a force—that allows that creature to draw upon the force of the universe, to take from it that living vitality which its nature allows it. It is this energy, this force, that we need, for our nature is such that unless we continually renew our supply of such force he dies in agonies inconceivable to lesser beings. But fully charged with this life-force, we can tap the basic vitality of the universe for powers and abilities that you, as you are now, cannot yet conceive."

"The Ritual."

"The Ritual is necessary—not the movements, the gestures, or any of the outward physical manifestations, but the absorption which is at its core is necessary. And, think—had you believed Janesha to be what she at first appeared to be, would you have been afraid of her? Think—how did you feel when you lay down on the altar? Were you afraid? Were you unhappy? Did you feel any regrets, frustrations, anger that your life was soon to be over?"

"No." He had not feared her. Why couldn't she have been what she'd seemed to be? "But I knew she was—that she wasn't what she pretended to be. I fought her."

"Because you were Lha. Had you been human you would have trusted her, you would never have fought."

"But the knife, the blood—. No. It's still cruel. Like torturing someone who's asleep."

"The knife, the blood—they are there for a reason. The Lha feels the pain of the Ritual, feels the pain that the human does not. The outward form of the ritual is symbolic; it gives form to the Lha's otherness from humanity. With the knife he kills his human host-parents again, declares himself other than they are.

When he drinks the blood he drinks his own blood, the blood of his own dead humanity."

"No. I can't. I won't."

"The Ritual is just a rite, a way of symbolizing a change. Long before we participate in it, we begin absorbing life-force. As you yourself long ago began absorbing human life-force."

"No. Never. I didn't."

"You did. Do you remember floating in a void filled with colored stars? Do you remember drawing them to you, making them part of you?"

"Yes," Lozan whispered. They'd been so beautiful, so—. They'd given him back his body, so many bodies. . . .

"I didn't want to hurt them. I didn't hurt them."

"You didn't hurt them. But those stars were the other orphans in the shaefi tubes around you. You yourself were in suspension and had no idea what you were doing; otherwise you could have refashioned your body and mind despite the suspension. As it was, you absorbed enough life-force to resist Janesha. To do that you had to tap a great number of minds."

"How many?" It had been so beautiful, so peaceful. So innocent.

"More than six hundred. Absorption demands close physical proximity, but in the twenty-seven years you were in your tube you were able to draw upon the infinitesimal amounts of life-force available to you from the more distant ones."

The number was too large to grasp. "I killed six hundred people," he said, trying to make sense of it.

"No. All but those closest to you are still alive. Your condition limited your power of absorption, and there is not very much life-force available from a suspended human. But you built up a large charge of life-force nonetheless; you will not need to absorb another mind for a number of years.

"In that you are lucky: normally a Lha must absorb a human life several times a year. That is the price we pay for our contact with the living vitality of the universe. But the other side of the coin is this: with an adequate supply of human life-force, we are immortal.

"Immortality, I was taught on Mig Mar, is a delusion; everything comes to an end, nothing endures forever. Perhaps. But that is a philosophy for the short-lived, for those whose lives rarely span a century, not for those of us who may live to see the stars that warm the worlds upon which we live grow cold and die.

"But I've said enough for now. Do you have any questions you'd like me to answer? I know this is hard for you."

"How much longer—until I need to, to do the Ritual?" Lozan asked.

"Not for a long time. No one will force you to make any decision you don't feel ready to make; you can wait as long as you want."

"How long?"

"Perhaps thirteen years, perhaps slightly less."

Thirteen years. He could barely remember the child he'd been thirteen years ago. It was another lifetime, beyond imagining. All he wanted to do was sleep. He said as much.

"Perhaps that would be best," Yag ta Mishraunal told him. "Lie back on your mat and allow yourself to relax. While you're sleeping I'll key you to Mishraunal's memory."

"I don't want—."

"No one will invade your mind. You will just continue to learn what you need to know to be free and take your place among us. What you already know but cannot remember yet."

Chapter Eight

VISIONS OF THE DISTANT PAST FLOWED from Yag ta Mishraunal's mind to the boy, and from his mind to hers. Furiously she fought to maintain consciousness of herself against the torrent of imagery, but she dared not let the other Lha know she was there, hiding in the depths of the boy's mind. Yag ta Mishraunal must not detect her resistance, must not learn she still lived.

It was no use. She could not fight the key memories any longer. She felt herself receding from herself, caught up in familiar sights and sounds—.

Lozan dreamed.

There was a tunnel leading through blackness and blankness to the heart of the world, and he was falling through it. Falling, he began to unravel, mind and body disintegrating, the strands of his being separating into isolated fibers until he was no longer a man, but only the potential from which one could be made.

Detached and disembodied, integrating separate viewpoints as he had once integrated his separate senses, Lozan floated above the world that was Rildan, observing:

A planet of jewel-like cities separated by wilderness, with each city a single work of art, a unified conception flowing from the natural contours of the land yet soaring out of that planet-hugging union to become a creation of pure artifice, fanciful and beautiful. Concepts and materials from myriads of worlds had contributed to the formation of something unique to Rildan, and in each city the grandiose and the fragile, the elfin and the grotesque, merged and fought, balanced and enhanced each other. The cities were as much gardens as they were creations of stone and metal and shimmering synthetics, and though this was true of all of them, yet no two were alike.

Lozan's multiple vision encompassed the world, its history visible in its present like some form meant to be glimpsed in the depths of a glass sculpture.

The Rilg were scholars, sometimes artists, a race of teachers; Rildan was the intellectual center of a vast interstellar civilization that had endured more than three hundred thousand years. Unlike the swarming, short-lived beings of most other worlds, the Rilg took little pleasure in pride and position, but lived only for the collection and synthesis of knowledge. Breeding seldom, they had never been driven to conquest by population pressures and they had little of the competitiveness of more sexually motivated species. When, after aeons of peaceful civilization on their own world, they had been motivated to seek out the stars, it had been from curiosity—mingled, perhaps, with an atavistic pleasure in flight inherited from their long-dead avian ancestors.

Empires came, fell; rulers were born, ruled, died. Rildan remained.

The Rilg were slim, tall beings who moved with quick, awkward grace. Their bodies and limbs were hidden by tight feathers, which changed color with their moods; they had four arms and two legs apiece, and the feathers on these were smaller and quicker to change color than those on their heads and bodies. Their fanged jaws, discreetly hidden behind feathered lips, were the last visible reminder of the herbivorous Rilg's distant carnivorous past.

Though the Rilg wore no clothing, each Rilg wore a double belt of jeweled metal around its waist and a similar band encircling its head. Though ornamental, they were only secondarily so: their primary function was as psychic amplifiers and transformers.

Many of the races the Rilg had studied on other planets were gifted with mental powers the more intelligent Rilg lacked: myriads of forms of telepathy, clairvoyance, levitation, direct control of energy flows, psychokinesis. The Rilg had duplicated some few such abilities by mechanical means; flight, mental control of machinery and pseudotelekinetic control of visible objects were relatively easy to attain, though the powers achieved were clumsy counterfeits compared with the natural talents of the races the Rilg were trying to imitate. But new senses were impossible in brains not designed for them, and it was new senses—with the consequent broadening of their conceptual horizons—that the Rilg craved most. All the Rilg brain seemed able to cope with was a form of mechanical telepathy in which only the speech center was stimulated, and even that required intensive training from birth.

And so the Rilg were a frustrated race. For millennia it had been clear to them that they were approaching the limits of what they could comprehend with their natural minds and senses. Their physical heritage was inadequate; mechanical aids were useless. The choice was clear: evolve or stagnate.

Lozan's multiple awareness encompassed the creation of an artificial symbiotic entity that would merge with its Rilg host to provide new sensory, manipulative and interpretive control centers. The symbiotically modified Rilg had complete control of his physical form and could modify the new neural structures in the light of experience. A side effect of this control was virtual immortality, but this was less important to the Rilg than it would have been to most other races.

Incorporating the symbiote, the Rilg took control of their evolution. Yet, as one by one they overcame their race's hereditary limitations, the thought of any kind of comprehension beyond their grasp became unbearable. When they discovered the Choskt, a race of limited intelligence but possessing a form of short-range precognition, the Rilg coveted the ability as another race might have coveted wealth, territory, or sexual merger.

The Choskt were studied until they were understood as well as they could be by a race itself lacking precognition. A Rilg was selected to be the first to evolve the new neural structures; linked with him in telepathic rapport, the massed mind of his race shared his consciousness as he brought his new sense of perception into play.

The combination of the unstable, hyperdeveloped Rilg mind and the Choskt sense of precognition was something new in the universe. Through that suddenly open channel, something—a force, a being, or something less imaginable—exploded into the linked minds.

In that instant, nine-tenths of Rildan died. Overloaded by the infinitely resonating experience of those deaths, the telepathic bond uniting the remaining Rilg burned out. Each Rilg faced the change occurring in himself as an isolated individual.

Lozan's mosaic consciousness shrank until it encompassed only a single Rilg teacher and his Offworld pupils.

Mishraunal was devoting most of his attention to his class, with only a small part of his mind on the Great Experiment, when the Change struck. An explosion of intolerable *wrongness* ripped him from himself, left his mindless body to crumple to the floor.

He lay there writhing and moaning, struggling with his fangs buried in the throat of a racial enemy extinct now for millions of years. With his four arms he tried to pull the creature only he could see from him, succeeded only in almost gnawing through one of his wrists.

Through the open window, his terrified students could see the city dying, its towers splintering and falling as the dying Rilg struck out in blind spasms of destruction.

The headless body of a Rilg floated in through the window, disappeared with a sound like metal striking metal.

Mishraunal jerked on the floor, rolling in a pool of his own blood. His feathers were colorless and matted; he whimpered as the channels of his mind were warped and fused into new patterns. His back arched in a final spasm; then it was over and he fell back, quiet now, and slept. His students gathered around him, unsure whether he was dead or alive and afraid to touch him to find out.

Mishraunal awoke to ugly twilight, though through the open window he could dimly sense Rildan's blue-white sun high in the sky. His body was a deadness, an unresponsive weight, yet each of his nerves felt as though it were being scraped across a jagged surface. And in his mind there was only silence where his fellow Rilg should have been. He was alone, cut off from the community mind for the first time since his race had taken its evolution into its own hands, and he was afraid.

He tried to heal himself but could not make his body respond. He could reconstruct the room around him from memory, then match the dim shapes he could perceive with those he recalled, but he could perceive nothing of the city outside. His attempts brought only new confusion, and more pain.

Timidly, afraid of piercing through to the thing that had hurt him so badly, he tried to break through the wall of telepathic silence that imprisoned him. He could sense nothing. He was trapped alone in his bruised and broken body.

He tried to contact his students, but even their simple minds proved beyond his reach. What little he could sense of them was garbled and incomprehensible, overlaid by a vividly hallucinated pattern of luminous spheres.

Yet he had achieved some contact, however garbled. He motioned all but one of his students—Azquan, recognizable by his bulk—away, squatted with him on the floor. Three of Mishraunal's hands were useless; he ran the fingers of the fourth over Azquan's rough features, trying to learn by touch alone that which his other senses could no longer tell him.

Keeping his fingers pressed to Azquan's concave face, Mishraunal tried to force himself into rapport with the other, but the more he tried to concentrate his awareness on Azquan, the more the image of a sphere of violet fire interfered with his perceptions.

He tried to ignore the hallucination, but the more he tried, the larger, the more intrusive the sphere became. Without warning it rushed at him and exploded.

Mishraunal found himself within Azquan's mind, experiencing it with an intimacy and intensity beyond anything he'd ever known before. Then the other's mind faded and he was in a sea of caressing violet, washed clean of fear and pain. Floating all around him were bobbing balls of colored light and in his newfound delight he drew them to him, rejoicing as each in turn exploded and altered the texture and taste of the sea in which he swam.

At last he was lost in a flood of multicolored ecstasy, tasting colors which crawled through his body and transformed him into a creature of shimmering rainbow. He basked and pulsed in the heart of a liquid sun, and time had no meaning for him.

I've pierced to the heart of the universe, he realized. *Through all the surfaces, all the appearances. And the universe is alive and I'm part of it, part of its life. I'm alive.*

When time again resumed its passage he was no longer the being he had been before. The room around him still blazed with a splendor he himself seemd to radiate, but elsewhere the blinding light had given way to a clarity in which his perceptions functioned as never before. Myriads of senses he had never before been able to distinguish from one another were coming

104

into play; everything he perceived seemed to caress him, yet it would have been the work of an instant to count the grains of sand on a beach on the far side of the planet.

He searched Rildan for other survivors. Some of the Rilg were dying, others were still caught in the agony of the Change; but most of the survivors were as he had been—prisoned by mismatched senses and walls of telepathic silence. Not even his newly augmented abilities could pierce the walls separating them. He felt their pain and despair as if it were his own but could not make them feel his presence.

Then, in cities on the far side of the planet, Mishraunal touched nine minds already brilliant with the same rainbow vitality that animated him. The ten merged, lost themselves in a bliss that would have been inconceivable to the being he had so recently been.

Another mind broke through to ecstatic transformation, reached out in search of others. The tenfold individual that Mishraunal had become encompassed it, merged with it, made it a part of itself.

When at last the eleven separated again, each contained within himself the being formed of their union, each knew that he could merge with the others at any time.

All over Rildan dulled minds were beginning to surge with new splendor as the Rilg found or were taught the key to transfiguration. Sitting surrounded by the dead bodies of his former pupils, Mishraunal was bathed by wave after wave of transcendent joy. He realized that it had been their deaths which had triggered his transformation; their memories were his now, their lives a muted song in the back of his consciousness. To the Mishraunal he had been, the knowledge would have been horrifying; but to the being he had become, that knew itself part of the living essence of the universe itself, the deaths of any number of non-Rilg seemed small enough price to pay for the rebirth and transformation of his race.

For the birth of a new Rilg, a Rilg who could tap, who could manifest, who could merge with the living essence that was the Universal Core, the wellspring of Creation.

Mishraunal's triumph faded. There was only sensationless void, without anticipation, without impatience, without memory. Another consciousness impinged on Lozan's awareness. He extended to it, sank into it, was lost in it.

The mind he had merged with knew itself to be Mishraunal, but it was not the same mind Lozan had entered before. For this Mishraunal, nine thousand of Rildan's long years had passed, and in that time the Rilg's mind and body had both changed almost beyond recognition.

Mishraunal was completing the absorption of another being and his thoughts were suffused with ecstasy. Over the millennia his capacity to control his mental processes had evolved to the point where he could now absorb a mind without any loss of self-control or consciousness of the external world.

He was concentrating on his body.

His external form was similar to that of nine thousand years before, but he was no longer muffled in feathers. Soft yellow scales covered him, each scale a complex synesthetic sense receptor. The whole surface of his body comprised a single multiplex sense organ. Though he could have apprehended his environment perfectly well without any bodily sense receptors, he preferred to keep his sensory mosaic as rich and varied as possible.

Internally the changes were more radical. Most of his internal organs had been dispensed with: when each individual cell can be supplied with nutrients and drained of wastes by teleportion, blood, a circulatory system, lungs and viscera all become unnecessary. Mishraunal's abdominal cavity was filled with neural tissue, but even this was different: the bulky, inefficient nerve cells with which his race had had to make do for most of its history were gone, replaced with compact substitutes that increased his neural capacity a thousandfold.

The body of the Aol whose mind he'd just absorbed floated in the air in front of him, slowly collapsing in on itself as he emptied it of the substance he needed to complete the slavebrain he was growing around a core of his own nervous tissue.

The thoughts of his race murmured in his mind as he worked:

. . . Deviants, frozen in some sort of temporal stasis at the moment of Change . . .

. . . impossibility of proving the universe sentient in itself, but failed to take into consideration . . .

. . . with highly developed paraphysical abilities, though their lack of mechanical technology has limited them to the surface of their planet. They have accepted my presence but still seem suspicious of . . .

. . . limiting factor intrinsic to all purely projective teleportion; unless the teleport can attune himself to a proper receptive matrix no amount of projective force can . . .

. . . have refused our offer to end their agonies. They seem to have gained some mastery of the Choskt modalities still beyond our grasp, and if the modified symbiote enables them to break free of the Change it seems almost certain that we will have found the bridge which has so long evaded us to the trans-temporality which the Choskt and Ashlu modalities imply. . . .

The slavebrain was structurally complete, a smooth gray sphere floating in the air in front of Mishraunal. He allowed what remained of the Aol to vaporize, fed vitality into the slavebrain's waiting tissues.

. . . flickering in and out of the present in their attempts to evade the modified symbiote, but their limited temporal control makes it statistically certain that. . . .

Mishraunal was programming the slavebrain for study of the mildly interesting Aol culture when he became aware of a change in the telepathic background murmur. Thoughts were coming in to him blurred with a shifting distortion—a distortion faint at first but growing worse even as he became aware of it, as though the thoughts he was receiving were vibrating slightly out of phase with themselves. The vibration was not a constant thing; it changed, shifting from thought to thought and mind to mind, accelerating and decelerating, expanding and contracting, but growing, growing all the while, intensifying, becoming ever more pervasive as it took up residence in his mind and body—an agony that shook his very cells until he thought he would be reduced, cell by cell, to a smear of yellow-gray jelly. Yet there was nothing he could do.

And he was only participating secondhand in the agonies of others. The vibration crawled through the network of thought linking Rilg to Rilg like a living thing, and wherever it touched a mind flared up, screamed, then faded as it died.

An infinite number of vibrations were crawling from mind to mind, and in their wake those minds that had escaped direct contact with them found time altering and fragmenting, so that a single thought came to them both rapidly and slowly, or at innumerable different rates simultaneously. Meaning was lost in anticipatory and echoing superpositions and resonances. Each mind found itself experiencing its existence at a rate shared with no other mind, and that rate was not constant but shifting.

Mishraunal was burning, being eaten away by acid, shattered and shredded and pulled apart as hundreds of millions of Rilg in whose minds he shared went down into death. Yet even as he felt their agony as though it were his own, another part of him was greedily drinking in their liberated life-force; he was gorging himself, bloating his spirit on life-force until he feared his mind would burn itself out from the para-doxical overload, and he had no control over the part of him that was doing this.

Then the searing vibration and resonating deaths

108

were gone as though they had never been. There was only the ecstasy brought on by Mishraunal's absorption of so much life-force and it was so intense it terrified him, yet he could not stand against it and he was swept away.

Finally that, too, dissipated and he was left with his loss and confusion. For some reason, he seemed to have come out of his ecstasy before the other survivors and for the moment he was alone.

Had this been some nine-thousand-year delayed aftermath of the Change, perhaps brought on by their attempts to integrate the Deviants back into the racial mind? Had some unwary Rilg made contact with some unsuspected new kind of lethal alien mental structure?

Mishraunal's newly programmed slavebrain lay at his feet, burnt out. All the slavebrains were burnt out. There was silence where before billions of telepathic recognition patterns had competed for attention.

Mishraunal could sense the other survivors mastering their ecstasies. His mind reached out to theirs and he entered into a strange rapport, in which each Rilg's anger and fear met and resonated with the fury in the minds of his fellows, becoming colder, more implacable, sinking so deeply into the shared substructure of their racial mind that their hatred of whatever had done this to them became as basic to them as their lust for knowledge and their need to absorb other minds. And underneath, the anger, the ecstasy, linking them, lending its strength to their fury.

To their linked minds came a whisper of thought, a soft, loathsome projection, so weak that the Rilg had to strain to apprehend it . . . but they knew its very weakness to be an alien mockery, for they could sense that it was coming to them from an infinite distance and that at its origin it was powerful beyond belief.

We greet you as kin, the alien voice whispered, *though it is not a kinship of which we are proud. We are the Votrassandra, the Time Binders; those whom you knew as Deviants before your efforts to force them*

109

into your image created us at the sacrifice of so many of your own lives.

As the Deviants we were, we chose to endure the Change, rather than repudiate all that was good in us and live as parasites and predators. We could do nothing to halt what you were doing; we had not the power. Now you have given us that power and we have used it.

Nowhere in the universe but on Rildan do any Rilg survive. We have destroyed your off-planet teleportation matrices and placed a barrier around Rildan. It will destroy any Rilg attempting to penetrate it, yet is harmless to all other life forms.

Those sentient beings you held captive have been taken from you. For fresh victims you will have to rely on whomever you can entice to visit you, for the barrier will keep you from going to them.

Yet it is not our intention merely to condemn you to a lingering death. Had we wished only your destruction you would already be dead. Instead we offer you an alternative.

The Rilg were once a noble race; somewhere within you the potential for that nobility still survives. Become somehow other than you are—become something other than Rilg—and the barrier will be no barrier to you.

If this seems impossible, consider: the potential to become Votrassandra lies within you, for like you we are products of the Change. So we offer you the chance to become as we are, and survive. As Votrassandra you will be free to leave Rildan, free of the need to absorb other minds, and endowed with understanding and powers beyond your present comprehension.

But the transformation from Rilg to Votrassandra must be undertaken willingly. Should you resist once the transformation is in progress, you will be torn apart by your own misguided strength. We will not deceive you; the transformation is perilous and not all who undertake it will survive.

110

We have seeded Rildan with our adapted symbiote. You need merely desire the transformation and our symbiote will merge with you.

We will not interfere with you again. Should you reject our offer, you are free to devise a transformation of your own. But you must change or die.

The whisper was gone. In cold deliberation the Rilg began to test its assertions.

No barrier was apparent to their senses, but when the first Rilg tried to levitate free of the planet he died in the same agony that had killed the others.

Another Rilg levitated to a height just below that at which the first had died, and teleported himself as far from Rildan as was possible without a teleportion matrix to receive him. He, too, died; the Rilg recovered the bodies and studied them, but learned nothing.

Slavebrains were constructed and attempts made to pass them through the barrier. They died. The Rilg tried to focus their energies beyond the barrier to create a slavebrain that would not have to penetrate it. They failed.

Attempts to devise mechanical means to take prisoners or life-force from other worlds and bring them back to Rildan failed.

Individual Rilg were already suffering from life-force deprivation, Mishraunal among them. The few animals remaining on Rildan were collected and drained of their minuscule charges of life-force.

A Rilg attempted the Votrassandra transformation. Mishraunal shared his growing horror as he became alien to himself, could only agree when he decided it was better to die than to suffer the loss of everything he valued in himself. The Rilg resisted the transformation.

His death was a prolonged torture to which the other Rilg eventually had to shut their minds.

The Rilg were not cowards. A second, a third, Rilg attempted the transformation, with identical results.

Investigation proved that any attempt to alter their

basic nature would produce the same result. The Votrassandra alternative was no alternative.

Shaefi tubes sufficient to house the entire race were constructed. When an individual Rilg found the agony of life-force starvation unendurable, he entered suspension, there to await whatever solution the race might devise.

Attempts to devise mechanical replacements for the system of sixty-four linked slavebrains which were at the core of their teleportion matrices failed. Attempts to find and contact other teleporting races elsewhere in the universe failed.

The Rilg did not accept defeat. If the barrier prevented them from making contact with the outside universe, it did not prevent that universe from contacting them. With shaefi suspension, they could wait. A plan was devised. Work began.

Mishraunal took little part in it. His life-force exhausted, he had taken refuge in one of the brightly lit suspension vaults. There he floated in an indestructible tube filled with thick orange gas, his body paralyzed but his mind free to follow the work of his race.

Rildan became a trap. The Rilg symbiote was modified to transmit itself like a disease, and Rildan was seeded with it. Any being walking unprotected on the surface would be infected with it, and the result for those who survived the infection would be a being equivalent to the Rilg, yet of a different race. Different enough, the Rilg believed, so that to it the barrier would be no barrier. Yet all such beings would share in the Rilg's group mind and through the help of such beings the Rilg could win free of Rildan.

The bait for the trap was knowledge. On a billion worlds Rildan had been known as the universe's greatest repository of knowledge; on far fewer worlds had it ever been known that the Rilg now lived by the deaths of other intelligent beings, and on none of those worlds were the reasons behind that fact understood. In time there were sure to be visitors, investigators who would ignore the vague warnings of legend and concentrate on the rewards those same legends promised.

Though the Rilg would be in suspension, their group mind would still be active.

It was not a plan they would have chosen had there been other alternatives available, but every other alternative they had been able to conceive had been tried, and had failed.

Before entering suspension, the Rilg altered their outward semblances, each taking on the appearance of a member of some alien race the Rilg had once contacted. If the vaults were opened by members of a race hostile to the Rilg, they would find, not Rilg, but members of many races, and perhaps their own. They might revive what they thought to be a member of their own race.

Mishraunal emerged from suspension long enough to take the form of a brown-skinned biped with only two arms. He was in acute pain and thankful to return to his tube.

Hungrily, yet with infinite patience, the Rilg awaited release.

Ages passed. A few aliens arrived, sickened and died, or departed and were lost to the Rilg mind. Not even shaefi suspension could totally halt the Rilg's expenditure of life-force; over the aeons their racial consciousness faded until the Rilg slept, millions upon millions of them in their separate tubes.

Blackness. Drifting. A slow coming together of things which had been separated. Two minds returning to consciousness of themselves.

Chapter Nine

SHE WAS CALMER NOW, WITH A CALMNESS she'd forced on herself. Even before she'd been caught up in the memory sequences, she'd seen the futility, the danger in her senseless attempts to turn the boy against Yag ta Mishraunal. No, not altogether senseless—she'd needed that reassurance of her own potency, her own reality. But that kind of reassurance was a luxury she could no longer afford.

Though would Yag ta Mishraunal really have detected her if she'd continued? He still thought as a Rilg—the memory sequence had reminded her of that—and would any Rilg have done what she was about to do? No, and it was on that alone that she based her hopes. She must not be suspected until the boy's body was hers.

It was a pity she'd have to destroy him; the thought of killing any Lha, even one who had never merged with her in Night, horrified her. But what choice did she have?

None. What she'd done had been an accident, a mistake. Certainly they'd known that. How dare they condemn her? How could Yag ta Mishraunal denounce her as he had when he had approved her selection of the boy? When he himself had absorbed Mishraunal?

Once she had a body of her own again, she could break through this silence, merge with the others again. Then they would understand, then they'd have to admit she was still one of them, still Lha, as much Night as they were. They'd have to take her back.

But if she failed and the boy survived? Would he call himself Lozan ta Janesha and remember her with nostalgic regret, even with love?

No! She fought down the panic she could not afford. There was nothing to fear. She would succeed.

But she could feel her will wavering. She was beginning to identify with him. How much longer could she maintain her identity?

She knew it had begun. One by one, her memories were slipping from her. Only a few so far, and those inconsequential, but with every loss she felt herself dwindle, her strength diminish.

How could she be sure? Would she even know if she lost some vital memory, some bit of information that would give her plan away? How could she be sure?

She could wait no longer. She began.

Slowly, far too slowly, she established a network of subtle controls in the boy's mind. She worked with precision, stealthily, using minimal energies; but even so she knew her work would never stand close scrutiny.

When she had done all she dared do with the boy, she turned her attention to the hawk, damping the sudden influx of energy and strength she felt when its brain became hers again. Too much joy could give her away as easily as too much fear.

At last the hawk was ready, though she hoped she would never need to use it. There was nothing more to be done until Yag ta Mishraunal left the boy alone. Reluctantly she allowed her awareness to go unfocused, conserving her dwindling energies.

Yag ta Mishraunal and Lozan were walking across the green and black plain, wandering from pool to pavilion, pavilion to statue, statue to building. Occasionally the Lha would point out something of interest, but for the most part they walked in silence. Lozan's thoughts were elsewhere, fascinated by the searing brightness that had been Mishraunal, in comparison with which his own thoughts were so stunted and insignificant that they hardly seemed worth thinking.

Mishraunal, the Lha—all of them—they're so much more, more alive than human beings. More different than Sren is from a cow, even an insect. And they don't die. I won't die. Human beings, people, everything else dies. That's why they need their religion. So they can believe they'll be reborn.

I won't have to die. I won't ever have to die. I can be like Mishraunal and I won't ever have to die.

The hawk flew above them, only appearing for brief instants when it dipped from cloud into the clear air beneath.

So bright. Like a fire. How could I ever be like that? He tried to shake free of his paralyzing sense of his own insignificance. *Think like a Lha,* he told himself.

The hawk caught his eye suddenly, and he remembered: . . . *fashioning it from my own substance, letting life flow into it until it was as much myself as I was, then flying free in the clouds, swooping and soaring with joy, liberated for the first time from all my human heritage and limitations. . . .*

"The hawk—," he asked as it disappeared back into the crimson cloud, "It was part of Janesha, wasn't it?"

"Yes. She shaped it from her own flesh, gave it her own life. It remains a part of her. Now that you've absorbed her it is a part of you, as she is a part of you. When you regain your memories you'll understand how to take its identity."

"Would I be—just a passenger, or would I be in control?"

"The hawk's body would be as much yours as the body you now inhabit. More—you have not yet really learned to control even your own body."

"When can I—become it?"

"When you've assimilated enough of Janesha's memories. Do you remember any more yet?"

"A little. The dream helped some and I keep re-membering fragments, but—nothing important. Just flashes, little things."

"Then you're not yet ready. But it shouldn't take you too much longer."

They'd been walking for hours without pause, but Lozan was neither hungry nor thirsty. His steps were as effortless as though gravity had lost its hold on him, yet he was intensely aware of the smooth cool pressure of the plain against the soles of his feet. The crisp air, rich with the scent of the distant jungle, brushed his skin, clearing, defining the interface between himself and his environment.

Mishraunal's memories were still settling into place among his own, slowly becoming less awesome, more accessible. Lozan was beginning to fit the formless intuitions he had always felt into the Rilg's perceptive structure, and the more he assimilated of these new modes of structuring his perceptions the more he became aware of the meaningfulness of sensations he had always ignored or rejected. Slowly, with faltering steps, he was coming to grasp a whole new way of apprehending the world around him.

"Had I told you yesterday," Yag ta Mishraunal was saying, "that we were a race at war, a race in hiding, you would not have been able to understand that it is for this reason that we must be—you must be—free to discover for yourself your own way of doing things. We are still a young race, and our future lies not in any premature attempt to fit ourselves into some preor-dained mold but in the exploration of our unknown potential. We do not yet know our limits, whatever they may be; we have not yet discovered our unique strengths. Ultimately, none of us can dictate to you how you should use your abilities, for we are still ignorant of their true nature. But, remember, we have enemies."

"The Votrassandra."

"And the Terran Hegemony. A child can be destroyed by something that a mature adult would only laugh at."

"The Temple. Here, the Refuge. Lavelle told me that human beings would never build anything like it. That's why he suspects you're here, suspects you stole the children from Mig Mar."

"Then Lavelle is a fool. Human beings could have built the structure that the Refuge appears to be from the exterior. Even his own computers tell him as much."

"Yet he still suspects you. He told me the story of the Pied Piper of Mig Mar, how you stole the children—."

"And thought his feeble mind-block would keep you from revealing his secret."

"No, what I want to know is—you were Yag Chan and that was Mishraunal in the tube? Then why did Mishraunal try to absorb you? Even if you weren't a Rilg?"

"He had been too long in suspension. Like all the Rilg. He was too close to death, unable to perceive the differences between myself and my human companions—no easy thing to perceive, for I myself thought I was a human being.

"So he died, as Janesha died. But three million years of shaefi suspension had dissipated his energies to a point where he did not know what he was doing. I honor his memory, as I honor him within me."

"But Lavelle suspects you're here," Lozan said. "Even if he shouldn't."

"True. They've discovered Nal-K'am, but they do not yet know what it is they've discovered; and though they suspect us, they don't know enough to know what it is they should truly suspect. I told you earlier that the Refuge is the Temple. That is not strictly true—we are far beneath the Temple, buried where they will never find us. The Temple itself is an elaborate sham."

"Lavelle asked me if the priests were human."

"The priests *are* human, without exception. The symbiote with which some of them have been inoculated is indetectable until it begins to kill its host; its material extension masquerades as an unexceptional protein molecule. And since the coming of the Terrans, all host priests have been taken here, inside the Refuge, where the Offworlders will never discover them."

They sat down by a small pool. Facing them from the opposite shore was an iridescent blue statue of a standing Rilg with outstretched arms.

Blue. The color of joyous creation.

The statue had been fashioned from something that resembled feathers as much as it resembled stone or metal, and as the breeze played over it it sang with a voice like hundreds of tiny flutes.

On the bottom of the pool, transparent crustaceans endlessly stalked tiny red fish. The fish always escaped. Lozan wondered what the crustaceans ate, since they obviously couldn't live on a diet of uncaught fish. Beside him, Yag ta Mishraunal sat perfectly motionless, staring into the pool as though fascinated by the perpetually unsuccessful hunt.

Yesterday Lozan had been consumed by hatred and suspicion; today he felt a trust for Yag ta Mishraunal that he had never before felt for any being. The trust he could understand, accept; it was the previous day's suspicion, the lack of any transition, that worried him. He was changing rapidly; he knew that. But could a day's growth render the previous day's feelings so alien that they were incomprehensible?

Was it because I knew he approved Janesha's choice of me for the Ritual? But even as he asked himself the question, he knew he'd have to look elsewhere for his answer. It would have been sufficient reason, perhaps, but he knew it had not been his reason.

Then why the hatred, the suspicion? Why couldn't he remember?

He focused all his new-found perceptive abilities on

the alabaster Lha, alert for any betraying tension, any wrongness that might lurk behind the other's tranquil facade, but there was nothing, no sign that Yag ta Mishraunal was anything but what he appeared and claimed to be—or, indeed, than Lozan wanted him to be.

But isn't that what I expected? What I already knew?

And he did know. Novice though he might be in the use of his mental abilities, he knew he was not deceiving himself.

Maybe I distrusted him because I didn't dare admit I needed what he was offering me.

He realized Yag ta Mishraunal's attention was on him.

"Dorjii—," he began, found he couldn't continue. He moistened his lips, tried again. What could Dorjii mean to him here, now? "At the orphanage I had a friend. His name was Dorjii and—he was my friend. But he was Lavelle's friend, too."

"You forget that I've been in your mind. I know about Dorjii—though I'm glad you decided to tell me. It shows you're beginning to trust me.

"But there's no need to worry: the Refuge's walls will block any attempt Dorjii might make to signal Lavelle or anyone else outside, and there's nowhere else he could learn anything dangerous to us."

"I wasn't worried about us—not just about us. I was worried about him, too. He was chosen for the Temple; I heard a priest tell him he was. I think he was meant for the Ritual. I don't want him killed. Can you save him? For me?"

"Certainly, if he's still alive . . . and if he really was meant for the Ritual. We can arrange to have him conditioned to forget anything he may have experienced here and release him, even send him as a special envoy of the priesthood's to other planets, if you'd like. I know how you both wanted to escape Nal-K'am.

"But, Lozan, have you forgotten that it's been

twenty-seven years since your Naming Day? If Dorjii was taken for the Ritual, he may have played his part in it long ago."

Twenty-seven years. Such a short time for Mishraunal but . . . so long. Twenty-seven years. He could be old already.

"And, if he is still alive and was destined for the Ritual, there's something you should consider. We Lha channel our human sexual heritage into absorption and thus we usually absorb humans of the opposite sex. Janesha chose you, you would choose a girl, and so on. But that's more custom than necessity. If you were to absorb your friend's mind, you'd be granting him the only rebirth possible for a human: rebirth as part of yourself. That way you could keep him with you always, as I'll always have Mishraunal with me."

"No." He found he was shaking his head. "Not Dorjii."

"As you realize more of your Lha nature, you may change your mind."

"No." He couldn't bear to have Dorjii there inside him, accusing him, blaming him. "Not like it was with Janesha. I couldn't."

"That was because you were Lha."

Lozan changed the subject. "You said the Rilg are still on Rildan. Why haven't you rescued them?"

"Fear. Not only are there still humans there, but the Votrassandra might learn of our existence."

"Mishraunal was revived without alerting them."

"As far as we know . . . but he never attempted to leave Rildan. I left Rildan, and I wasn't Rilg. Even now, we try to make sure we never become too like the Rilg, for until we understand how the Votrassandra defeated the Rilg we dare not face them."

"Yet you do plan to rescue the Rilg someday?"

"Of course. Our matrix needs only to be activated to connect the Refuge with Rildan, and the human population of Nal-K'am is already almost numerous enough to satisfy the Rilg's immediate needs."

They wouldn't really die, not exactly; they'd be like Mishraunal and Janesha. Part of us. It's not the same.

If it's not the same, then why do I feel the way I do about Dorjii?

"We know more about the Votrassandra than the Rilg did—we know they used the energies of time itself, though we do not yet understand how to do so ourselves—but we dare not try to confront them yet. We are the result of the union of two races, we have powers and potentials denied both our progenitors, but we are still in our racial infancy. Already we know that some MigMartian techniques work better for us than those the Rilg used—we can make use of mudras, gestures that focus and direct our nervous energies, in ways the Rilg could never have done, for example— but we do not yet know enough to do more than attempt to take from the two sciences what we can best use. In time we will create a science of our own, and it will be far beyond that of either the Rilg or the MigMartians. Until then, we must remain hidden."

Yag ta Mishraunal stood. Lozan followed him across the green and black plain.

Walking, Lozan found his sense of identity changing. Only a short while before he'd felt himself extraordinarily solid, but now, as he used his new sense of perception to observe his own body, he realized that his skin was only a bag filled with muscles, bones, organs and fluids. How could you speak of a body as though it were one solid thing (and that thing him) when he was so many different things—a beating heart; kilometers of veins, arteries, capillaries; ducted and ductless glands, each different; coiled intestines; a brain itself composed of innumerable individual cells? He realized that what he really was was a rather large and amorphous entity like an ethereal jellyfish or a giant cell in the center of which his organs hung suspended, that part of him within his skin being only the cell nucleus, but his consciousness encompassing the cell as a whole.

Intrigued, he studied himself, looking within and

beginning to learn the patterns and rhythms of his body. His nervous system fascinated him and he followed various nervous impulses from their sites of origin to their ultimate destinations in his brain. After a while, it occurred to him to try to discover the origin of his sense of perception itself. In this he failed; parts of his cortex would be excited as though stimulated by trains of nervous impulses, but there were no impulses he could detect. He gave up and went back to studying the more comprehensible workings of his brain and body.

Some hours later he sighted a structure of curving white stone and shimmering translucent forms. As he and Yag ta Mishraunal approached it, Lozan could make out tapering pillars rising to varying heights, each topped with a shimmering globe. Spiraling ramps emerged from tunnel mouths and coiled around slender columns. Glistening translucent forms hung unsupported in the air.

Closer still, he began to notice brilliantly colored specks darting around in the translucence. Curious, he tried to focus his new senses on them.

At first the lack of a clear visual image he could use to focus his other senses left him unable to organize his impressions, but he persisted until he found the logic. The specks' identity became obvious: they were fish, and the translucent substance was water.

"What keeps the water like that?" he asked.

"The fish."

"The fish?"

"Of course. They're no more natural creations than the hawk is; when Janesha created them she gave them the ability to maintain the water in the shapes she wished to retain."

"When can I try the hawk?"

"Tomorrow, if you do well with the fish."

The floor of the structure was a network of tiny pools, all housing fish. The fish were of all shapes and colors, alike only in the eccentric brilliance of their coloration.

"Their minds are very simple," Yag ta Mishraunal said. "It should be both simple and safe for you to merge with them."

"Safe? You never mentioned any danger."

"Sit down, there, where you can look into that pool." Lozan sat. "Do you remember the two Lha dressed like priests?"

"Yes."

"I told you their identities were obliterated by premature contact with the Goddess. Night is more than the sum of those portions of our minds we contribute to Her being; She is alive, with a mind and will of Her own. The two you saw, and others you did not see, tried to open themselves to the full force of Her before they were strong enough to maintain their individuality while merged with Her. Now She alone animates their bodies."

"This could happen to me?"

"Easily. You were lucky your mind was not more sensitive to Her when you absorbed Janesha. Had you been more open you would have been lost.

"But now that you are learning to open your mind a bit more, any direct contact with Her—or even with another Lha in rapport with Her—could be fatal to you. So I have blocked your telepathic channels. Only my mind is open to you, and that only in a very limited, and hence safe, way."

I must have sensed him blocking me off, Lozan thought. *Closing me in. That's what felt wrong to me about him.*

He felt himself relaxing.

"I don't like having to be protected," he said. "Like a child. Can you teach me how to do what has to be done myself?"

"Soon. I'll give you some of the basic techniques today and the rest will come to you when you assimilate Janesha's memories."

"When will that be?"

"Soon. The fish and then the hawk will help. How soon, I can't tell you exactly; no Lha has ever absorbed another Lha before. But when I absorbed Mishraunal the shock knocked me unconscious for a while, but I had most of his memories assimilated by the time I recovered."

"It's taking me longer."

"I had already been trained as a MigMartian adept. One of the Bon-po—not a follower of the Vajrayana, but it probably helped.

"Now, for your training. As a Lha you have a mind which is partially independent of your physical brain. You must learn to foster and make use of that independence. Think of your symbiote as an immaterial second brain into which you can transfer yourself, or as a body with no characteristics which you cannot change at will. By operating from within your symbiote, you can reach back and modify the structures of your physical brain."

"Show me how."

"You are already doing it a little. But since you have not yet modified your material brain to conform to the Rilg model you cannot yet interpret your new perceptions except as extensions of your old senses. You will learn to change this, but it is a slow process.

"Now. Concentrate on what you are. You are not your body. You are not your brain. Everything you are—your feelings, thoughts, memories, sensations—can be concentrated into a single point. Yes. Now move this point out of your brain into other parts of your body, then out of your body altogether. There is nothing to fear; you can always return to your body, and enough of you will always remain behind to keep it alive. Now let the point you have become float just above your head. Good. Ease yourself back into your brain. Allow yourself to take up residence in your body again.

"Feel that body. Make yourself aware of it as a whole, make yourself conscious of your whole nervous system. Concentrate on your arms. Hold them out in front of you and concentrate on what holding them that way does to your entire nervous system, to the total patterning of your energies. Do you have it? Then cross your arms in front of you with the left arm over the right. Concentrate. Can you perceive the pattern? Now cross your arms with the right over the left. Can you perceive the difference? Good.

"We can use those differences, those patterned energies, in ways the Rilg never seemed to understand. We call that use mudra, after something the adepts on Mig Mar do which is somewhat similar.

"Now, remain sitting as you are, but clench your fists—not too tightly—and cross your arms, right over left. Keep your eyes open and stare into the pool. Do you see that fish near the center, the red and purple one with the long golden fins? Study it carefully with your eyes and mind, then close your eyes and with its image still clear to you reach out for it with your other senses—."

Lozan's visualization of the fish gradually clarified. He was not sure whether Yag ta Mishraunal was helping him or not, but as he concentrated he began to sense the play of the muscles beneath the fish's bright skin, began to comprehend the workings of the organs those muscles sheathed. At last he was aware of each bone, organ, gland; he knew when a neuron fired and a blood cell died.

". . . concentrate on the nervous system. Participate in the impulses flowing from the eyes to the brain, from the swim bladder, from the lateral lines running along your sides. . . ."

For an instant he felt the touch of Yag ta Mishraunal's mind.

"Try to attune yourself to the rhythm of the impulses. Identify yourself with the fish's perceptual field. Now concentrate yourself in a single point again and move this point into the fish's brain. Allow yourself to expand into the fish. . . ."

Lozan translated the impulses he felt in his swim bladder into comprehensible terms, became aware of the pressure of the water surrounding him, the clicking sounds the other fish in the pool were making. The sounds seemed to come from within him and to reverberate throughout his entire body.

He concentrated on the organs of his skin and became aware of movements and vibrations, of smells and tastes—the total feeling of the water in which he was swimming. Then at last he managed to identify himself with the whole and *was* the fish, straining water through red gills, flexing tail and fins—.

Abruptly he found himself sitting on the edge of the pool, feeling a twinge of dull excitement. He opened his eyes and saw the red and purple fish floating belly up, its long golden fins trailing dispiritedly behind it. He looked at Yag ta Mishraunal.

"As you can see, contact with other minds can be dangerous."

"What happened?"

"You absorbed its mind. Had you been in contact with another Lha when the reflex was triggered, you would have been consumed. As Janesha was consumed.

"Now try the same thing with another fish, but terminate your contact with it before you kill it."

The surfaces of three pools were littered with dead fish before Lozan mastered the technique of leaving a fish's mind without absorbing it. He became a moon-shaped fish with protruding eyes and an underslung jaw filled with jagged teeth, swimming around near the bottom of a deep pool.

His field of vision was much wider than it had been in his human body, so extensive that only a sixty-degree cone of space behind him was hidden from him. Colors were very bright and subtly different; he could only see a short distance in any direction before his vision blurred. The entire surface of his body could smell/taste the water, and as he adjusted to his new sensory mosaic he found his sense conveyed more important information to him than did his vision. Deep within himself he could hear the other fish feeding, and

127

though they were too distant for him to locate them visually, he was able to approximate their position—just below the surface and to the far side of the pool—from the movements he sensed in the water around him. He was having no trouble adjusting to his altered senses.

He ignored the other fish, content for the moment to remain near the bottom, darting back and forth or drifting motionless feeling and smelling and tasting the water. It was like flying, effortless, free from gravity, yet he was more intimately in contact with his environment than any burrowing animal could have been with the soil, more a part of the world around him than he had ever been in his human body.

Abruptly he sensed traces of blood and flesh drifting down like fine silt from the fish feeding on the bodies of the fish his earlier efforts had killed. His fish-brain reacted instinctively, the smell and taste overwhelming his rationality instantly, driving everything but the hunger from his mind. He rushed to the surface.

There he found the body of a small silver yellow fish being torn apart by fish smaller than himself. At his approach the smaller predators scattered, hanging in the water, watching him from a safe distance as his powerful jaws ripped at the dead fish's sides and belly. Occasionally one or more of the smaller fish would dart in and snatch morsels of food that escaped him. He ignored the small fish but kept alert for any fish large enough to dispute his claim to the carcass.

All at once he was satisfied. Freed of his hunger, he found himself swimming back to the bottom, rational once more.

I lost control, he realized, and tried to detach his consciousness from that of the fish. He could not pull free. Regretfully, he absorbed his host's mind.

"I couldn't maintain my identity," he admitted.

"I didn't expect you to be able to, not yet." Yag ta Mishraunal pointed to a crystalline-appearing torus which glistened in the air above them. "Do you see that fish, the one with the green fins and red eyes? I want you to enter its mind, only this time I want you to maintain some consciousness of your own body while you're in the fish's mind. I'll maintain the torus if you find it necessary to absorb its mind, though I hope you'll be able to restrain yourself."

Chapter Ten

NINE HOURS LATER YAG TA MISHRAUNAL took Lozan to the Place of Remembrance and left him there.

"I've closed the channels linking us so I can merge with Night." The Lha's voice sounded flat and expressionless. "I'll reopen them when I return. If you keep to the sequence of visualizations and mudras with which we've programmed you, you should have no trouble. Should you finish before I return, you might want to work with some of the electrical fish; I think they can teach you something more about expanding your perceptual mosaics.

"I'll have the hawk ready for the next stage in your instruction when I return," he finished, and stepped into the wall.

Lozan was alone in the silent, oval room. He walked over to the skull on its pedestal and ran his fingers over its uneven surfaces, building a tactile image. His fingers traced the spiral of green gems radiating from the right eye socket, the matching spiral of milky white coiling from the left. He closed his eyes and rested his hand on the clustered jewels set in the center of the skull's forehead, felt them warm to his touch.

Opening his eyes, he stepped back about two meters. He sat down, crossed his right leg over his left, and lifted his necklace and twisted it around so the bone disk rested against his forehead. It felt surprisingly cool against his skin. Staring into the skull's spiraling eyes, he felt his own eyes grow heavy.

He twisted his fingers together in the way Yag ta Mishraunal had taught him and closed his eyes again. He began blanking out his senses. First, the senses dependent on his exterior sensory receptors: taste, smell, hearing, vision. Next, the senses signaling his position in space and the arrangement of his head, limbs and organs. He felt as though he were floating. Then the interior senses. He could no longer feel his heart beating or his lungs expanding and contracting. He had only his sense of perception. He blanked that and became a point of blind consciousness, then triggered the sequence with which he'd been programmed.

Lozan, he thought, and projected the image of his seated body, visualizing it as completely as if it were being perceived by all his sensory systems. He allowed himself to expand into his visualization, identified himself with it.

Next he visualized Janesha's skull, projecting the remembered image into the nothingness surrounding him. The spiral eyes began to spin, glowing and flowing, until the skull was clothed in radiance. The light condensed, became flesh; where the skull had been he perceived the head of a young girl with green eyes and floating red-black hair. Her hair grew until it became a shimmering cloud. Within the cloud, her body took on substance, materialized, as slim and lovely as Lozan had remembered it.

Janesha—the illusion Janesha he'd seen in the arena—floated in the void with him. Her eyes were closed and she seemed to be asleep.

He concentrated harder on her. Her image clarified as she began to register on his perceptive sense. He perceived her totality now—living sinews, beating heart, strong bones. She was alive. She was real.

Her green eyes opened. At first they stared dully, but almost immediately they came alive, focused on

Lozan. There was something frightening in the look they gave him.

This is only an illusion, he reminded himself. *Something I'm projecting from my memories. Nothing to be afraid of.*

The girl's smile was terrifying.

Janesha, Lozan thought, helpless to alter the sequence. He felt his consciousness leave his illusion-body for hers. Her body felt strange but he had no time to explore that strangeness; looking out through her eyes he could see his own body changing. He fought against panic, reminding himself that he'd known that this would happen, but it was hard to remain calm while his body altered form and color, while its features changed and it became female.

Finally nothing of Lozan remained in the figure he faced. A crimson giantess. Janesha. The real Janesha.

She repelled him, as he knew she should not.

Janesha, he thought reluctantly, and felt his consciousness jump the gap to the tall crimson body. He was reluctant to identify with it and expand into it, and when he had done so he felt uncomfortable, as though the phantom messages its nerves were relaying to him were out of phase with his receiving consciousness. It was with a sense of intense relief that he saw the other body taking on his form.

Lozan, he thought, and felt his consciousness leap the gap once more. It was all over. He was back in his own body.

Yet he felt no influx of new knowledge, no rush of alien memories.

Perhaps it takes a while. He unblanked his perceptive sense so that the projection would merge with his true body image. He tried to open his eyes.

His eyes would not open. With mounting frustration he tried other muscles, other movements, until he was forced to admit defeat. Not one muscle obeyed him. He was completely paralyzed.

What had he done to himself this time?

He assessed his situation. He was still oriented in

space, still aware that he was sitting upright with his hands twisted together in his lap. He could feel the cold floor beneath him and the pressure his legs exerted against each other. There was no pain. His perceptive sense told him he was still in the Place of Remembrance. But taste, smell, hearing—every sense which would have given him a direct idea of what was happening in the world beyond his skin was gone.

Still, his heart was beating; his chest was rising and falling as his lungs took in and expelled air. Whatever he'd done, it hadn't interfered with the automatic functioning of his body. He was in no immediate danger. He'd be safe until Yag ta Mishraunal returned. There would only be the shame of having proven himself incompetent.

What had he done to himself?

He concentrated on his perceptive sense. Images beat in on him with great force, imbued with a paradoxical clarity which made them harder to translate into terms his mind could comprehend. Nonetheless, he gradually built up a clear picture of his body.

All his organs seemed to be functioning, though many of his bodily rhythms were drastically altered. But there were regions in his brain which eluded his attempts at perception, as though part of his forebrain was wrapped in a sort of mental shadow, a confusing darkness he couldn't penetrate. Yet within that darkness he sensed furious activity, a fire that was not a fire blazing.

Yag ta Mishraunal had blocked his—no! This darkness was new, was . . . wrong, somehow, and the shadowed areas were those he'd mapped out earlier as controlling the functions he'd now lost. This was something else, something new.

Something dangerous. If only he'd understood what Janesha had done to him when she'd cured him of his earlier paralysis. But he'd felt nothing then, and without her memories he had no idea what to do.

And he definitely had none of her memories. What had he done?

He dug into Mishraunal's memories but they were too alien, too irrelevant, to help. Perhaps a complete understanding of Mishraunal's knowledge would have enabled him to deal with his present situation, but he was far from that kind of understanding. Too far.

He checked again for Yag ta Mishraunal, then probed cautiously at the shadowed region of his cortex, was rewarded with an agony worse than anything he'd ever experienced, like the agony Mishraunal had felt during the Votrassandra attack.

No, he thought, *it was the same. I tapped into the agony he felt during the attack.*

I don't understand.

The agony continued, spread. His body was dead and his every nerve was being burned from the dead flesh.

Then the pain was gone. His eyes opened, though he had not willed them to open; and though he felt them opening, he was still blind, totally dependent on his sense of perception.

And the dark fire that was not a fire had uncoiled, escaped the shadows, was pulsing, spreading, flowing down into the free structures of his cortex. Lozan was a pool of liquid fire in which the free cells of his brain were suspended, a sensitive liquid entity without protection from the searing darkness that burned him, drove him back, forced him to abandon, cell by cell, the structures that had been part of him.

He was losing all sense of his body. The dark fire had taken his cerebellum, driven him from it; he had no sense of spatial orientation, felt no identity with the body he could detect with his sense of perception. He was a field of energy contained within and containing the free regions of his brain.

How much of his self was in the symbiote? Could he use it to take over the lost functions? He tried to remember the knowledge that had been his as Mishraunal, but even that was fading, fragmentary.

His hands. They were moving in a swift, complex pattern and his body was rising to its feet and walking.

Walking smoothly, though he had no control of its actions, no knowledge of its destination.

He was gripped by an almost-memory, a sense of acting on decisions once clear but now forgotten.

Nervous impulses were running to and from the shrouded regions of his brain. Had he split himself off, was he some tiny part of Lozan that had lost contact with his greater self? If he could visualize the visual cortex, mold the plastic potential of his symbiote into a duplicate. . . . No, he was losing touch with his sense of perception.

There. Visualize the whole thing, then shrink it to a single point. *Identify.* Make the proper connections with the rest of the brain—. *So. Yes.* Now, reroute the impulses from his eyes into that point-source of consciousness—.

He could see the matrix's red disk ahead of him. Then intolerable pain: he had tapped Mishraunal's memories of the Votrassandra attack again. He was blind. *Again.* He had failed.

But if the part of his mind that was directing his body continued blundering around without conscious control, he could hurt himself badly. Perhaps if he only tried to damp some of the control impulses from the shrouded parts of his brain, keep his body motionless—.

He fell heavily and struck the blood-red floor with his head; then the agony was back, going on and on and on, blotting out everything.

When at last it was gone, he found himself stepping out of a teleportion matrix into a room he'd never seen before. The room was huge, rectangular, windowless, filled with case after case of carved and faceted gems that coruscated with more than the glitter of reflected light. Lozan's body moved toward the far end of the room, where a single transparent case stood alone against the wall.

Lozan could not use the matrices, yet he had just done so; he had never been in this room before, yet he was moving through it as though he knew it well.

Whenever he tried to regain control of his body he was punished for his efforts.

He could deny the knowledge no longer; the mind motivating his body was no split-off fragment of himself, no part of himself at all. Yet his body was under the control of a functioning mind.

Whose, then? Yag ta Mishraunal's? Night's?

I trusted him.

The case opened to his fingers' touch. It was filled with dark, glistening gems, black lotus flowers half the width of his hand. His hand took one of the flowers and pressed it to his forehead, where it adhered.

Lozan went from case to case, selecting jewels without hesitation. A huge white lotus fitted itself to his bald crown. Two curving bars of orange and black replaced his vanished eyebrows. His hands placed a flat yellow lozenge on either side of the black lotus. His ears were sealed with two milky plugs. Lenses of green-gold crystal covered his eyes.

Around his neck snaked a coil of crimson and azure gems terminating in a tiny blue-black lotus. He placed a green lotus over his neck and a translucent black lotus, smaller than the first and flecked with gold, over his solar plexus.

Removing his kilt, he placed a purplish-red lotus just above the place from which his penis jutted out. His penis was erect and the hands wound it with a rope of purplish-red gems. Bands of azure and crimson covered his wrists and ankles. Small opalescent disks were scattered over his body and opalescent lines traced the length of his spine.

From a case at the center of the room he took sharp amber-colored claws and fitted them to his fingers. He began to dance, moving with strange, slow steps that never quite repeated themselves.

As he danced, his body's nervous system evolved strange, complex energy configurations. He could perceive the forces coming into existence, growing, focusing.

Mudra.

136

His body's clawed fingers sketched a complex gesture that left lines of slowly fading fire hanging in the air. His body laughed, and as it laughed, the shrouded mind's triumph escaped for an instant the shadows in which it had concealed itself.

And in that instant he knew her. *Janesha.* Of course.

Yag ta Mishraunal said she was dead. That I killed her.

Had that, too, been a lie?

Lozan was suddenly conscious of her presence.

—*Lozan.*

—*(?)*

—*I want your body. A body to replace the one you killed.*

—*You killed yourself. This is my body. Mine.*

—*No longer. (Confidence/Arrogance.) I can expel you from this brain so easily—but I would prefer not to do it. I don't want to kill you.*

—*(Skepticism.)*

—*I tried to absorb a human, not kill a Lha. Now that I know you for what you are, I would save something of you if I could. Preserve you as Yag Chan preserved Mishraunal.*

—*By absorbing me.*

—*Yes.*

—*(Absolute refusal.) Give me back my body. Have you forgotten the First Law? Or was that, too, a lie?*

Unbidden, the memory of Yag ta Mishraunal as Lozan had last seen him returned to him.

Janesha picked the image from his mind.

—*He took the hawk?* Lozan could feel her fear despite her barriers.

—*He did*, she answered herself, and abruptly her thoughts were again shielded.

—*Lozan, I must have your body. I can destroy your mind almost without effort, but I would prefer to absorb you—to retain something of you, for you are Lha and my enemy through no fault of your own—and to absorb you I need your cooperation. The First Law is real; unless you attempt to absorb me I cannot absorb you. So the choice is yours: cooperate with me or force me to destroy you.*

—*No.*

—*The choice was yours.*

With quick, complex movements, she began touching his clawed fingers to the opalescent disks on his body, then began drawing lines on his skin, carefully avoiding further contact with the disks. The jewels were flaming now and the flaming patterns were writhing, squirming over the body's flesh.

My flesh.

In a tiny area of his cortex the darkness seemed to dissipate. A sweet voice—his own, yet soft and lulling—came fountaining out of the place where the darkness had been. The voice filled him, gentled him, blotted out his fear and anger:

—*There is nothing to fear, nothing to fight against; . . . softly, think about softness, rest, floating, warmth; . . . your thoughts are slow, languid, joyous; . . . listen to yourself, your better self, your true self, listen . . . gently; . . . feel yourself here, know yourself here, here without memory, without plans, without fears . . . content; . . . remember the joys you've always felt among those who love you, who love you, who cherish you as the gentle tide sweeps you away, drifting to joy. . . .*

The darkness was pulsing, throbbing, expanding, gently lapping at the free parts of Lozan's brain. Entranced, he drew back, relinquishing cell after cell, structure after structure. The shadows pulsed and sparkled, singing to him.

. . . softly, slowly, without fear or anger . . . joy, only joy and the knowledge that you are cherished, loved, protected. . . .

Lozan felt himself fading as the voice was fading, dimming, falling to an inaudible murmur; yet still it held him, still it filled him.

He was dissolving into pastel confusion. He tried to ignore it, concentrate on the voice, but his thoughts and memories had become entangled. The darkness was the night sky, the flame Dusum held to pipe of Dakkini slivers, the shadow of Lavelle's hand on his old Go board; the voice was Dorjii's voice, Sren's voice, the voice of the bubble stream, *lying to him*—.

Lying to him! Anger shattered the trance, brought him back to himself. All that remained of his physical self was a small knot of cells deep in his thalamus. The darkness was the night sky and the voice was the taunting voice of the bully who'd just knocked him to the ground. Gaining strength from his fury he struck out at the darkness, picking up a rock and hitting the bully with it again and again while he pierced through the agony of the Votrassandra attack, pierced through the universe of blankness beyond it, fought the controlling will as he spat out broken teeth and drove Janesha back.

He was falling. Three other boys were holding him down while the bully kicked him again and again. One of his ribs was broken. He squirmed and fought, keeping his teeth clamped shut, trying to get free—even one hand free—so he could get at them; but they held him down and he had to get away, he was burning, burning—.

He was a dimensionless point, fleeing, abandoning brain and body. Yet now that he was outside his body, his thoughts were clear again; and from his new vantage point he could perceive the body that had been his, throbbing with powerful energies, sheathed in liquid fires. All his pain was gone. He could sense powerful forces seeking him, strikng out blindly—how did he know they were blind? but he knew—and though he knew the forces should have destroyed him, he felt nothing. Something shielded him.

A wave of dark force struck the place which he had defined as his location but did not touch him. Had Janesha been bluffing when she'd promised to destroy him?

No. His mind was working with cold clarity now, extracting meaning from his confused experience.

139

He'd fled his physical brain to take refuge in his symbiote. Janesha couldn't get at him to destroy him because Yag ta Mishraunal had blocked all telepathic access to the symbiote.

Yag ta Mishraunal had not been in league with Janesha. Did that mean he could count on the Lha's help when he returned?

Yes. But he had no idea when Yag ta Mishraunal planned to return.

The lines of fire faded from his body. Janesha was beginning to restore the lotus-gems to their cases. She spoke aloud; Lozan could perceive her words:

"I couldn't destroy you after all, Lozan; but without your body you're cut off from your life-force and you'll soon die anyway. Everything you do takes part of yourself now, Lozan, part of you. Can you feel it beginning—your memories getting dimmer, your thoughts fading, your will dissipating as you cannibalize yourself? Pretty soon you'll lose your memory of this conversation, Lozan. Then you'll consume what's left of you without any further help from me. Is that what you want, to eat yourself like a starving animal? Are you sure you still don't want me to absorb you? Can you still hear me, still understand me? Lozan?"

He would not allow her to destroy him. He had to find a new source of life-force.

The fish. He said I could work with one of the electrical fish.

He redefined his location and he was there, among the translucent globes. He could feel the fish-minds, simple, greedy, accessible.

He absorbed fish after fish until dead fish littered the surfaces of all the pools. He needed more. He reached out to a green fish in one of the floating globes, absorbed its mind. A tiny flash of satisfaction as he absorbed the fish's life-force.

The globe was only water, falling, splashing. Gone. If Janesha detected its loss, realized what he was doing—.

No. If she'd detected him she would've already reacted. He was safe as long as he kept himself from absorbing any more of the fish that helped maintain the structure.

He absorbed another fish. Another, as his brief exultation faded. Each fish had so little life-force. And without a body of his own to charge with that life-force, even the little he could absorb from the fish drained from him almost as soon as he took it.

There were only so many fish.

Could he pour himself into the brain of one of the fish? Would it hold him?

How long would he have there before Janesha found and destroyed his host?

He had no alternative. He entered the mind of a large blue-white fish with armored scales. It was ecstasy to have eyes again, to taste the water with his long barbels, to smell, feel, hear. But the fish's brain was not adequate to house him. Life-force was still draining from him, though not quite as rapidly as before. He could feel his thoughts growing sluggish. Soon he would be unable to think, unable to plan.

He absorbed more fish, took from them a moment of the clarity he needed. Deep inside his swim bladder he could hear the sounds the other fish in the pool were making. Could he divide himself, inhabit a multiplicity of bodies at once?

A black fish with a flat body and long sinuous tail swam by. Lozan tried to project himself into it without losing his identification with his original host.

It was surprisingly easy. A moment of fitting himself to the new configuration, then he was in two places at once. His new acquisition was blind, sensing its environment through minute changes in the electrical field it generated, and its brain was far more complex and unfamiliar than that of his original host. But though it could contain more of him than his first host, even the two together were insufficient. His thoughts were growing steadily fuzzier; it was becoming harder and harder to deal with two sets of conflicting sensory data, neither of them familiar, and to control two entirely different bodies at the same time.

He parked his blue-white host on the sandy bottom of the pool so he could give it minimal attention; but despite its more complex brain his new host was a more primitive type of fish, and he had to keep it moving to keep it supplied with fresh oxygen. He set it swimming in a circle, with the side of the pool always to its right.

He took over seven more fish, parking those he could on the bottom and sending the others to swim behind his second host. As long as the swimming fish followed the same endless course, he could coordinate them without too much confusion.

At intervals he sensed food appearing in the pool and would partially withdraw from his hosts' minds, waiting until they were satiated before reestablishing full identification. It was too difficult to try to coordinate all of them when they fed. Whenever he withdrew, he lost more life-force; to regain it he'd absorb the lives of fish in distant pools, then settle back into his routine, awaiting the moment when Janesha would find him and destroy his hosts.

Yag ta Mishraunal found him first.

Chapter Eleven

IT WAS WHILE HIS HOSTS WERE FEEDING and Lozan's identity was partially disengaged from theirs that he first sensed Yag ta Mishraunal. Lozan's sense of perception had atrophied in the never-ending repetition of rest-on-the-bottom, swim-around-the-side; he had lost all sense of time and had no idea how long the Lha had been standing by the pool with the crimson hawk on his arm.

There had been something about the hawk. . . . Lozan's mind was torpid, dulled by the never-ending loss of his vitality that his life as a school of fish could only slow, never halt. It had been . . . a long time since he'd had the energy for free thought. He couldn't remember if it had been Yag ta Mishraunal or some other that Janesha had feared.

Lozan. The warmth he remembered was there, the candor, a flash of joyous brilliance in the sluggish dullness of his mind. The barrier was no barrier against its creator.

—(?) He did not have the energy to frame a question.

—*We did not know Janesha was alive. We are sorry.*

—*What good are . . . ? My body. Give me back my body.*

—*Later. For now, you must wait.*

—*Now. I need it, I'm dying, I—give it to me!*

—*I was Mishraunal; I spent three million years dying. You can wait a little longer.*

143

—*No.*

—*It need not be painful. You can take this hawk's body while you wait. Janesha designed it with a brain of great complexity, and though she modified it into a trap for you I've corrected that. It is as good a brain as your human body possesses.*

—*I don't want. . . .Yes. I'm dying. It's killing me, even trying to talk to you like this; it's—help me. Please. I can't. . . .*

—*Open yourself to me.* Clarity and focus flowed from Yag ta Mishraunal into Lozan.

—*Can you make the transfer to the hawk yet?*

With Yag ta Mishraunal's life-force still flooding into him, Lozan attuned himself to the hawk, wedded himself to its nervous system. Yet the transfer was incomplete; some of him remained entangled in the lives of his former hosts. With little regret he stopped their hearts and freed his trapped selves.

It was like coming home to the home he'd always imagined but never had to find himself once again in a single, sight-oriented body with four limbs, . . . and if two of those limbs were wings, wasn't that the fulfillment of a lifelong dream?

The hawk's mind occupied only a tiny portion of its capacious brain; the rest was Lozan's and within it he felt whole and at peace. Within seconds he had taken the knowledge he needed to fly from the hawk-mind and was aloft, wheeling and soaring, all else forgotten in the glorious freedom of flight.

—*There is no time for that now. You are needed.*

Almost reluctantly, Lozan landed on the Lha's wrist.

—*Do I get my body back now?*

—*Not yet, but we must begin the process which will return it to you. You will accompany me while I talk to Janesha. Withdraw to the portion of the brain you share with the hawk's mind so I can shield you without arousing her suspicions.*

Lozan relinquished control. The world lost all color,

feeling; he was once more totally dependent on his sense of perception.

—*I'll leave the channel between us open.*

With the hawk on his wrist, Yag ta Mishraunal began to descend a spiral ramp into one of the tunnels. The faintly greenish water of the pool formed a cylinder around which the ramp coiled, and curious fish peered at them as they descended.

The tunnel ended in the red metal of a teleportion matrix. Yag ta Mishraunal made a complex gesture with the fingers of his left hand, stepped through into the Place of Remembrance.

It shocked Lozan to perceive his body sitting crosslegged before the skull, a slight smile on his lips, his eyes closed.

No. Her eyes are closed. She's smiling. Not me.

Opening her (his?) eyes, Janesha glanced up at Yag ta Mishraunal, ignoring the hawk on his wrist.

"You were gone a long time."

"I had to help prepare someone for the Ritual. Everything went well?"

"I think so. I'm still confused about a lot of things, but it's all beginning to sort itself out."

"Good. But I don't think you'll be ready for tele-pathic contact for a while yet, no matter how confident you feel. I'll leave you shielded."

"I should be ready for the hawk now." She stretched out her arm and the hawk flew to her. "I have enough of Janesha's memories now."

Yag ta Mishraunal shook his head. "Not quite. I examined it and found that Janesha must have been using it to practice maintaining her identity under difficult conditions. She must have been afraid of losing herself in Night. I'll have to reprogram the bird before it'll be safe for you."

No relief showed on Janesha's face.

"Do you remember Jomgoun?"

"A little younger than Janesha? I can't get a clear picture of her."

"Him. He comes of age today and it's customary among us for all Lha to attend a first Ritual. We are so few and it is such a rare and precious thing when one of us can transcend his human ancestry and take his place among us."

That's where she'll try to do it, Lozan realized. *It'll give her the perfect opportunity to announce she's still alive and one of them. Just as if she were completing her own Ritual.*

"You'll find that watching a proper Ritual will give you a less distorted idea of what the Ritual is really like," Yag ta Mishraunal continued. Lozan felt the words were directed at him more than at Janesha. "Experiencing it as you did, it must be hard to believe that it is not cruel, but joyous."

"It is hard to believe. . . . You're sure that Dorjii will not be selected?"

Lozan hated her for that, for the smug way she was counterfeiting concern for Dorjii to give herself more time to make sure he was dead.

"Yes."

"Will I be able to perceive the Ritual, shielded as I am?"

"The shield is necessary for your own protection, but you should be able to sense enough to correct your earlier impressions despite it.

"I'll take the hawk with me." The hawk transferred itself back to Yag ta Mishraunal and all three of them stepped through the matrix to the arena.

Music was all around them, throbbing and insistent. Janesha stood among the giants of the upper tier; Yag ta Mishraunal was in the bottom tier.

—*What happened to the haze?* Lozan asked, as much to test his ability to communicate as to get an answer.

—*What you saw was the result of your untrained perception of the energies gathered here. Your shield keeps you from sensing most of them now.*

A stocky dark-skinned girl with a bald head was standing in the set of rings in which Lozan had once

146

found himself. She could have been any of the female orphans whom Lozan had seen in the shaefi tubes. She looked up at the three tiers of Lha, then turned her back on them and prostrated herself to the Goddess's triple statue.

—She feels no fear.

—None? Not even of us? For an instant Lozan saw the Lha around him as he imagined the girl was seeing them, as grotesque demons. *Then what does she feel?*

—Pride that she's been chosen for mortal life, regret that her best friend was not chosen with her, some embarrassment that she is naked—though she tells herself it makes little difference because we are only S'in-je—and contempt for us. We are here to watch and envy her and she is very aware of that fact.

—But why Naming Day? All the promises, all the lies?

—We are in hiding and must keep our actions hidden. But more important, the preliminaries serve to intensify the human's experience of the Ritual—to intensify her pride and pleasure, not her fear or pain— and this intensification makes the Ritual more fulfilling to both participants. You will see.

The iron black being with the dancing manikins on the pedestal of its neck was sitting to Yag ta Mishraunal's left. It seemed to Lozan that one of the manikins now bore a suspicious resemblance to himself, while the other looked like Janesha, as she had first appeared to him.

The two figures were making love.

—When do I get my body back?

—After Jomgoun's Ritual.

Two swellings appeared on the flat surface of the black being's pedestal neck. The skin split and drew back, revealing two moist eyes. The manikins picked them up and trained them on the girl in the arena.

The Lha seated themselves with a single movement, Janesha following a calculated instant later. A Lha appeared in the second set of rings. He was at least four meters tall, chrome yellow. In the center of his forehead a scarlet lotus glittered; a spiral of green and white gems wound up his right forearm and a small black lotus glinted on his chest. In his left hand he held the skull-flower, the red gems flashing in its eight golden eye sockets, while his right hand gripped the Knife of the Ritual.

The girl turned from the statues of the Goddess to stare at Jomgoun.

The voice Lozan had heard when he'd faced Janesha sounded, repeating the same words.

—*What is she seeing now?*

—*(A boy dressed in red, his hair cut short, his whole aspect radiating strength and serenity. His eyes glow golden in his dark face and behind him the arena fades into golden mist. . . .)*

It happens so quickly. The girl and Jomgoun walk to the center, face each other over the white stone. She kneels, facing now not Night's triple figure but the watching Lha, and says, "To you, O Goddess, I relinquish my life."

Lozan hears the truth in her voice.

She rises. Jomgoun hands her the knife. She makes a deep incision on the inside of her left arm and offers the bloody blade to the watchers. The blood is suddenly gone from the blade. Her wounded arm does not bleed.

Jomgoun takes the knife and hands her the skull-flower. She holds it beneath the wound. A single drop of blood falls into the cup. She kneels once more and holds the skull-flower in front of her, offering it to the watchers.

Jomgoun takes it from her and places it in the recess in the white stone.

She rises. All this time, her face has been transfigured by bliss.

She lies upon the stone. Jomgoun takes the blade and makes careful incisions in her limbs, neck, and body, working the blade back and forth so the blood flows freely. It runs down her body and into the waiting channels of the rock, dripping through the tiny hole and slowly filling the skull-flower. The knife's jeweled pommel and blade are blazing steadily brighter.

Yag ta Mishraunal suddenly links Lozan with the girl.

There is no pain, only a voluptuous lassitude. She sees Jomgoun as he is now, yet what she sees is no different from the Mother bending over her to take her soul and deliver it from Nal-K'am. The girl knows that everything in her existence has been only preparation for this moment of supreme fulfillment and she is content. Her memories come alive for her and she relives them, relives her whole life, each incident dissolving into sacred all-forgiving flames which are sheer, unbearable ecstasy, growing, growing—.

As suddenly as it had come, Lozan's contact with her was gone. On the floor of the Place of the Ritual, Jomgoun had begun to drink from the skull-flower. The girl held the knife poised over her breast, then plunged it into her heart. She was smiling.

For an instant Jomgoun was shrouded in shadow, then the pure yellow of his body was broken by tracings of black and silver while some subtle change took place in the shape of his ears. His new colors reminded Lozan of some of the fish in Janesha's pools.

—She felt no pain.

—You told her she would be reborn as a human. You lied to her.

—Perhaps, but there was no cruelty in our deception. And she lives on in the only way a human can survive the death of its body. As part of one of us.

Jomgoun took the knife from the girl's breast. The blade was clean, its jewels again dull. The girl's body grew misty, indistinct, faded away. There was no blood on the stone.

—And Jomgoun, what does he feel now? Like a god?

—He feels humble. For the time he truly under-

149

stands what it is to live life as a human being, what it means that he too participates in humanity and must transcend his origins.

—*Link me to him.*

—*I cannot. He is one with Night. But prepare yourself: Janesha's judgment is at hand.*

There was no sense of transition, but Yag ta Mishraunal and the hawk that was Lozan were in the set of rings that Jomgoun had been in a moment before. Janesha stood in the other set, her mouth open in unsimulated surprise.

—*Remain here.* Lozan felt tiny and vulnerable in his hawk's body. The black floor was cold beneath his clawed feet.

Yag ta Mishraunal walked with measured deliberation toward the center. The light was suffused with drifting shadows. The watching Lha sat immobile, unmoving—statues of bright metal.

Darkness was gathering around Yag ta Mishraunal, solidifying, taking on substance around him, hiding him. Where before there had been an alabaster Lha, there was only darkness.

From the darkness Night spoke. "Janesha, your crime is known. You have taken into your hands the judgment which is Ours and Ours alone. You were of Us, and you have plotted murder against that which is of Us. Do you have anything to say in your defense?"

"My defense? Why mock me with words, as though we were human beings? Open Yourself to me, let me merge with You, then You will know what I've done, why I did it. Then You will be able to judge me. But not this, these words. Not this mockery."

"Our mind must remain closed to you."

"Then I killed him for nothing?" She paused, brushed at her upper lip, scowled. With a shock Lozan recognized the gesture as his own. "I was dying. You think you know what being absorbed is—and maybe You do, for a human being or a Rilg who's already only one step away from death. But I, I was alone, alone for

150

the first time in my life . . . and I was dying, I was dissolving, he was destroying me. I killed him to survive.

"I gave him what choice I could—to let me absorb him or be expelled from his body. He refused to let me absorb him. I didn't want to kill him, I didn't even want to absorb him, now that I know what it means for a Lha to be absorbed, but I had no choice. Can't You understand that? Look into me, experience the choices I faced, then judge me if You wish!"

She was poised, tense, waiting for a response. When none came some of the life seemed to drain from her. "You've already condemned me. Yag ta Mishraunal told the body so; I heard him. What else could I do? Appeal to him—when he himself had already absorbed Mishraunal as Lozan had absorbed me? He would have left me to dissolve!"

Some strength returned to her. "But I thought that if only I survived, if he was gone beyond recall, then You might let me live. I am Lha, a Lha who had to face alone and without guidance a choice none of You has ever had to face. If I chose wrongly—if I am flawed, incomplete, unworthy—make me over, help me. I am one of You, part of You. Let me merge with You, let me lose myself in You forever, but don't cast me out. Please let me merge with You again."

"The boy is still alive."

"Alive?" Her eyes caught the hawk, stared. "That's him? There?"

"Yes."

"Then I didn't need his body to survive?"

"No."

"I didn't know. Open to me, look within me. I didn't know."

"None of Us knew."

"But then"—she rallied—"why mock me like this? Why this trial, if he can have his body back and I can have the hawk?"

"You cannot have the hawk."

"You'll kill me then? Even though he's still alive?"

"No. We would never kill a Lha, not even one so flawed as you, not even a Lha who has broken every law of Our kind, and that from stupidity, without thought or reason.

"Why were you so sure We'd condemn you to absorption? We could have given you a new body. Why were you so certain of your own guilt that you put yourself beyond the reach of Our forgiveness and Our help?"

"But You didn't know a Lha could survive without a body."

"No. But *you did,* for you had already done so. We could have programmed a slavebrain to absorb your mind so that you could have animated it and grown yourself a new body. Or We could have removed that portion of the boy's brain housing your consciousness and grown a body around it."

Cut out part of my brain. For her. Lozan stretched his wings, scraped one claw slowly across the chill black stone. This was sounding less and less like the vindication he'd been promised, less and less like the judgment Janesha deserved.

She tried to murder me. And they were going to forgive her.

"You proved yourself unable to act in any way better than a human would have acted without Our support. So for you We have devised a special Ritual: you must learn to transcend your humanity on your own, in isolation; you must prove yourself Lha without Our help. Only then will We allow you to merge with Us again."

Janesha slumped, defeated, exhausted. Seeing her, Lozan had to fight back sympathy, though her punishment seemed mild enough to him. All she had to do was learn to live the way he'd lived all his life.

"In what body?" Janesha asked.

"In the body you now inhabit."

Lozan tried to yell, "No! Wait!" but all he could force from the hawk's mouth was a shrill scream.

152

—*Yag ta Mishraunal!* he projected. *Wait. Please! Give her the hawk. I want my body back. You promised. You promised you'd give me my body back!*

"The two of you will share the same body," the voice that was many voices said.

—*No! I don't want her there.*

"Which is one reason why the two of you will share your body. You must learn to live together if you are ever to merge together into Our mind. Now that you, Lozan, no longer have Janesha's knowledge to draw upon, you will need instruction to fit yourself to Our way of life. Janesha will provide you with that instruction."

Shadow reached out to cloak them. They slept.

Chapter Twelve

SOMETIMES WHEN LOZAN SAW HIMSELF RE-flected in a faceted crystal or a mirroring pool he would glimpse the flattened back of a huge crimson swamp spider clinging to the back of his neck, its mandibles and hollow legs buried deep in his flesh so that his blood flowed through it and its through him. . . . The spider was always just a suggestion of crimson, a shape seen out of the corner of his eye as he turned his head.

In the center of an empty room with dull black walls Lozan sat staring with unfocused eyes. A green lotus gem shone on his forehead.

. . . *Mishraunal is running his fingers over two touch-tapes submitted to him by a blind, warty creature from a high-gravity world far from its parent sun. The creature will not be allowed to study on Rildan.* . . .

. . . *Mishraunal examines the ruins of Pransitthaja. It is not worth rebuilding; a new city will have to be created. He concentrates, abolishing the wreckage.* . . .

. . . *Mishraunal is a student, barely out of the egg, with the soft green tongue of the very young. There are only three other students in his class; for the ninth year Azeid has failed to meet its breeding quotas.* . . .

. . . *Mishraunal flies high above the vast gray-purple jungle, wearing the twin belts and jeweled headband which provide him with limited control of matter and energy. A flock of white-winged birds bursts from the jungle below and for an instant he wishes that he too had wings, that he could fly without mechanical aids. . . .*

. . . Mishraunal senses the aliens' life-force through the ever-increasing agony. He reaches out, takes one, then the others, only when it is too late and he feels himself being absorbed, realizing that one of the aliens is the alien Rilg for which his race has waited so many aeons. . . .

Lozan's concentration broke. The light in his forehead lotus flickered, died. Angry, he plucked it from his skin, then shook his head, trying to clear away his fatigue. He put the lifeless jewel in a pocket of his kilt.

Another wasted session. He could no longer find his way among Mishraunal's memories. It was as though what he had experienced that first night had been only the seed of what was to come, for ever since the Rilg memories had grown in detail and complexity, remaining separate from his own yet still a part of him, until now when he tried to probe them he lost himself in an infinity of branching associations, unable to follow any thought through to its conclusion without being diverted into something else.

Like a senile old man.

Janesha appeared. Her back seemed to touch the wall; her posture exactly duplicated his. His eyes registered the presence of a slim amber-skinned girl with windblown hair even while his sense of perception told him he was alone. Though he knew her appearance was only an illusion tailored to deceive him, the sight of her affected him like Dakkini wood; he could feel his muscles tighten; there was sweat on the palms of his hands. An excitement he could not suppress, could not deny.

She smiled, and the falseness of her appearance, the helplessness of his response, infuriated him. He remembered the arena.

—*Why can't you look like you really do?* he demanded, surprising himself with the extent of his anger. *I know what you are. What you really are.*

—*Do you?* Her smile intensified but he could feel the anger behind it. *Good. I thought you thought I was a giant spider.*

—*No.*

—*I no longer have a form of my own, Lozan. You took that from me.*

—*You lost it yourself.*

—*Perhaps. It makes no difference. But I'm here to train you, so I've chosen a form you find attractive.*

—*No.*

—*But I got it from your mind, Lozan. It's because you find it attractive that you refuse it.*

—*So? You can't change how I feel. Don't try. Don't try to lie to me.*

—*How would you know if I was lying? You deny everything I tell you.*

—*That. It's a lie. That's not how you look.*

—*It's how I look for you. How you want me to look. Part of what I have to teach you is how to harness and redirect your human sexuality, or you'll never learn to control your mind. When we grow me a new body it'll have to be attractive to you, and I have to prepare you to think of it as me.*

—*Don't expect it to happen any time soon.*

—*You need my help. Let me help you. Please.*

—*I don't want your help.*

—*If you let me help you, you can have your body back.*

—*I'd rather keep it now. Why don't you crawl back in my head where I can't see you?*

—*Like a swamp spider?* Her bitterness reached into him, twisted at him, but he shut it out, readjusted his shield to shut out everything but her voice and image, over which he had no control.

—*Yes. Just like a swamp spider.*

She continued to smile. —*But I'm always in your*

head, Lozan, always watching over you, even when you're asleep.

—I hope it makes you less lonely. Leave me alone. I have work to do.

—You can't do it, Lozan, not without my mind to draw upon. That's why it's not working for you. You'll have to accept my help if you ever want to get rid of me. Why not now?

—Not now. Not even to get rid of you.

—You're too tired to work. Just give me a few seconds of control and I'll fix things so you'll never need to sleep again.

—You'd like that, wouldn't you? Just a few seconds of control.

—So I can prove you can trust me. What are you so afraid of?

—Nothing. But I don't like you doing things to my mind.

—Then you'll have to get some sleep.

—I like sleeping.

—Don't try to lie to me. I know what your dreams are like.

—Then I hope you enjoy them as much as I do.

She vanished. Lozan stood up, stretched, then took the green lotus back out of his pocket and put it on his forehead. He sat down, positioned himself correctly, and tried to concentrate, but it was hopeless; he was too tired; the jewel remained dead. He put it back in his pocket.

In the month he'd spent here, he'd gained some control of his body's production of fatigue poisons, but, even so, he was weak from lack of sleep. Since his first awakening he'd only slept nine—no, eight—times. While he slept, his mind and body were no longer under his conscious control, and though he'd been promised Janesha would be unable to take control of either without his consent, he found it impossible to trust such assurances completely.

It was not that he was afraid she'd try to steal his

body again, or that she'd destroy his mind. Not now, not with Night aware of her. What Lozan feared was something more subtle—thoughts whispered to his sleeping mind, alien attitudes and values supplanting his own, his will to remain himself weakening until he gave in to her and—.

And what? He didn't know, didn't even know if it would be good or bad. What he did know was that he had nightmares, strange complex nightmares filled with alien scenes and characters, with colors that were somehow evil, odors and sounds that were subtly—frighteningly—wrong. He had dreams in which he watched, laughed, as he dismembered himself, gorged himself on the putrefying flesh of his corpse, dreams in which there was nothing with which he could identify or sympathize, dreams frightening in their utter incomprehensibility. But worse than these were the sexual dreams, the couplings in which he was both male and female or in which he was an animal coupling with strange beasts while S'in-je looked on, waiting until he was totally committed to his sins before they began to torment him. But it was the dreams of traitorous ecstasies, the dreams in which he reveled in his own violation, his own degradation, that frightened him the most.

Was Janesha forcing his dreams upon him or were they the result of some sort of seepage from her mind to his? Or were they his alone, the product of his attempts to deal without help with Mishraunal's memories?

He was tired; he could push himself no farther. He had to sleep. Something about the golden lotus island seemed more inviting than the rooms in which he'd been sleeping recently.

He stood in front of the teleportion matrix, moving his hands in the proper gestures while he visualized the one matrix he'd been taught to use—the one connecting the interiors and exteriors of these sealed buildings. He stepped through the metal into the open air.

In the jungle he caught sight of the crimson hawk. The thought struck him: his exhaustion was purely physical, wasn't it? Wouldn't he be just as refreshed if he spent the time his body was asleep in the hawk's brain? Maybe more refreshed, since there'd be no nightmares to torment him and Janesha wouldn't be able to get at him.

Was it safe to leave her alone in his body? *As long as I don't give her control she can't take it for herself, even if I'm not here.*

And he'd be free of her, alone with himself at last. If it worked he'd never be driven by the sluggishness of his tired thoughts to turn to her for help he didn't want. He could—.

No. I'll have to let her in sometime. But not yet, not while he was still so weak, so ignorant, so easily fooled.

It was not his fear alone that made him want to keep her out of his mind. There was anger, too, anger and hatred and even contempt. He despised her for her arrogant self-righteousness, her assumption that she understood him better than he understood himself. What right did she have to feel so superior, when she couldn't even care for herself? She'd been sentenced to her own company because she'd failed as a Lha— because she'd been the only Lha ever to fail as she had—and solitude seemed little enough punishment for what she'd tried to do to him. Let her endure it.

—*You are not here to punish me. Neither of us is being punished. We're here to learn to live with each other.*

She'd been eavesdropping on his thoughts again; he must have let his shield slip. He gestured with his left hand, tensed certain facial muscles, restored the shield.

—*You're here to learn to live with yourself,* he thought at her.

—*Then why am I here in the same body with you?* He had no response.

The light was dim as he crossed the silver bridge,

159

only the luminous twilight which passed for night illuminating the hall; and the fish beneath the surface of the water were merely vague shapes. Lozan wondered if they'd been programmed to stay where they'd be visible from the bridge.

Calling the hawk to him, he lay down on the hard golden surface, surprised again at how comfortable it felt. He closed his eyes, located the hawk with his sense of perception, and transferred himself to it.

It was like an explosion of energy and awareness. His exhaustion was gone, abandoned. He could see his body sleeping peacefully, its mouth half-open.

He let the hawk mind retain control, content for the moment to be no more than a passenger.

He was flying back to the jungle. The crimson cloud was only a veil of almost transparent pinkish mist through the hawk's eyes, and he could see perfectly well in the twilight. Hidden in the mist, Lozan glided silently just above the tree tops, watching for the birds and small animals that were his host's customary prey. But though Lozan enjoyed the hawk's hunting exhilaration, he did not intend to let it attack any birds. He had a sentimental fondness for birds.

The hawk saw something, swooped down on it before Lozan could react. The hawk perched on a branch while it devoured the small furry animal, bones and all.

I was too slow. I wouldn't have been able to stop it in time to save a bird.

When the hawk again took flight, Lozan was in complete control. Golden light was beginning to shine through the clouds. As it grew brighter, Lozan felt a sudden curiosity about its source. He began to climb, flying in ever-widening circles, the crisp air parting before him.

His flight took him out over the lake. Far below, the golden lotus gleamed in the bright morning light, his body an insignificant blotch of brown at its center. He continued to climb.

For the first time he saw the Hall of the Crimson

Cloud in its entirety through his own eyes, was able to experience the full beauty of its design.

It's too beautiful. I could never do anything this—like this.

He thrust the thought from him, continued his ascent. The floor was lost in the pink haze. Drifting tendrils of golden gas were beginning to appear, like threads of molten metal in a pink wool rug. The drifting gold glowed with its own soft warm light, but when Lozan's wing brushed a tendril it was shockingly cold.

Then he was above the pink, lost in chill brilliance. Dazzled, intoxicated, he continued to climb.

An immense expanse of darkness overhead, cutting him off from the sky, closing him in. He had reached the roof of the hall, was trapped beneath it.

The hawk was untired. Lozan did not want to stop climbing. He circled around and around beneath the great dark domed ceiling, feeling its immense weight pressing down on him.

There was no escape from Janesha's hall, no way to climb free of it. And—there was no escape from Janesha. He had been lying to himself. He would have to make his peace with her sooner or later, and the longer he waited the harder it would be.

The changes he feared—how could he be sure they weren't the very changes which Night intended for him? There was no escape, no real evasion—he was here, in the Refuge, beneath a roof of stone, and he might have to live here for thousands of years. Denial was cowardice, lies. He began to spiral downward.

The Temple—he was here, in the Refuge, beneath the Temple. He thought back, remembering what the Temple had meant to him, how he'd feared and loathed it; and suddenly the hawk's body was alien and unfamiliar. The floor of the hall was beginning to reappear as he lost altitude, but now its very beauty made it seem hostile and unnatural, incomprehensible. What could he have in common with a mind which could conceive *that?*

For a moment all he wanted was to be human again—lonely and angry and afraid, yes, but surrounded by things he understood, difficulties he could overcome. Now that he knew he had no choice but to commit himself to Janesha, he felt a weariness, a despair of ever learning what he had to learn that his earlier feelings had masked. He missed the fields, the swamps, the skies in which the birds were only birds. He missed Dorjii, Dusum, even Sren.

The lotus island was becoming visible. By a trick of light, the bridge was invisible against the shimmering silver water. The golden flower looked totally isolated from the shore, and his body looked like a tiny spot of rot in its center. Lozan felt very alone, incapable of facing Janesha. He altered his descent to land on the shore.

He perched in a tree overlooking a pillar of pink crystal, trying to come to a decision. Without warning, he thought, *Why not wake Dorjii?*

True, he was not even sure that Dorjii was in the Refuge or alive, but if he was, why not? Lozan was forbidden contact with Lha other than Janesha, but Dorjii was human. And when they freed him they were going to erase his memories anyway; this would just give them a few more memories to erase. Dorjii could be a link with Lozan's past, a friend where he had none, until the time came when he'd progressed too far, become too inhuman. Then Dorjii could be returned to the outer world to become an envoy to the planets of the Terran Hegemony. Lozan almost envied him.

That is, if he was still alive to be envied.

And if he wasn't, if Lozan found that he's been killed by one of the other Lha? Could he still go on trying to be like them?

I have to know if he's still alive.

Lozan crossed the lake, perched on one of the lotus's inner petals.

—Janesha?

—(?) A tiny girl with hair like dark fire appeared, seated on his sleeping body's forehead.

—*I think I'm willing to cooperate with you, if you help me with something first. But I need to know what you want from me.*

—*You'll give me full cooperation?*

—*What do you want me to do?*

—*I want a body of my own. I want to be able to merge with Night again.*

—*I can't help you with that. Night put you here to learn to live your own life, without Her help.*

—*But I am also here to teach you what you need to know to live among us. I cannot teach you anything until you stop shielding yourself from me and agree to share control of your mind and body with me.*

—*Will you leave me alone, let me be by myself, when I need to be?*

—*Yes.*

—*Then I accept.*

—*Are you sure? Think. You must cooperate willingly, and what you have so far agreed to do is only to allow me to help you. You must also agree to help me. You know that you are to be the judge of my progress, as I am to be the judge of yours. But what kind of judge will you be? How fair have you been to me so far? You've done everything you could to make my life with you intolerable. How do you think it feels to share the body and mind of someone who refuses to see you as anything but a bloated swamp spider?*

—*I'll do everything I can to help you, but that's all I can promise. I can't promise to change the way I think. When I think about you I think of you as a swamp spider, that's all; it's not a choice I made, it's just how I see you. Do you think I like it any better than you do?*

—*Yes. Because you did choose. Perhaps not at first, but whose decision was it to accept that image of me without trying to change it, without trying to learn better? You chose to reject me, to learn nothing about who or what I am, and you've been forced to live with the result of that choice. You must choose to open yourself to me, merge with me, as much for your own good as for mine. But before you can open yourself to me, you must choose to accept me.*

—*Yag ta Mishraunal warned me I would be engulfed if I tried to merge with another Lha.*

—*Another evasion. All Lha are channels to Night, and hence dangerous to you. All except one: myself. Even so, there are dangers, but do you think I am unaware of them? My fate is linked to yours; I dare not harm you. What we do, we will do gradually, cautiously, taking no risks.*

—*Agreed.*

—*Good. But you have not yet told me what you want from me, nor have I agreed to it. What do you want?*

—*I want you to find out if my friend Dorjii is still alive and here in the Refuge. If he is, I want you to bring him here and awaken him.*

He could feel her surprise. This time he forced himself to keep from shielding himself from her emotions.

—*Why?*

He tried to project his loneliness, tried to make her feel how empty he felt.

—*I need a friend, someone to connect me to things the way they were before. So I can feel comfortable and relaxed, not always—scared. Alien. Like I don't belong here.*

—*But you're Lha—.*

—*And he's human? True, but how much of a Lha am I yet? That's all in my future; right now I still think like a human and I need a human friend. I need Dorjii.*

I can tell—you're contemptuous of me because I'm still so human. Maybe that'll change when I get more like you, but I still have to live here with you now, and here and now you can't supply the companionship I need.

—*So you're not as independent as you claim.*

—*Maybe not.*

—*I don't like it. He'll slow you down, keep you human. And the longer you stay human the longer I'll be trapped here in your body.*

—*You'll have to take that risk. Otherwise I won't cooperate.*

—*How much are you going to tell him?*

—*Not about the Ritual, or the Lha, or you. Not that I'm not a human being.*

—*What will you do when the time comes to grow me a new body? It'll take a long time. Months. And you won't be able to keep the changes in you secret:* (Lozan lying on his back, a shapeless growth pushing its way with agonizing slowness out of his left side, growing larger, taking on form, developing a body, legs, arms, a head, becoming a slender girl with red black hair and green eyes.)

—*I won't let Dorjii interfere with what I've promised to do for you.*

—*What you've promised to do with me.*

—*With you, then. You'll get your body as soon as possible.*

—*What if he's already dead? What if he was never brought here at all?*

—*I'll cooperate with you until I learn enough to check for myself. After that, I don't know.*

—*Give me control. If I find him, I'll bring him to the Place of Remembrance.*

Chapter Thirteen

—HOW MUCH LONGER?

—*Soon. (A grid of coordinates superimposed on the image of a body in a shaefi tube.) You're shielding again.*

—*(Apology.)*

—*Better. Project: (Images/Sensations/Feelings), not just words. Like Mudra.*

—*When? (Dorjii picking himself up off the floor, smiling at Lozan.)*

—*Soon.*

Lozan set the tray of hot meatrolls on the floor by his unconscious friend. Dorjii lay still, seeming scarcely to breathe. When Lozan tried to probe his mind, he found only a frightening emptiness, like a bodiless hunger.

—*What's wrong with him?*

—*You. You drained him of most of his life-force while you were in suspension.*

—*Like a swamp spider. (Lozan with his teeth buried in his friend's side, bloating as Dorjii shrivels.) Is he going to die?*

—*No. You may have saved his life. (Lha after Lha examining Dorjii, rejecting him in favor of other orphans with more life-force.)*

Lozan stared at his friend's healthy-looking body, sensing the emptiness behind the closed eyes.

—*Can I give him back his mind? Give him some of my life-force?*

—No. Let him eat and sleep, regain what he's lost as any animal would.

—Will he recover? Be as he was before?

—Probably. But you'll have to take control of him until he does, make him feed himself.

Lozan tried to probe Dorjii's mind again, sensed only that terrifying emptiness.

With Janesha's help, he took control of Dorjii's de-energized body. Lifting the food to Dorjii's mouth, he felt as though he were moving through thick frond-tree sap; as he chewed and swallowed the food it seemed only more sap, thick and tasteless. When the meal was over he lowered Dorjii's body back to the floor and returned to himself.

—He'll be like that for months. You'll have to feed him and clean up after him. I'll arrange his diet so there's little mess. Lozan detected a hint of amusement in her thought.

—Why are you so happy?

—Because he won't interfere with your progress until he recovers. And the more progress you make, the more you can do to help him.

Dorjii improved slowly. Within three weeks he could feed himself on command and control his bowels if commanded to, but he was no more conscious of himself than a plant would have been. He ignored food put in front of him until Lozan commanded him to eat it, then spooned it clumsily into his mouth and chewed and swallowed it mechanically.

Within five weeks he could answer simple questions, but he seemed as empty of self as ever. He still would not eat until commanded to do so.

"Where are you?" Lozan asked him one time.

No answer.

"Do you know where you are?"

"No."

"Who are you?"

"Dorjii?"

"Do you want to know where you are?"

No answer.

Dorjii had lost none of his memories, but they were without force or meaning; he had no conscious thoughts and few dreams. Lozan soon gave up probing him; the hungry emptiness he found in his friend was too painful. It was increasingly hard to remember Dorjii's courage, the friend he'd once been—even to recognize him as a person. Feeding him was a routine requiring little attention and less time; Lozan's thoughts were elsewhere, concentrated on what he was learning.

At first he only practiced conversing mind to mind with Janesha. Lozan slowly learned to drop his shields, to project the fullness of what he thought and felt without censorship and evasion, to encompass and accept the totality of her response in the same way. He no longer saw Janesha as a bloated swamp spider; he had come to accept the body she projected for him as her true form, to feel that she was the only person he had ever truly known, the only one who had ever known him.

There were periods of relapse, of anger, suspicion or fear, when he'd lash out at her and close himself off behind his shield; but as the weeks passed such moments came less frequently, and meant less and less when they did.

Lozan was changing, but the change was nothing to be feared or endured; it was a growth, an easing, as if he were finally escaping from a life too cramped and bleak to one rich with possibility. As if he'd lived his life shut up in one tiny closet, afraid to leave the security of the dust and darkness, only to find when at last the door was opened that it opened onto the throne room of a palace, and that the palace was his.

As Lozan learned what it was to be Janesha, to feel as she felt and see through her eyes, he realized that despite her vast knowledge and awesome mental competencies, despite the great size and mature development of the body in which she'd first confronted him, she was somehow almost fragile, young and—innocent. It was a strange way to think of her, but it was the only word he could find that described her openness, the unquestioning trust he found in the deeper layers of her mind.

—*How old are you?* he finally thought to ask.

—*Sixteen standard years, about a year less by the Nal-K'am calendar.*

Somehow the fact that he was a year older than she made a difference. And as he learned more about what it meant to live in total openness and intimacy with another Lha, he realized that he could have had no real idea of what it had meant to her to be cut off from Night.

Her hunger to return to Night shaded her every thought, intruded upon her every joy. Lozan found that as he began to comprehend the anguish of her separation, to realize with what strength she endured her exile, the contempt he had felt for her vanished.

I was always so proud I could endure more pain than other people. But all I ever knew were little pains, easy pains. Easy for me because I'm Lha. Nothing was ever that bad for me.

It did not at first seem strange to find himself getting angry at the Lha for the way they were treating Janesha.

—*It's not fair to punish you like this. Could any of the other young Lha have done any better?*

—*Lozan, I am not being punished. I'm here to learn to bear the pain of my exile, to function as I should be able to function despite it. What I learn to do we will all be capable of. I did not understand this at first but now I know how important it is. Nothing like what I tried to do to you can ever be allowed to happen again.*

—*But I already know how to live without Night. Use my knowledge.*

—*You have no knowledge to share; your strength is only ignorance. Chordeyean, Dawa Tsong, Yag ta Mishraunal—they all endured existence as humans ignorant of their true natures. Their experiences were*

useless to me. Not knowing something is not the same
as knowing how to live with its loss.

One morning, as Lozan was setting a tray of food on the floor before Dorjii, Dorjii said, "Lozan."

"Dorjii!" Lozan was totally unprepared; he had almost ceased to regard Dorjii as a sentient being.

"Lozan," Dorjii repeated, then lapsed back into his silence. Lozan attempted to probe his thoughts, sensed something there that had not been there before, as though a little—a very little—of his friend had returned from some far-off place; but the hunger and the emptiness were still there, still too painful to endure. Lozan withdrew.

—If I pry into his mind it'll change things too much; we won't be able to be friends as we used to be.

—What you mean is you won't be able to playact at being the same kind of friends you were as easily. You're not who you were when Dorjii knew you, and you're not going to be able to tell him who you really are now. You'll just be using him to play a game with yourself.

—In a way. But I'm still his friend; I still care for him and want to do what I can to make his life happier.

—Then don't awaken him here. He won't be happy in the Refuge. He can't be.

—I still need him. He's all I've got left of what I used to be. I'm not ready to let go of it all, not yet. Not quite yet.

Lozan watched Dorjii's face closely while he fed him his evening meal, but did not probe his mind. Dorjii remained oblivious to him, though he seemed to be eating less clumsily. Lozan finally left him.

That night he grasped for the first time the techniques necessary to use his Rilg memories. Before morning came he could dip into Mishraunal's vast fund of experiences and retrieve any specific experience of whose existence he was aware, but Mishraunal's memories were available in much the same way the books in a library would have been; he could consult them but they were not yet a part of him.

170

—Give yourself time, Janesha told him.

Dorjii was still sitting staring at the wall when Lozan entered with his morning tray of meat rolls, but he was wearing the kilt that had lain ignored within easy reach for weeks. His back was to Lozan.

"Dorjii?"

Dorjii turned slowly, stared up at Lozan, then down at the tray of food Lozan had put beside him. He picked up a roll and ate it, chewing each bite slowly. He picked up the second roll, ate it with the same slow deliberation.

"How long . . . have I been here?" His words were as slow as his movements.

"Nine weeks. Do you remember anything . . . how you got here?"

"There was . . . a tube. They put me in a tube." He paused, continued haltingly, "I couldn't move. Everything was orange. Nothing moved. Nothing ever moved . . . but there was a hole in me. Just a little hole, that's all, but I drained out of it until there wasn't any of me left anymore."

I did that to him. To six hundred people.

"It was like . . . when the priests killed my mother and father. But it was me they were killing and it went on and on. . . . You said—nine weeks? Only nine weeks?"

"Nine weeks here," Lozan said. "Here with me. But we were in the tubes for twenty-seven years. Both of us. I was there with you."

Dorjii clenched his fists, looked up at Lozan. "I'm not that old." He opened his hands, examined them carefully, put his hand to his smooth cheek. "I can't be that old."

"You're not. Neither am I. We didn't get any older in the tubes."

"I could feel myself draining down that little hole. . . . Lozan, I'm so weak, so—. Only I'm not weak, but—. Like there's just a little Dorjii here inside my body and it doesn't fit me anymore, there isn't enough of me left to fill me up. . . ."

171

"You're still you, Dorjii. You were asleep for twenty-seven years, that's all. It's going to take you a long time to wake up."

"Sren. . . . The priests that told me mother and father were dead. Maybe they're all dead now. Even—. Even—." He shook his head, confused. "I can't say—."

"Don't try to talk about it," Lozan said, remembering the way Lavelle had twisted their minds so that any attempt to speak about him was lost in a confusion of unrelated memories. "You're safe here with me."

"Lozan, where are we? What is this?" His words were coming faster now as he stared around the small square room, seeming to notice the black-silk panels with the green and white lotus flowers on them for the first time. "They dressed me in red and I knew they were going to kill me, and then they killed me before I could. . . . I can't remember!"

Lozan put a hand on Dorjii's shoulder, felt the tension knotting the flaccid muscles. "You weren't dead, Dorjii. Just asleep. That's all. Just a different kind of asleep, and it makes you feel a different kind of tired when you wake up. But you're safe here, with me. I promise."

"Are we—hiding here? From the priests?"

"No. We're somewhere where there aren't any priests. Would you like to see what it's like outside?"

Without waiting for an answer Lozan visualized the necessary coordinate and made the corresponding gesture. "Follow me," he said, and stepped through the teleportation matrix to the outside. A moment later Dorjii followed him.

"Lozan, how did you. . . ." He broke off, staring around him in stunned wonder.

"It's a special kind of door. I'll tell you about it later."

Dorjii wasn't listening. Lozan said, "This is the Hall of the Crimson Cloud."

To their left they could see a fountain half-hidden in

172

the artful tangle of the jungle; to their right the black and green checkered plain stretched away into the distance. In the jungle, birds sang. Overhead hung the crimson cloud.

"Are we on another planet?"

—*Tell him yes.*

—*No.*

—*Why not? You're going to be lying to him about almost everything else and he won't remember anything you tell him afterward, anyway.*

"We're still on Nal-K'am but we're—we're in a place deep underground, where there aren't any priests. But it's not Hell down here as they say it is. It's not Heaven, not really, but it's like a Heaven."

"No priests?"

"None. You're safe here. Come along and I'll explain it to you." He took Dorjii by the arm, guided him along a path into the jungle.

"Do you remember those tests we had to take on Naming Day?"

Dorjii nodded.

"Because of them I was chosen to come down here. Not by the priests; the priests don't know anything about down here. They've got it all backward, they think this is Hell—."

"What about me?" Dorjii's voice was unexpectedly harsh.

"You were chosen to come down here, too. Like me. After we learn what it's really like down here we're going to be sent to other worlds, so we can tell the people the truth about what it's like here."

—*You're telling him too many lies, making things too complicated. Tell him he's on another planet.*

—*It's too late.*

—*I can blank his memories of what you've told him. Then you can start over, do it right.*

—*No. That would be as if—as if I was Lha and he was just a human. And I don't want it like that. Not with Dorjii.*

173

—It would be kinder.

—I can't.

"There aren't any priests here?" Dorjii asked.

"No. You're safe here. It's like—we're adepts here, underground, Dorjii. Not like your father, not like the adepts on Mig Mar, but adepts anyway. I'm not an adept yet but they're training me; I'll be an adept someday.

"We're down here because—the priests revolted against us and took Nal-K'am away from us and perverted all our teachings. They made the Goddess Night into a monster and forced us all to come down here where they couldn't come after us—."

"What you're saying is, you're a priest of Night now, but not the same kind of priest?"

—Blank his memories. Tell him he's on another planet. Or you'll have to keep on telling him more and more lies.

—No, I—. That's Lha.

—And you want a human friendship. What can that be worth, if it's all lies?

—You don't understand. We've spent our whole lives together.

"Are you or aren't you?" Dorjii demanded.

"I'm training to be an adept. I worship Night, but She's nothing like the Goddess Night the priests told you about; that's all lies the priests tell, like the lie that we're dead and in Hell."

"I don't believe you."

"Dorjii—."

"You're lying to me, Lozan. They made you a priest and now you're just like the rest of them. I can *feel* it in you."

—You've lost him. Unless you let me make him forget.

—Do it. Put him to sleep and do it.

Lozan caught Dorjii as he fell.

—You tried to share too much of the truth with him. You're trying to make yourself a little fantasy world in

*which you and he can be human together, but when
you try to mix in any of the truth you ruin everything.
If you want to live in a fantasy, fine, do it; but you'll
have to make up a fantasy world to do it in. Tell him
he's on another planet.*

—*He'll be happier if he thinks it's another planet.
He always wanted to get away from Nal-K'am.*

—*That's right, Lozan. He'll be happier. And you
won't have to keep on making up new lies all the time
to keep him from hating you.*

—*Janesha, I know what I'm doing. I'm not lying to
myself; I know I'm just pretending, acting out a fantasy. I know. But I need that fantasy because once it
stops, once I really give up being a human being and
become Lha, all Lha, then that's forever. It'll never
end, Janesha; good or bad it'll never end, and that's
frightening. It scares me. I need to rest, to give myself
time. Time that's going to end. Something that I know
is going to be over. Please. Help me.*

—*(Acceptance.) Do you want me to erase all his
memories of the Refuge? I can make him think he
remembers escaping from the Temple with you,
or—.*

—*No. Can you just erase them without—touching
anything else, without learning anything more about
him? The—fantasy—will be easier if I don't know that
all I have to do is just ask you if I want to know when
he's telling the truth. I want us to be human beings
together, lying and exaggerating and deciding to trust
each other without really knowing—do you understand? Can you do it?*

—*I can make his mind do it to itself. But I don't
understand; I feel something of what you feel but—
you're shielding. You don't really want me to understand.*

—*I want you to understand but not to—share. It's
like forever. If you're part of it then it's bigger than
me; it doesn't end; I can't just—stop. Like being a
Lha. If you share it, it's the same thing. Not separate.*

175

Not being a human being again, even a fake human being.

—Then you don't want me to give him any false memories.

—No. I'll lie to him. That's a very human thing, lying to a friend.

Chapter Fourteen

"Nal-K'am really was Hell, compared to here," Lozan said, gesturing at the jungle around them.

Dorjii nodded, too preoccupied to really notice his surroundings. "I don't—. After that priest came to tell me I'd been chosen for the Temple. I don't remember anything after that."

"What happened to me was, a priest took me to a room where the light was all bright and swirly," Lozan said. "Do you remember that?"

"No. . . . Just, I went through a door and it was light on the other side. That's all."

"They already had you in one of their . . . conditioning machines, I guess, and they were going to put me in next when Lavelle's people rescued us. Maybe that's why I can remember and you can't."

"But then why did he. . . ." Dorjii broke off, the familiar confusion on his face. "How come you can talk about . . . about *him,* and I can't?"

Lozan shrugged. "It's taken them a month to overcome what the priests did to you. Give yourself a little more time to recover; then they'll take care of the rest of it. Don't worry about it."

"And this is—where? What's the name of this planet?"

"I don't know. It's a secret place, where some of the MigMartian adepts train people like Lavelle . . .

and like us, now. So we can go back to Nal-K'am."

"You said—." Dorjii broke off again, scowling, then demanded angrily, "Why can't I remember things? I mean, not just what happened in the Temple, or what they did to cure me, but right now, when you tell me something—."

"Because of the conditioning machines. You'll be back to normal in a few weeks."

"They're really going to train me to be an adept? The same way they're training you?"

"Yes. But your father was training you in the Vajrayana, so you're going to have to wait a little longer, until a Vajrayana adept comes from Mig Mar. There aren't any here now, just Bon-po adepts like the one training me."

"How much longer?"

"A month or so. You need more time to recover before you can start, anyway."

"And then, how much longer till we go back to Nal-K'am?"

"When they're done with us. My adept won't tell me how long that'll take."

—*So many lies,* Janesha said.

—*Not now. Wait until he goes to sleep.*

Ahead of them, the path turned aside to avoid a sheer cliff of smooth stone banded like a giant agate, and widened out into a clearing beside a deep quartz-bottomed pool fed by a small but noisy waterfall. In the clear water green and silver fish darted. Lozan could feel the warm golden light from the cloud above on his bare shoulders.

"You look tired. Let's sit down a while," Lozan suggested. Dorjii looked like he was about to protest. "You've got to get your strength back before you can do anything else," Lozan added, and Dorjii nodded unwillingly and sat down beside him on the mossy ground, where they could stare at the waterfall.

Every now and then an insect would skim too close to the surface of the water and be snapped up by an alert fish. In the distance Lozan could hear a chorus of tiny flutes: the wind playing over one of the singing statues.

A small blue hawk with a gold crest on its head and white wingtips swooped down on the pool, emerged with a struggling emerald fish. The hawk landed on the far shore and began to devour the fish.

Dorjii was staring at the bird in fascination. Lozan was caught up again in the memory of that first time he'd seen Dorjii with a bird perched on his arm. It would be so easy; all he'd have to do would be reach into the bird's mind, make it love Dorjii—.

No. But why not? He couldn't lie to himself, pretend he was a human being, not when he could hear the thoughts of the birds in the trees, not when he could feel the insects burrowing through the mud. What he could do was make Dorjii happy, give him a taste of that happiness which Lozan would never again be able to share, and enjoy it through him.

"Do you think you can call it to you?" He half whispered. "Like the birds at Agad?"

Dorjii looked sad. "I don't—."

"Try."

Dorjii took a breath, sang a few tentative, quavering words—and as he did so Lozan reached out for the hawk, impressed his command on it. The bird gulped down the rest of the fish, walked deliberately around the pool and up to Dorjii, then pecked him amiably on the cheek.

Dorjii laughed, surprised and pleased, but very quietly so as not to startle the bird. The hawk regarded him out of russet eyes. Dorjii slowly brought his arm around under the bird's chest and the hawk hopped up onto his wrist. Very slowly Dorjii lifted it free of the ground. When the bird remained perched on his wrist, he brought his other hand around, gently stroked its feathers.

The hawk gave a little screech of pleasure. Dorjii tried to imitate it. The hawk screeched again. This time when Dorjii tried to imitate it there was a faint resemblance between the two sounds.

The hawk took flight. Dorjii watched it in anxious silence as it circled the pool, then dived for another fish; but he was smiling happily when the bird returned to his wrist and ate its catch there.

"You seem to have a friend for life," Lozan said softly. The bird looked at him suspiciously.

"I'll name him Ja-mi-zan," Dorjii said.

"He's the wrong color for the King of the Dragons."

"But he's got wings and scales—even if they are on his feet—and he eats fish." He stroked the hawk a while longer, then said, "I've had enough rest. Show me around some more."

Lozan spent the rest of the day showing Dorjii the Hall of the Crimson Cloud, avoiding only those places, like the Place of Remembrance, that he would have had difficulty explaining away. Dorjii seemed curious and open-minded, impressed by the beauty of everything he saw. Ja-mi-zan stayed with him, riding sometimes on his arm and shoulder, flying sometimes overhead.

When evening came, they entered a room with a surabha in it. Dorjii stared for a moment at the painted screens covering the walls—Lozan could tell they reminded him of the tutelary demons guarding the Temples and Shrines—then walked over to the surabha and knelt beside it, examining the jeweled landscape inside the crystal globe.

"It's nice," he said, straightening, "but I thought you brought me here for dinner." He jumped back as two plates of food and two cups of tea snapped into existence on the woven-wire table cupping the globe.

"You did that?" he asked.

"The machine did it."

"But you controlled it." He took a bite of one of his rolls.

"Yes."

"Can it make anything? Anything you want?"

—*Janesha?*

—*Within certain limits. Nothing too massive, and you have to be able to indicate the molecular structure*

180

for anything the surabha hasn't already been pro-grammed for.

Lozan repeated the information, adding, "I only know how to make it make a few things. Do you need something else?"

"No, but other people do. In the village I grew up in a lot of people starved to death every time they had a bad year. With this machine they could have been fed."

Lozan shook his head. "No. It takes an adept to operate it."

"How much training do you think you've had, Lozan? Three weeks? A whole month? It takes years to learn to be a good beggar!"

"I know, but—. Not everybody can become an adept. Anyway, the priests would've never allowed it. If the people weren't starving to death, they'd never believe they were in Hell."

Dorjii nodded. "It'll be different after. . . ." He lost his train of thought.

". . . after the Terrans get there," Lozan finished for him.

Dorjii nodded, changed the subject. "And it's that mysterious adept of yours who's training you to use it, along with all the rest?"

"Yes."

"Then why haven't I seen him? Why haven't I seen anyone?"

Lozan reached into the memories Yag ta Mishraunal had given him of his life as Yag Chan for an explanation. "There aren't many people here and they're all Bon-po right now. You're Vajrayana."

"So?"

"The Bon-po adepts are all hermits. They avoid contact with anybody else except when, well, when they've accepted you as a student."

"This training you're getting—could you teach it to me? You're not a hermit."

"Not yet. But you're Vajrayana."

"You could ask your adept."

"All right. The next time he allows me to ask him a question."

Dorjii frowned. "You never used to be like that. Waiting for someone to give you permission to ask him a question!"

"Things are different here. It's not like Nal-K'am."

"No."

There was no real reason not to ask Janesha; he'd given up trying to pretend he could fool himself into thinking he was human.

—*Do you think I could actually teach him something?*

—*We use some MigMartian techniques, but they take years for humans to learn. And you'd just make your little fantasy that much harder to maintain.*

For a moment he was tempted to tell her to go ahead and erase Dorjii's memories, put him back in suspension until they were ready to send him offplanet.

—*I won't need him much longer.*

—*It would be a kinder—.*

—*I know. I know I'm doing this for me, not for him.*

"You know my father started to train me—," Dorjii was insisting.

"In the Vajrayana," Lozan finished, cutting him off. "I know. That just makes it harder. But I'll ask my adept anyway. As soon as he lets me."

Dorjii scowled but let the matter drop.

Chapter Fifteen

IT WAS AS THOUGH EVERYTHING HE SENSED became part of his body and subject to his will. It was a little like becoming a fish again, sensing the world around you by touch, living in intimate connection with everything you perceived. Like becoming a fish that had become the sea in which it swam.

—*How long have we been here?* Lozan demanded abruptly.

—*I don't know,* Janesha admitted. *Without my body, I have little sense of duration.*

—*It's late. (Bright golden light striking the pavilion's green dome, beginning to warm the chill stone.) He must've already left the lotus-island.*

—*So? He won't hurt himself.*

—*He must be hungry.*

—*Not very.*

—*You're not—.*

—*No. He just had that long to get hungry in. Use your sense of perception to locate him; that shouldn't interfere with your fantasy too much.*

—*It's not like that anymore; I know I can't even pretend to myself that we're still human beings together. But I still need him. Maybe to remind me that I'm not human anymore. And I want him to be happy.*

—*He was never happy.*

—*Why? Why (Dorjii telling Lozan and Lavelle about his parents' deaths/Tsong refusing to wear the glasses*

183

he needed so the blind in other Hells could have the vision he was sacrificing/the Nagyspa Lozan had seen kill the priest being broken on the blasphemer's rack) are we so cruel to them here? Why make them live in Hell?

—That other colony ship, the one we arranged for the Terrans to find, was filled with the followers of a leader preaching much what we have our priests teach. We did not invent the religion of Night; we merely turned it to our own uses. And our priests are programmed with only the conditioning necessary to make them believe in Night and carry out those duties necessary to our existence; the rest—their cruelty, their fanaticism, the pleasure they take in their power over their fellows—they chose for themselves.

—Why not condition them out of it, then? Why allow them to continue?

—Camouflage. Human rulers are always cruel. (Sren whipping Lozan with the knotted cords.) We dare do nothing to call attention to our existence.

—Lavelle told me humans would never build anything so big as the Temple.

—They might never have built it, but we found the plans for the Temple—only larger, of course, and not nearly so well designed—on the same ship. Its height was supposed to convince the damned of the total effort they had to make to escape Hell.

—But letting people starve—.

—It is necessary. As you told Dorjii, who would believe he was damned and in Hell if nobody starved or did without the necessities of life?

Lozan let the subject drop, still unconvinced, and reached out with his perceptive sense for Dorjii.

—I've found him. (Dorjii prying furiously at the flimsy panels of an octagonal structure in the middle of the checkered plain with a length of branch broken from one of the trees in the jungle, trying to force his way in.)

—He's bored. He suspects the Terrans of hiding

184

something from him, and you of going along with them. You've got to give him more to occupy his attention.

—You're right.

—Can you leach the strength from those walls so he can break in? That way (Dorjii yelling in triumph as the wall gives way) he'll at least feel that he's accomplished something.

—I think so. . . . Her tone had been ironic, but the idea made sense. Lozan reached out to the structure, grasped its patterning in his mind and began modifying its molecular structure, weakening it. . . . *(One of the panels breaks loose. Dorjii rams the branch in farther, twists harder, and the panel breaks off. Dorjii scrambles into the building through the hole he's made, searches the empty interior, finally climbs back out again and fits the broken panel back into place to hide what he's done.)*

—You can't just leave him here like that. He needs something to do. Some sort of goal.

—Can you free him to talk about Lavelle with me? That way I can find out more about what Lavelle promised him, what he expected, and arrange things better for him.

—If you want. It'll make it even harder for you to keep your explanations straight.

—Do it anyway. At least it'll give him one less thing to be frustrated about.

"Did you ask your adept?" Dorjii demanded. He took a spoonful of barley mush, swallowed it.

"Yes. He said your adept would be here in three weeks—."

"And I just have to wait until he arrives."

"Yes. He said I don't know enough yet to teach anybody anything." He paused an instant, then asked, "What's wrong, Dorjii? It's only three more weeks."

"This place. No rain, no sun, it never gets too cold or too hot, all the animals are too friendly to be real. . . . There's never anything to do, nowhere for their

185

starships to land, no people or machines, nothing. It's like—."

"Like what?"

"Like it's all fake. And I can't even take care of myself; you have to follow me around, help me as if I were some sort of baby. . . . You can get what you want from that thing"—he gestured angrily at the surabha—"but I can't even ask you about Lavelle—." He broke off, realizing what he'd just said.

"You're coming out of it," Lozan said. "As I said you would."

Dorjii nodded.

"So you can ask me what you want, now."

"I don't want to ask *you* anything. I want to ask Lavelle, or that mysterious adept of yours . . . somebody who really knows something."

Lozan shrugged. "Try me. Maybe I already asked the same questions."

"All right. What is that adept training they're giving you for? What're you supposed to *do* back on Nal-K'am?"

"The same thing Lavelle was doing, until the Terrans take over. You remember what the priests did to us in Testing, with the bubbles?"

Dorjii nodded.

"That won't work on me anymore. Pretty soon I'll be able to handle the machines they used on you in the Temple."

"And that's all?"

"Of course not. I can use the surabha now. When they get rid of the priests they're going to need some way to keep people fed before they get things organized again. . . . That sort of stuff."

"You remember getting here?" Dorjii demanded. "The starship, landing here, everything?"

"Not much. They put me to sleep for the trip."

"But you remember landing?"

"Yes."

"Where?"

"They've got a starport somewhere on the other

186

side of the world. They brought me here in a flyer."

"And it's all like this? The whole planet?"

"Not what I saw. Mostly just black rocks and deserts. This is sort of a garden they built. For the adepts."

"You could see the sun?"

"From the flyer, when we were high enough. It's a lot yellower than our sun. Why?"

"Nothing . . . Everything just feels so—artificial here. Like none of it's real. . . ."

"It's a different planet, that's all. That's why it doesn't feel right."

"Maybe. . . . You think they're going to train me to do the same stuff as you?"

"I don't know." He caught the look on Dorjii's face, asked, "Did Lavelle promise you something different?"

Dorjii nodded, looking suddenly more vulnerable. "He said that . . . maybe . . . if we got through this alive, both of us . . . that he was going to be someone very important on Nal-K'am and that he'd adopt me. As his son. But if he meant that, he wouldn't have just shipped me off here, without even any sort of message for me—."

"I told you I didn't get to see him, that they had to sneak me onto the starship before the priests had a chance to discover what they'd done in the Temple. He'll get a message to you when he can; I'm sure he will."

When they met for evening meal, Dorjii said, "Could you teach me just how to get in and out of buildings and feed myself? That way, you won't have to be taking care of me when you could be learning more of those mysterious secrets your adept doesn't want you to share with me."

"It isn't like that."

"Yes it is."

Lozan hesitated.

—*Janesha?*

—*I can make a slavebrain to do it for him. I'll need*

187

a full day and complete use of your nervous system. You'll have to stay in the hawk.

—*The isolation won't bother you?*

—*A little.*

—*I'll return at mealtimes, to help with Dorjii.*

"I'll ask my adept," Lozan promised.

Dorjii was looking at him speculatively. "Can you get that thing to make Dakkini wood?" he asked finally, indicating the surabha.

—*Can we?*

—*Easily. Give me control.*

A Dakkini-wood twig snapped into existence on the surabha's wire rim. Dorjii picked it up, sniffed it, scraped a sliver free with a fingernail and jabbed it into his skin.

"Thanks. Can you ask him to teach me how to make Dakkini wood along with the food?"

"I'll ask him."

Lozan spent the night in the body of the hawk, flying high above the crimson cloud in the cold golden brilliance just beneath the roof. He was finding that long periods spent in the bird's body helped sharpen his sense of identity with Mishraunal.

The next morning Dorjii still seemed groggy from the Dakkini wood he'd used the night before. But he asked for a second log half again the size of the first one anyway, as well as some food for the birds and animals he said he was befriending. Lozan gave him the log with some misgivings, though as far as he knew Dakkini wood was completely harmless and would serve to keep Dorjii occupied and out of trouble.

He told Dorjii his adept had agreed to provide Dorjii with a talisman that would enable him to use the doors and surabhas, but it would take a day to get it ready. Dorjii thanked him with such a profuse and insincere show of gratitude that Lozan was worried.

I'll look in on him later, make sure he's doing all right.

Dorjii left for the jungle with the food he'd saved for the animals he was befriending. Lozan returned to the hawk. But the bird was ravenous and Lozan found its hunger too distracting to allow him to concentrate on Mishraunal. He hadn't given the hawk much chance to hunt the last few days and had avoided taking it with him to meals, where Dorjii's less impressive hawk would have inevitably suffered by comparison.

Lozan flew out into the jungle, freeing the hawk-mind from his control and reducing his role to that of a passenger in its brain.

The hawk found a smaller bird, killed and devoured it. Lozan hesitated when it finished—he could go back to concentrating on Mishraunal or he could look for Dorjii—finally decided to look for Dorjii.

Dorjii was sitting on an artfully fallen log, sucking on the wooden part of the Dakkini twig Lozan had given him while he carefully stripped the hair-fine splinters from its dry inner bark and jabbed them, one by one, under the skin of his forearms and inner arms.

There were only a few splinters left, which surprised Lozan: he'd expected Dorjii to pace himself so as to remain intoxicated all day.

Dorjii never did anything halfway. And at least, totally withdrawn like this, he wasn't any danger to himself or anyone else.

He suggested to the hawk-mind that the hawk land in one of the branches overhead. Dorjii glanced up at the hawk, grinned wryly, then returned to his concentration on the final splinters. He shoved them in under his skin, checked to make sure the others were dissolving correctly, then sat for a moment in perfect stillness, as though listening.

He absentmindedly ruffled Ja-mi-zan's neck feathers, then closed his eyes. He slid slowly off the log, upsetting a place piled with food that had been resting by his foot, to lie sprawled and unconscious while Ja-mi-zan, unconcerned, hopped around tearing pieces off the meatrolls he'd spilled.

Lozan's perceptive sense told him Dorjii's body was still functioning perfectly, but this was an effect he'd never seen from Dakkini wood. By rights, Dorjii should still have been in the rational stage of his intoxication, despite the high dosage.

A moment later Dorjii opened his eyes again. He smiled, started to get to his feet, then seemed to think better of it and twisted around to sit propped up against the log. He took the bare Dakkini log from his mouth and put it in his kilt pocket, then carefully put all the food he'd knocked from the plate back on it. He glanced around once more, then sat back very still, waiting.

A small feathered biped, yellow and four-armed, came swinging down out of the trees. Lozan was impressed: choolahs were among the few unmodified animals in the Hall of the Crimson Cloud, and they were exceedingly timid.

The choolah tugged at Dorjii's left arm with two of its hands, while it used the other two to snatch a roll from the plate. Dorjii scratched it behind the ears, and it curled into a ball by his side and seemed to go to sleep.

A large six-limbed carnivore with a bright blue muzzle sticking incongruously out of the bristly black hair that covered the rest of its face and body entered the clearing. Dorjii clucked at it and it padded up to him, resting its heavy head in his lap and half crushing the choolah in the process while Dorjii fed it the remaining rolls. The choolah wriggled out from underneath, protesting, and scampered to Dorjii's other side, where it again curled itself into a ball.

There was no need to worry about Dorjii; he seemed happy enough and he was far more skilled with animals than Lozan could ever have imagined. He released his control on the hawk, freeing it to resume its hunting.

Dorjii saw the hawk leaving and closed his eyes. Lozan felt an abrupt feather-touch at the hawk's mind, a quiet caress, a suggestion of warmth.

Dorjii was telepathic.

Lozan kept himself sealed off, waiting to see how the hawk would react. Blurred images of the hawk returning to Dorjii began to drift from Dorjii's mind to the hawk's, accompanied by reassurances about the choolah and the blue-muzzled carnivore, which seemed to have gone to sleep. Lozan disengaged himself entirely from the hawk-mind and, shielding, projected: —*Janesha, can you be disturbed?*

—*(Assent.)*

—*Is Dorjii Lha?* (The animals clustered around Dorjii/the telepathic feather touch at the hawk's mind.)

—*(Absolute denial.) His parents survived his birth. You drained him of most of his life-force.*

—*But then what is he?*

—*A talented human who's had some training.*

—*Then what makes us so superior to them?*

—*They are ephemeral, with no control over their bodies and natures, no ability to surpass their individual selves.*

—*But does that make it right to treat them the way we do?*

—*We do what we must, for our own survival. The Ritual is kind, and the Religion of Night is their own invention.*

—*The Rilg regarded the unChanged members of their race as their brothers.*

—*And were destroyed by them. We must learn from their mistakes, not repeat them.*

—*Yet—.*

—*Not now. Your friend, at least, is safe for the moment; we can discuss this further later.*

Dorjii was asleep again, a ribbon of drool running from the corner of his mouth. The animals were beginning to drift back into the forest. Soon only Ja-mi-zan and the crimson hawk remained.

He never told me. And he had thought Dorjii incapable of keeping a secret from him.

He'd been trying to resurrect the lost simplicity of their human friendship . . . and all the time it had been a friendship between a Lha making unconscious use of his powers and a human telepath hiding his abilities.

Whatever they'd been together, it had undoubtedly been something very other than a normal human friendship; for all that, neither of them had realized how different it had been.

—*I've completed the slavebrain. You can return to our body.*

—*Janesha, they're too like us. It's not right.*

—*(Dorjii lying unconscious, drooling.)*

—*Yes! Like Lha without training. Without Night. As I was.*

—*We have no choice. None of us can survive without absorbing other minds. You'll have to absorb another mind soon yourself, and there are no nonhuman intelligences on Nal-K'am.*

—*I have thirteen years.*

—*(Denial.)*

—*(?)*

—*You would have had thirteen years if you'd had my mind to draw upon. Now with the two of us in one body we need far more life-force than a single Lha, and it will take still more life-force to animate a new body for me.*

—*How long do I have?*

—*Less than a year. I'll need to absorb another mind myself as soon as I gain my new body.*

Dorjii opened his eyes and pushed himself clumsily to his feet. He started walking, stumbling repeatedly but keeping going.

—*He's going to hurt himself! Teleport us there.*

—*Give me control.*

They met Dorjii coming around a bend in the trail.

"There you are," Dorjii said, looking at them with unfocused eyes, a patently false ingratiating smile. "I need some more wood."

"No. I've given you too much already."

"You're just afraid to let me have any more." Dorjii attempted to twist the slack muscles of his face into a scowl.

"I'm just afraid you'll hurt yourself."

"No, you're not. You thought it would keep me

busy. Out of trouble. But I've been watching you. Watching you when you're not around. The wood helps me see. When you're with me you're Lozan—."

"Of course I'm Lozan."

"But not quite the real Lozan. And when you're alone you're not Lozan at all. You're something else, like Lavelle told me about. The animals remember. You stole Lozan's body and you're just pretending to be him. Just like you're just pretending we're not in the Temple."

—*Put him to sleep. You've lost him.*

—*Janesha, transfer to the hawk. I want to try one last time.*

—*Will you put him to sleep if it doesn't work?*

—*Yes.*

"Who am I now?" Lozan asked.

"You seem like Lozan—only different, just a little different. But you're just being careful now you know that I know who you really are."

"No. I'm Lozan—. You know I'm Lozan; otherwise you wouldn't be talking to me like this. But someone sometimes shares my body with me. The adept who's training me. And I seem different because I'm becoming an adept. That's all. I'm still Lozan, Dorjii."

"Sometimes Lozan wasn't there at all."

"I can—put myself into that red hawk you saw." Lozan said. "That's one of the things he's teaching me."

Dorjii seemed to be wavering. "You always loved birds," Lozan said. "Don't you want to learn how to *be* one? I can fly now . . . and when I'm away from my body I sometimes let the adept use it. I let her use it so she could make the talisman I promised you."

Lozan reached into his kilt pocket for the tiny black ovoid that was the slavebrain. "With this"—his hand coming out of the pocket, opening to show the slavebrain—"you'll be able to make yourself all the Dakkini—."

Dorjii's eyes wide with horrified recognition, Dorjii screaming, in his mind the scream, Dorjii screaming in his mind: —*HERE, THE TEMPLE, THE VAMPIRES FROM THE VAULT*—.

—*Control!* Janesha's commmand like a whiplash. Stunned, he relinquished control.

The screaming stopped. Dorjii fell. Slowly. It took him a long time to reach the ground . . . to hit, rebound slightly, settle back. To lie there unmoving.

Dead.

—*You killed him!* Lozan snatched control back from Janesha, knelt down and touched Dorjii's face.

Dead.

—*He was betraying us. There was no other way.*

The ground shuddered. There was a distant explosion, and the birds in the jungle took panicked flight. Another explosion. Another.

—*We're under attack! Merge us with Night!*

Lozan ignored her. "I'm sorry," he said. "I'm sorry, Dorjii."

—*Merge us!*

—*No.* But Night's dying thoughts thrust aside his flimsy barriers, flooding him:

THEY ARE USING THE RILG AGAINST US. DO NOT ACTIVATE THE DOOR TO RILDAN. BREAK RAPPORT; TRY TO ESCAPE AS INDIVIDUALS. . . .

(Jomgoun's headless body still leaking slow blood. In one hand he holds the skull-flower; the Knife of the Ritual lies half-hidden beneath his body. Above him floats a metal sphere: inside it a man, his head completely enclosed by a jeweled helmet, flanked by two octagonal green crystals, the one on the left containing a gray, many-tentacled Rilg, the one on the right holding a white-furred, four-limbed, fanged Rilg.)

DYING, TRY TO—.

(Chordeyean, eyeless, the manikins on his neck drooping like flaccid balloons, stands with fists clenched on a plain of white crystal. Three metal spheres float above him; a fourth lies crumpled at his feet. A green mist forms around him, crystallizes. Two of the spheres vanish.)

Janesha was pleading with him for control. He gave

it to her, felt his hands strip his kilt from his body, as his mind visualized a complex system of matrix coordinates and his hands moved in quick, complex gestures.

Everything was frozen, orange. Still. He did not have a body. On every side of him endless rows of shaefi tubes, in each tube the nude body of a hairless orphan.

—*I've shielded us with a layer of human-seeming thoughts,* Janesha told him. *We'll be safe here.*

Chapter Sixteen

—YOU KILLED DORJII. BUT HIS ANGER AND loss were receding, slipping away from him. He fought to retain them, to hold on to his pain, but the shaefi suspension robbed him of his feelings, left him nothing but cold rationality.

—There was no way to destroy the slavebrain (the tiny wrinkled ovoid lying hidden in Dorjii's brain, using a trickle of his life-force to remain concealed until the time came for it to drain him of his remaining life-force, to use his stolen life to power its telepathic broadcast) without killing him. And the slavebrain would have killed him anyway even if I hadn't interfered.

Lozan pictured Dorjii sitting with Lavelle in the tea shop as Lavelle reassured him, promised to adopt him as his son, then led him trusting to the Terran starship and implanted the slavebrain in him.

Killed him.

Cannibals.

He dismissed the thought, asked: —How . . . ?

—The Terrans have found a way to enslave the Rilg. (The Rilg embedded in the octagonal green crystals/ the human operators in their jeweled helmets.) They're trying to do the same thing to us. . . .

—(The green-mist crystallizing around Chordeyean?)

—Yes. Give me control: I can use your senses better than you can.

A moment later: —*It's some kind of suspension . . . almost like shaefi suspension but it paralyzes the will as well as the body, so the human operators can use those helmets to draw on their captive Rilg's powers. . . .*

—*Are there any Lha still free?*

—*No. There were too many of them, too few of us.*

—*Night?*

—*Destroyed*. It was only a fact to her, something to be taken into consideration when she made her plans. She knew how anguished she would have been had she not been in suspension, but that too was only another factor to be taken into consideration.

—*Their helmets are like the old Rilg mechanical telepaths; they can't have much sensitivity. I think I can risk mental contact with one of the human operators if—*.

She broke off suddenly. —*No. A Rilg—they're directing the Rilg to absorb the orphans in suspension. . . . They don't realize we're any different. Merge with me, quickly. . . .*

Memories floated to the surface of their united consciousness at the Rilg-mind's touch—simple human memories from Lozan's childhood. He felt Janesha selecting from them and taking those she chose, fashioning them into a ball of amber fire into which the Rilg reached greedily—.

Only to be itself absorbed. Lozan and Janesha's linked minds absorbed it as it had sought to absorb them, as it had already absorbed all the orphans in the tubes around them, sucking out its vitality and that of its human operator, drinking the flames of their lives and leaving a dead sphere to bob uncontrolled in the air above them.

—*We're lucky there was only one Rilg in that sphere*.

Then the energy was cascading through them, the flaming rainbow ecstasy that swept them away despite their suspended condition. New memories spun dizzily through their minds.

And winding through those memories, a dark serpentine thread, the human operator's lust for the ecstasy he shared every time the Rilg he controlled absorbed another life, the hunger that made him willing to become an operator despite his fear of losing control of his Rilg and being absorbed by it like so many of his fellow operators had been.

Cannibals, Lozan thought again. *At least we respect our own kind. That's where we're different from them.*

The energies swept him away again.

—*Can we do anything to stop them?*

—*No. If we try, they'll know that a Lha is still free.*

Memories swirled through them.

—*Could they have detected us when we absorbed that Rilg?*

—*I don't think so, but I don't know how much they've learned, what they can do. . . . That Rilg was strange. As though its will itself had crystallized. But it was still conscious in a way, just not . . . free.*

—*Can we preserve it alive inside us, give it a new body later?*

—*No. It's already being assimilated. The suspension they had it in left it in very delicate condition.*

—*What about the others? Can we free them, use them to free the Lha?*

—*I don't know if there's any way to remove them from suspension without killing them. It's not like shaefi suspension.*

Memories swirled, flared.

Connected.

Lozan remembered Lavelle sitting at a control console in the starship hovering over the Temple, wearing a jeweled headband that enabled him to maintain mental contact with the operators in their jeweled helmets as he directed the attack. Remembered that Lavelle was going to be appointed the Planetary Governor as his reward for having defeated the Lha.

He shared his memory with Janesha, asked; —*Can you touch his mind without giving us away?*

He felt her probing, making tentative contact with one of the surviving operators, then following the man's thoughts back through his telepathic linkage with Lavelle.

Felt the texture of Lavell's thoughts, his fanaticism, his absolute conviction that what he was doing was right.

—*It would have made no difference to him if we'd been doing everything possible to aid the humans we ruled*, Janesha told Lozan. *Any alien which thinks itself equal to a human must be forced to submit, any alien which thinks itself superior must be destroyed. And yet he places very little value on individual human lives, even his own.*

Lavelle was beginning to realize he'd lost contact with the operator they'd absorbed. It took him a surprisingly long time to verify the fact, even longer to decide to send another operator to investigate.

—*Can you influence him without being detected?*

—*As long as I don't try to go against his basic conditioning.*

—*Can you alter (Dorjii's face, his sudden look of vulnerability as he tells Lozan about the way Lavelle had promised to adopt him as his son if they both survived the conflict) and make Lavelle believe that I was the one he'd promised to adopt . . . and that he'd really meant what he'd said?*

Janesha studied Lavelle's memories a moment longer, then: —*Yes, I've aroused his curiosity. He's maintaining close contact with the operator he's sent to investigate, looking out through his eyes. . . .*

Lozan's perceptive sense detected the new sphere as it winked into existence in the air alongside the sphere containing the dead Rilg and human operator.

—*He's recognized you . . . and he remembers his promise to you. He's sending a team to get us out of here.*

In Lavelle's mind as he looked through the operator's eyes at Lozan naked in his tube full of orange gas, the confused idea that somehow, through his treatment of Lozan, he was going to make up for all the other deaths he'd caused.

"There it is," Lavelle said with satisfaction, pointing through the flyer's transparent side at the Governor's Palace glowing with a thousand soft, shimmering colors below them. He ordered the blue-skinned pilot to circle it slowly so Lozan could examine it from all sides. Light rippled and flowed over its domes and spires, its curving walls, sculptured columns, towers and turrets and minarets. Surrounded by landscaped gardens, groves of trees, pools, fountains, streams and lawns of modified Terran grasses, it soared to a height of over three kilometers, yet for all its massive size it seemed almost too fragile to endure, as though it would come crashing down with the first breath of wind.

"It's beautiful," Lozan said, making himself look properly impressed.

—Janesha?

—It's all there. The memories of having thought about you for years, the decision to adopt you as his son if he ever saw you again. And they have a policy of training natives to take over the administration on newly rediscovered worlds. He's going to have you tested to see if you have the abilities required for his eventual successor. All this in the belief that everything he's going to do for you is to the Terran Hegemony's ultimate benefit.

—Are you satisfied?

—I left no evidence of my tampering that any of them will be able to detect.

Lavelle was explaining how the Palace had been built in a single day. Work had begun on it even as the first Lha was being captured, so confident had he been of his eventual victory. Of course, the Temple's ruins still dwarfed his Palace almost to insignificance, but—.

"For the moment that's all for the best, anyway. The Temple was alien—do you remember how I once

200

told you and Dorjii that no human beings would ever build anything that many kilometers tall? The Palace's comparatively modest size will make it clear to the people of this planet that they're free of Nal-K'am and that this is Jambu-lin, the World of Mortals. And when we destroy the Temple—in a single day, the same way we built this Palace—they'll realize just how much more powerful we are than the aliens who ruled them were."

The flyer settled softly to the landing stage atop the Palace's tallest tower. Lavelle got out, followed by Lozan, then paused and looked back at the grounds, hesitating. Lozan read what he had in mind, nudged him mentally into continuing.

"Do you see that spot, just outside the main gate?" Lavelle asked.

Lozan nodded.

"I'm going to put a statue of Dorjii there. A monument. Not just because he was a hero, the first man to die in our attack on the vampires, but because he'll stand for all the other orphans the vampires killed. You know we only found about fifty of you still alive, out of the thousands they had in those tubes."

Because you gave the rest to your captive Rilg to keep their operators happy.

"You said . . . the vampires killed him while he was trying to get a message out to you?"

"Not exactly." Lavelle was watching him closely now. "Or rather, that will be the official story, but what really happened was that getting the message to us killed him. We implanted something in him that one of our captive vampires grew for us. Like this headband I'm wearing, only organic. But it was a vampire, too, in a way, and it killed him when he used it."

—*They don't know we killed him first,* Janesha commented. *Even with their mechanical linkages with the Rilg they aren't sensitive enough telepathically to tell the difference.*

"You wanted to put one in my head, too," Lozan said.

"Yes. I would have implanted one in myself if I'd thought it would do any good. No individual is too important to sacrifice for the good of humanity.

"You know how much I care for you, Lozan. And I cared as much for Dorjii as I do for you. I didn't want to ask either of you to enter the Temple, but I knew it was necessary and I did it. So he has a statue and you have lost your best friend and I—I have lost someone who might have become a son to me as you have become a son to me. . . ."

"Why are you telling me this?" Lozan demanded, letting just the proper amount of his real bitterness and anger show in his voice and expression.

"Because you would have learned about it sooner or later. I didn't want to start off lying to you, then have you hate me later when you learned the truth. Can you still live with me, live with the knowledge that I caused your best friend's death?"

Dorjii died because of you. I helped kill him, Janesha helped kill him, but he died because of you. And for that I'll never forgive any of you.

Aloud he said, "You did what you thought you had to do. I can't hate you for that, but—."

"But you can't accept it either."

"No. I don't ever want to have to make decisions like that."

"You may have to, someday. For the good of humanity. And you won't like them any more than I did. But we'll talk some more about that sort of thing tomorrow, after you've been tested and we've got a better idea of just what sort of position and responsibilities you're suited for."

Lozan followed him into the Palace. Though it had been built in a day, that had been the outer shell alone, the parts that could be seen from the exterior; furnishing and equipping it was another matter. Lavelle took him through mazes of unfinished corridors past the empty rooms that would eventually become dining rooms, salons, game rooms, galleries, conservatories and offices, past the blue-skinned alien workers, their minds so thoroughly programmed that they were little more than organic machines, until at last they came to the wing in which the Terran psychotechnicians were waiting for them.

It was like the Testing he'd undergone on Naming Day back at Agad, only the Terran methods were far subtler and more sophisticated, a hundred times more thorough, than those the priests had used.

And with the information Janesha had gleaned from Lavelle's mind and the minds of the technicians who tested them it was easy, unbelievably easy for them to give the machines the data that proved Lozan had all the qualities which Lavelle's eventual replacement would need.

Chapter Seventeen

LOZAN'S BODY LAY FLOATING IN THE AIR above the conditioner's padded bedbase, but he had left it only enough awareness to record and respond to the conditioner's whispered orders and questions. His attention was kilometers away, following a ragged procession leaving Temple City and beginning to wind its way across the hills toward the Palace: men and women left starving by the breakdown of the Temple's food-distribution system who'd heard that everyone who came of his own free will to the Palace to pledge his loyalty to the Terrans would be fed and given work.

And conditioned; but that's something most of them'll never guess, ever after they've been through it themselves.

The conditioner's singing whispers died away; the waves of pleasure emanating from Lozan's brain's overstimulated pleasure center faded. Lozan returned to his body as it began its gentle descent to the bedbase. The last of his basic conditioning sessions was over.

Lavelle was standing, watching him. Lozan opened his eyes and sat up, pretending to be surprised at the sight of the Governor there in front of him.

Lavelle had shed his appearance of age. His face was unlined, his body strong and youthful, his movements without their former old man's hesitancy. He wore a tight-fitting uniform with Jambu-lin, as it appeared from orbit, worked on the chest in scintillating jewels, and over the uniform a bright emerald cape: a style of dress chosen, he'd told Lozan, to provide the greatest possible contrast with the priests in their anonymous black.

"How do you feel?" Lavelle asked. Lozan could perceive the networks of surgical scars, the sagging tissues and aging organs beneath the smooth skin and youthful exterior. Like the stench of rotting meat imperfectly masked with cloyingly sweet perfume.

Lozan scanned his thoughts, saw nothing to indicate he needed to call Janesha's attention back from the technicians and scientists charged with the Rilg and Lha whose minds she was studying, trying to find a way to release the Rilg and Lha from the human's modified suspension without killing them.

"Sort of warm and . . . content," Lozan told him slowly, as if searching for words. "Safe. But that's all. I don't feel any different."

"You never will," Lavelle assured him. "All our conditioning does is help you dominate your instincts and bring out the higher self you would have otherwise had to struggle years to develop."

Lozan could feel Lavelle's sincerity, the utter trust in his conditioning that had been conditioned into him with the rest.

—*He's been so thoroughly conditioned there's no way to change his attitudes without first breaking his mind*, Janesha had told Lozan. *That's why Terra trusts him with such complete control of this planet: he himself is completely controlled. And that's also why we'll be able to dominate him so easily—he's been conditioned to accept his certainties without questioning their meaning or origin, even when they seem to contradict the reality around him.*

—*Like the priests*, Lozan had replied.

—*Except that we were still in control, able to modify our priests' conditioning whenever necessary. But Terran conditioning is always determined by men who have themselves already been totally conditioned, and so are incapable of changing the imperatives with which they program others, in any way whatsoever.*

It's as if their conditioning itself were a sort of parasite, reproducing itself through the medium of its human hosts, its survival ultimately more important than their own.

—If we could get control of that system, modify their conditioning—.

—Then it would be just as it was here again. Only we wouldn't need to imitate human rulership, human cruelty.

It had been a measure of the way that Lozan's attitudes had been changing that, fully conscious of the way he would have once rejected Janesha's ideas, he'd found nothing to object to in them. Human beings were obviously worse to one another than the Lha had ever been to them.

"And that's my last session? It's all finished?" Lozan asked.

"The last of your primary conditioning sessions, to make you a full Hegemonic citizen, yes. You haven't started the special conditioning you'll need as a gubernatorial trainee."

"It's still hard to believe you trust your tests enough to make somebody like me Governor on the basis of them."

"We don't, but we trust them enough to accept you as a gubernatorial candidate. How old do you think I am?"

"Sixty? You don't look that old, not now; but if I really spent almost thirty years in the Temple—."

"I'm closer to three hundred and sixty—and I have another two hundred years to go. I'm a longspanner, Lozan. Everybody else you've ever met has been a mayfly, a shortspanner—they live fifty, sixty, maybe a hundred years, and then they die. But there are ways to extend men's lifespans, though population pressure forces us to limit them to those people truly important to humanity. People like me . . . and like you, now.

"So you've got another two hundred years to count on before I die and you take over as Governor. More than enough time for us to discover anything about you which would make you unfit for the task, and to prepare you for it in every way possible. Until then, your presence as my adopted son and intended successor will help show this world that they're truly a part of the Terran Hegemony, and not just subject to it. That their rulers are men like themselves now.

"Though there's another thing about your tests. They answered the one real question I still had about you when they revealed just how much parapsychic ability you had. That's why you refused to spy on the priests for me, isn't it? Because you could see through me?"

He's testing me again. To see if the conditioner had the proper effect on me.

"I've always had hunches, been good at guessing, that sort of thing. And I could tell you didn't really want me to do what you were asking me to do, not really. It wasn't so much that the priests scared me, but there was something horrible about them. As though they'd given up their humanity. I didn't want to become like that."

Lavelle nodded, satisfied. "That's what I thought. You didn't lack courage—you just saw through me. A useful ability in a future Governor."

If Dorjii hadn't believed you he'd still be alive.

"If I'm really supposed to start training to be the next Governor—."

"You are."

"—what am I supposed to do?"

"You'll start with education and indoctrination—six hours a day of encephalotapes, plus another two hours with the conditioner."

"So all I have to do is study?"

"I didn't say that . . . and it's not like studying, anyway. As soon as you're ready you'll be accompanying our reconstruction teams out into the more isolated areas as the Hegemony's spokesman. But for the moment most of your duties will be taken care of for you. Here, I'll show you what I mean—."

Lavelle walked over to a control console beside the

conditioner, activated the holo-display. The far end of the room became a window opening onto what looked like the interior of a courtroom in which a black-robed priest was confessing his sins.

The scene shifted and Lozan found himself staring at Lavelle and himself. The two of them were addressing a gray-robed group of village elders.

"That never happened," Lozan objected.

"Of course not. It's a computer simulation, like that priest's confession. You'll be ready to go out with the reconstruction teams when you can do the same thing in person."

The Lozan in the holo-display was describing the horrors of his captivity in the Temple, how the vampires had forced him to watch their cannibal feasts while he awaited the time when he, too, would be consumed.

As he spoke the backdrop changed, showing scenes the Terrans had recorded during their attack on the Temple: Chordeyean being defeated, the discovery of the hall with the thousands of ranks of shaefi tubes in it, Lozan being taken from his tube, the priests who'd tried to defend their masters being taken prisoner—.

Lavelle switched the display off. "You'll memorize that speech tomorrow. There's no point in listening to it now."

"Do the vampires really eat human flesh? I thought that was just a story."

"It is just a story, but it has a basis in fact. What do you think you were doing in that tube? They were going to do something to you a lot worse than just use you for meat. They feed on men's souls.

"There's a planet about twelve hundred light-years from here. That's where we found the vampires, hibernating in tubes like the one we rescued you from. One of them took over a human body—we're still not sure how, though we're getting close to an answer—and escaped—."

"Yag Chan. The Pied Piper of Mig Mar. You told me about him."

"So I did. Remember, I've had twenty-seven more years than you've had in which to forget things. Anyway, the vampire that took over Yag Chan's body never went back to Nosferatu to try to rescue the others. I guess vampires don't have much loyalty to one another.

"After that we were more careful. We used robots at first, then conditioned aliens, and finally condemned criminals—."

Lozan was following the conversation with only a fraction of his attention as he scanned the Palace around him. A group of brightly clad minor officials was being swept past the suite they were in by the corridor's moving floorway; three blue-skinned workmen were finishing installing the wood paneling in a small nearby dining room; a technician was checking out the hidden monitors that reported everything going on in the Palace back to the security computer. Nothing to worry about for the moment.

". . . and at first all the MigMartian adepts who tried contacting the vampires' minds were killed by them. But then we developed a way of modifying their way of putting themselves in hibernation which enabled us to take control of their powers for ourselves. After that the MigMartians were able to make contact with their minds. Or, not their minds exactly, not even their memories—we're just starting to do that now— but some center of the will which enables us to control their actions.

"For a long time only the MigMartian adepts could do it, but when the MigMartians finally began to understand their minds a little better, we learned how to make the telepathic amplifiers which allow Terrans without adept training to control vampires."

"Could I learn to do that?" Lozan asked.

"Of course." Lavelle looked pleased. "We took almost three hundred vampires alive, and Terra's allowed us to keep most of them. There are millions of them on Nosferatu, of course, and thousands more on Mig Mar, but there aren't any others anywhere else except here. So if there's as much to be learned from them as we think there is, Jambu-lin may well end up the third most influential world in the Hegemony."

"Good." He scanned Lavelle's surface thoughts idly, suddenly noticed something he'd overlooked.

—Janesha!

"You won't need a helmet to control them, either," Lavelle continued, remembering. "You've got enough paraphysical ability to become an adept yourself. I just learned that the MigMartians are sending a team of their highest-ranking adepts to train you. They should be here in eight weeks.

—We can't face the MigMartians like this, Janesha told him. *We won't be able to conceal my presence in your body.*

Through a window in the wall behind Lavelle, Lozan could see the ragged procession from the city hesitate before Dorjii's statue, then continue on past onto the Palace grounds.

Chapter Eighteen

IT WAS A SMALL FARMING VILLAGE ABOUT three hundred kilometers from Temple City and surrounded by half-flooded fields. Thirty or so long, low, cramped buildings of yellow gray stone, each containing three or more families, all grouped around the central square where the threefold image of the Goddess Night had once stood.

The villagers stood around the fallen statue or sat on the low stone benches surrounding it; one adolescent couple, greatly daring, was sitting on a fragment of the Mother's broken forearm. All of them were slack-jawed and giggling from the euphorics the reconstruction team had put in the food they'd been handing out since they'd arrived in their flyers at dawn to declare the day a holiday. Technicians were setting up and testing equipment, ostensibly for the demonstration that had been promised for later that day of just how the priests had faked the miracles of Eclipse Day. Dressed like Lozan in shimmering emerald-green uniforms—though only Lozan's had Jambu-lin's globe worked on its chest in sapphires—the team members circulated among them, talking, answering and asking questions, getting to know the villagers and putting them at ease. Preparing them for the mass conditioning session that would accompany the Eclipse Day illusions.

The other team members deferred to Lozan, asked his advice, pretended to take orders from him. His

211

coloring, the shape of his ears, his accent, everything proclaimed him to the villagers as one of them: living proof of the fact that the Terrans considered the people of Jambu-lin as human as they were and their equals, even to the point of taking orders from a former orphan like Lozan.

One of the technicians signaled Lozan. Everything was ready for his speech.

He climbed up onto the fallen statue's back, gestured for silence.

"People of Jambu-lin, Mortal men and women," he began. "The priests of Night taught you that you were dead and damned and living in Hell. All your lives you have suffered and slaved, but they told you that this was only justice, because your sufferings were punishment for the sins of your past lives. They told you that only the Goddess Night's mercy kept you from the infinitely greater torments you deserved.

"People of Jambu-lin, Mortal men and women, they lied to you. They have always lied to you. You are not dead, you are not damned, you have been punished all your lives for sins you never committed. Their merciful Goddess is only another lie, and this is not Nal-K'am, not Hell, but only a world like any other.

"Though I am one of you—an orphan raised at Agad and destined for the Temple—I come to you now as the representative of the Terran Hegemony, of mortal men and women united for the good of all humanity, to help free you of these lies and the false tyranny they upheld. To end your suffering."

The technicians adjusted their equipment as he spoke, measuring the villagers' responses to Lozan's images and concepts, the way he used his voice. One of them gestured unobtrusively, signaling Lozan to shunt his speech off onto one of the alternate lines of development he'd been prepared with.

"But though the priests of Night were the ones who taught you the lies, they themselves were only puppets—puppets not of the Goddess they pretended to

212

serve, but of alien monsters worse than any of the S'in-je with whom they threatened you. . . ."

The technician nodded. Lozan let the speech roll on automatically while his attention returned to the Palace, three hundred kilometers distant, where Joseph Lavelle was speaking to his wife. The distance posed Lozan no problems; ever since he'd absorbed the Rilg with its memories and the life-force it had stolen from the orphans it had killed, he'd found his powers increasing and developing with astonishing rapidity.

"Yes, but I'm worried about Michelle. She didn't want to come here, you know." That was the Governor's wife, Margaret Lavelle, talking to her husband while a machine applied the thick blue and green velvet of her sprayon. She'd been on Jambu-lin two weeks now. Her two youngest daughters were due to arrive on the ship from Terra the next morning, and the mixture of anticipation and tension with which she awaited them was clearer to Lozan than it was to her husband.

"Why should she? She's never known me; I'm just a name, a few tapes and a lot of outdated holo-displays to her."

"That'll change when she gets here. You're her father," she said while she hid the thermostat to her sprayon beneath another layer of velvet.

"Still, why didn't you want to let her stay on Terra? She could always have joined us later. It's not that I don't want her here—I do, you know that—but she's only a year short of legal age and you could have arranged some sort of guardianship. If she didn't want to come—."

"I could have arranged a guardianship, but I wanted to get her away from her friends. She's taken up Metallique now, and I don't like it."

"Metallique?" Joseph Lavelle frowned.

"A mayfly life mode. One we've encouraged to help keep their population in check. They wear metallic sprayon and try to appear expressionless—you'll see when Michelle gets here, I'm sure." She paused and regarded herself in the trumirror, rotating the image so that she could see herself from all sides. The sprayon clung to her cosmetisurgically perfect body in swirls of shimmering blue and green.

"It's not just the fact she's adopting a mayfly life mode, though that would be embarrassing enough. The problem is, the Metalliques are devoted to electroencephalostimulation."

"I thought that was illegal."

"They changed the law. Population pressure."

"Still, her longspanner conditioning will keep her from participating, won't it? So there really can't be anything to worry about."

"I'm scared they've found a way around their conditioning."

"They? Who are they?"

"Her friends. I told you. She spends all her time with other failed Terran adept-trainees from the MigMartian academy. They're all longspanners who've adopted Metallique. I'm sure they've discovered a way around their conditioning."

"That's supposed to be impossible," he reminded her. "Though there were rumors that some of the MigMartian adepts. . . . Anyway, she'll find very little opportunity for electroencephalostimulation—there must be a better way to say that."

"It's called cephalization."

"Thank you—for cephalization here. No equipment."

"That's what I was hoping."

"But tell me some more about this group of friends of hers. You say they're all Terran?"

"I think so."

"I've heard the Hegemony suspects the MigMartians of discouraging non-Tibetans from completing their training at the Academy. If they try to prevent Lozan from becoming an adept—."

"Joseph, we were discussing Michelle."

"I'm sorry; I thought we'd finished. After all,

there's no danger of her getting involved in cephalization here.''

"Nonetheless, I'm sure she'll be neither ready nor
willing to take her place as part of the family here.''

"There's no hurry, is there? When I was her age, I
was caught up in the revival of sadism—.'' He broke
off, seeing his wife's expression. "I'm sorry. I know
you don't want to be reminded. What do you want me
to do about Michelle?''

"I was hoping you could help me arouse her interest
in Lozan. He's about her age, he's smart even if he
isn't at all educated yet, and he's got an interesting
face. Besides, you said that he's about to start adept
training.''

"I doubt if she'll be interested in him.''

"Why? He's not neutered, is he? Or homosexual?''

"No, but if Michelle's so bored with what life on
Terra has to offer that she's resorting to cephalization—and I'm not that sure she is—what's she going to
find in Lozan to distract her? I've told you how
puritanical this planet is; I don't think the boy's ever
had any real sexual experience at all. . . .''

—(!)

Lozan faltered an instant in the delivery of his
speech, regained control and asked:—*What?*

*—That's how we're going to grow me a new body!
Inside that girl, disguised as a baby. (Lozan and the
girl moving together in the rhythms of sex—she is
faceless, a mere female receptivity. He climaxes, ejac-
ulating not true semen but the fluid medium for a
bioconstruct, which attaches itself to the wall of her
uterus and begins to grow. The faceless girl goes
through a seemingly normal pregnancy and Janesha is
reborn as her baby. The baby grows into a slender
woman with green eyes and red black hair.)*

Lozan felt an instant's hesitation, even fear, as he
remembered the idealized fantasies and Dakkini-wood
hallucinations that had been his only personal sexual
experiences; then the irrational fear was gone, banished by the wealth of sexual memories he had gained

from the human operator's mind when he absorbed it along with the Rilg the man controlled. As those memories integrated themselves into his conscious experience, he realized a defect in Janesha's plan.

—*They take steps to prevent conception. A baby would be suspect.*

—*Their contraceptive methods must fail sometimes, by accident or design. We'll make sure they don't examine what happens too closely.*

—*What about the adepts? Can we continue to tamper with the minds of the people here without being suspected?*

—*That's the least of our worries. Besides, it's already too late; we have no choice. We don't have the time to think of something else; the fetus must be ready for me before the adepts arrive.*

You'll have to impregnate her by the day after tomorrow. Give me control.

Lozan finished his speech, stepped down. The Eclipse Day illusions held everybody's attention.

He concentrated on Margaret Lavelle, beginning the modification of her attitudes that would prepare her for a pregnant daughter. Deep within him, he could feel the changes Janesha was beginning to make in his body.

They waited for Michelle and Umber on a hillside of modified Terran grasses. On Terra, as Margaret Lavelle explained to Lozan, where even a longspanner could ordinarily spend only four days a year in any of the continental parks, a natural setting was the height of elegance. Rich men—and in this context rich meant they owned planets outright—entertained in tiny domed parks, the upkeep and taxes on which were greater than any other expenses they were likely to incur. So Lozan and his foster parents sat on the grass, served from a hovering pavilion by blue-skinned servants.

One side of the Governor's tight synthavelvet trousers was white, the other black. His shoes were green, like the grass. Lozan was similarly dressed, in trousers of lemon and violet, his body a shiny black filigreed with silver lines that made him look a little like a metallic skeleton. Margaret Lavelle was dressed in a blue and green sprayon similar to the one he'd seen her applying the day before.

A hovercar appeared in the distance, a shimmer of brightness against the black backdrop of the Temple. Lozan could sense the excitement of one of its passengers, the studied indifference of the other.

He plunged into their minds. Umber, the elder daughter, was the excited one. The openness excited her. She had always felt cramped in the close confines of Terra, in the sealed cities that shut out the sun as well as the poisonous air.

She had been a failure as an artist there. Forced to work in miniature when she wanted to create monumental forms, she had been frustrated, unfulfilled. Here she would have the room she needed. She pictured huge works of art, drifting cloud sculptures and evolutionary storms of the kind long banned on Terra that would dwarf the hills below them. There would always be the tremendous bulk of the Temple to overshadow her creations by the mere fact of its massive presence, but—no. They were going to destroy it. A pity: the sheer physical effect of such hugeness excited her.

In Michelle's mind, Lozan found a studied boredom, an elaborate indifference to the world around her which masked her fear and anger, her longing to return to Terra. She should not have been forced to come here—here where the unnatural openness, the distant horizon, the incomprehensible immensity of the Temple all terrified her. She could not bear to leave the close, comforting ways, the solid comforting walls, the thronging people.

But she was here on this world to meet the father who had not even bothered to be present at her conception and the brother adopted without her consent into this family she did not want. Umber, beside

217

her on the seat, was a vapid nothing, and Michelle ignored her the same way she would have ignored her mother, had Margaret Lavelle been present.

"Here they come," the Governor said to his wife, who had been looking in the opposite direction, away from the Temple, at a flight of red-winged garudas, and had missed the hovercar's silent approach. There had been no birds on Terra for thousands of years and she knew the garudas would fascinate Umber.

Umber had seen the garudas and was staring out the window at them. Michelle sat slumped in her seat, feeling empty, incomplete and lost. She needed Jason, Carla, Shino, Robert, Mischa—all of them. Her friends. But more than she missed her friendship, she missed—no, she needed—the ecstasy they'd shared together. If she'd been on Terra, she would've been sitting with them right now, their hands joined, concentrating with them until together they achieved with their minds alone what their longspanner conditioning prevented them from achieving any other way. But here, alone in this hovercar with Umber, she felt the emptiness, the terrifying void lurking behind and beyond ordinary reality, and which had driven her from adept training. She pressed a wombcube to her arm, felt the calm excitement cascade through her.

The hovercar settled to the crest of a hill. Its canopy folded back and the two passengers stepped out onto the thick mat of grass. The sun burned white overhead.

Umber ran to embrace her parents. She was tall and slender, with long hair and almond-shaped eyes, another triumph of cosmetisurgery. Her sprayon was white velvet, its simplicity hidden in the cloud of shapes and colors projected by a device she wore at her waist.

Michelle stood just outside the hovercar, making no move toward the others. She was small and muscular, with wide shoulders, a narrow waist and firm youthful breasts. She wore a sprayon of shiny metallic black, which covered her hands and feet as well as her face.

Her eyebrows had been removed and her face sprayed a shiny copper. It was a beautiful, inhuman mask, totally expressionless. Her hair was a metallic silver, each hair tipped with an iridescent bead.

The Governor introduced Lozan and Umber while his wife talked to Michelle in a low voice. Leaving them to make conversation with each other, he walked over to join Michelle and his wife. He started to bend over to kiss his daughter, thought better of it, and straightened.

"You must be my daughter Michelle. I know we've never actually seen each other before—."

Michelle gave him a tight, wary nod.

"—and I'm sorry. All I can say is that I've been waiting a long time for this meeting and I hope I can make our long separation up to you. Welcome home, daughter."

Michelle said, "Hello, father," in an utterly disinterested voice, her face still an expressionless mask. The Governor smiled down at her, but Lozan could read the distress behind his smile.

Eventually he led Michelle over to where Lozan, Umber, and Margaret Lavelle were discussing the statues of the tutelary demons surrounding the Temple. When they greeted each other Lozan mimicked her impassive countenance and bored voice while subtly manipulating her reactions to him.

The Governor saw their apparent lack of interest in each other and allowed his distress to show for an instant. Margaret would be displeased.

Michelle saw a MigMartian boy who seemed somehow very young, though actually he could not have been much younger than she was. His face was impassive, which she liked, but she could sense something behind that impassivity, an energy and aliveness that impressed her despite herself, though she was careful to let none of her reaction show.

After a few minutes' desultory group conversation, in which neither Lozan nor Michelle volunteered a comment that was not an answer to a direct question,

219

the party started out on a tour of the grounds. They were on foot, the better to appreciate the landscape, though floaters followed them, ready to pick them up if they tired. Despite Lozan and Michelle's manifest indifference to each other, Lavelle managed to split the party into two groups, walking ahead with Umber and his wife while Lozan and Michelle followed at a short distance.

Though the three in front were engaged in an animated conversation, laughing often, Michelle maintained her bored pose. The wombcube's effects had worn off and she was once again fighting her fear of open spaces. For some reason, she was unwilling to dial another wombcube from her belt dispenser, so she had little relief from her distress until Lozan's mention of the fact that he was due to begin adept training in a few weeks distracted her. He sensed the spark of interest that flared up in her, fed it and watched it grow as she realized that here, just possibly, was someone who could take the place of the friends she'd left behind.

"I've had some adept training," she admitted, volunteering information about herself for the first time.

"On Mig Mar?"

"Yes."

"What's Mig Mar like?"

"Cold, and empty. Not many people, just . . . everything is too far away from everything else and there's nothing in between. I hated it."

"I had a friend who wanted to go to Mig Mar and become an adept. The vampires killed him."

Michelle was silent a while, then said, "If they're sending a team of high-ranking adepts to train you they must think you have a fantastically high potential. Especially if they're Bon-po adepts. The Bon-po are more interested in siddha, in powers."

"I think it's because I'm a gubernatorial trainee."

"No. Mig Mar's too proud. There must be something very special about you or they'd have just told you to come to Mig Mar. Did they rate your potential?

They must have, if they accepted you for training."

"I'm a K'an-po. No one explained what that means."

"It means a lot of things, but in your case it just means you've got a very high parapsychic potential. Still, they wouldn't send a team all the way here just to train a K'an-po. There must be something else, some other reason they're coming."

Though she kept her elation hidden, she felt hopeful for the first time since she'd left Terra. With proper training a K'an-po could take the place of her whole group.

"The vampires?" Lozan suggested.

"Of course. They've come to study the vampires. You're only—well, partly their excuse." It was perfect. With the adepts busy with other things she should be able to win him away from them when he reached the crisis in his training.

But without the circle, there was no way she could introduce him to the ecstasy, let him share in it before teaching him how to induce it. She needed some kind of hold over him, something to make him willing to break with the adepts when she wanted him to.

She realized she'd fallen silent. He was looking at her. She rarely spoke more than a few words at a time anymore; it was becoming a strain to keep up her part of the conversation. She dialed herself a loquator, a drug whose effects she generally despised, then offered one to Lozan, showing him how to press the cube to his neck.

Lozan was telling her about the first time he had ever seen an unveiled woman when the answer came to her: sex. Of course. This was a backward planet, and Lozan could have had none of the supervised sexual training every Terran child went through between the ages of eleven and fifteen.

He might even be a virgin.

He was, she decided a few minutes later. She remembered all the training she had had to enable her to distinguish sex partners from lovers, to avoid the

221

patterns of dominance and submission that had been so fashionable a few generations earlier and had caused such problems before they'd been outlawed. She understood the use of sex as a means of power abstractly, though until now her understanding had been no more relevant to her real life than her understanding of viral medicine; yet the knowledge was there now that she had a need for it, and she knew she could use it to bind Lozan to her.

She dialed them both light aphrodisiacs.

As the loquator and aphrodisiac reinforced each other, her conversation grew steadily more animated, more intimate. Expression began to appear on her copper face and she began to touch Lozan in casual emphasis of her words. Lozan responded as she'd hoped he would and she felt their chemically induced intimacy growing.

By the time they excused themselves and took a floater back to the Palace, the Governor and his wife were beaming.

Chapter Nineteen

MICHELLE STILL SLEPT, EXHAUSTED BY their night's lovemaking, but Lozan only feigned sleep, as he had every night since Michelle had come to share his bed. Almost automatically, he monitored her sleeping mind and soothed her troubled dreams. Slowly, night by night, he was stripping from her that extra awareness the MigMartian academy had so disastrously awakened in her, that half-talent which only showed her the deceptiveness of surface reality without giving her the means to penetrate to the substance beneath the illusion. She no longer awoke to stare helplessly up at the glowing ceiling, or to reach out for Lozan and hold him to her as if to reassure herself of their mutual reality. And as she lost her gift—lost it gently, imperceptibly, without realization of her loss—the world took on new richness for her, and she found her fear of the abysses lurking beneath her every thought receding. And for Michelle sex was no longer a means to an end, a way of dominating Lozan; it had become lovemaking, one of the certainties upon which she based her new life.

A comfortable lie, to keep her happy.

Janesha interrupted his thoughts: *—The fetus is ready.*

—Today then, at the execution?

—Yes. Neither of them knew for sure whether Janesha would be able to leave his brain without help; she might have to be driven forth, as Lozan had once

been. He reexperienced his own expulsion and exile, dipping into Janesha's memories whenever he found his own information insufficient.

The room pulsed with light, every surface flashing forth in a compelling rhythm that penetrated Michelle's eyelids and brought her painlessly awake. A cool breeze, containing a number of mild stimulants, blew through the room as the wall opposite their bed faded to transparency and revealed the landscaped grounds of the Palace to them.

There was a tiny flash of crimson in a nearby grove of nearoaks. The hawk? There was nothing else Lozan was familiar with that was quite that shade of red—. He reached out, effortlessly encompassed the crimson hawk's mind. It had been searching for him ever since it had escaped the ruins of the Refuge.

For a moment, he considered keeping it at the Palace. He could say it was a bird Dorjii had trained.

—*Twenty-seven years ago?* Janesha asked. *It's too unique; it might arouse somebody's curiosity. We can't keep it around.*

—*You could use its body if the fetus doesn't prove right.*

—*If we need it I can find it again. I can do much more as a human being than as a hawk.*

—*I'll send it away,* Lozan agreed reluctantly. He impressed the command on the hawk's mind.

The conversation had taken a fraction of a second; Lozan and Michelle were still drifting gently down to the cushioned bedbase.

Weight returned to them. They lay still the prescribed moments, letting their bodies readjust, neither moving nor speaking. Michelle's copper face and silver hair shone in the bright morning light.

"Some music?" Lozan asked, kissing her.

"No. Not today."

"You'll have to show your real face today, you know. There can't be any confusion; the priests were masked and we are not. The distinction has to be kept absolutely clear."

224

"You're starting to sound like father," she said. "I'll wear a white spraymask; no one will be able to tell the difference."

"Then why not expose your face?"

"If you'd grown up on Terra, you'd understand," she said. She closed the door of her dressing room behind her.

In his own dressing room, Lozan stepped through the sonic shower and put on the clothing that had been laid out by his valet for him—a one-piece emerald uniform, a white cape with a blue and green representation of Terra on it, long white gloves, and white sandals which revealed the brown of his feet.

He dressed himself, preferring to avoid contact with his dead-minded blue valet whenever possible. Though the cape had been designed with Jambu-lin's climate in mind, it still felt heavy and awkward. As he surveyed himself in the trumirror he saw that his hair was growing back satisfactorily.

Waiting for Michelle in their dining room, he reviewed the recordings of his previous night's activities that the various surveillance devices had made. As usual, there was no need to edit them.

Michelle had designed the dining room herself. Everything in it was silver—walls, carpets, chairs, chandeliers, candlesticks, even the table off which they ate—and the red gleam of her copper spraymask was usually visible wherever she looked.

She entered, accompanied by a train of three of the blue-skinned servants and wearing a cream spraymask. Lozan had to admit that from a distance it would pass for her natural skin. She had on a dark-green gown, which, though tight-fitting, had not been sprayed on, and in which she both looked and felt uncomfortable.

"You look good," he told her, changing her perception of the way the fabric felt against her skin to make it a little less irritating to her. "But not happy."

"Of course not." Two of the servants seated her while the third stood watching, waiting for any further commands. The three remained behind her chair while others served breakfast. As always, Lozan found the food unfamiliar—no two meals he'd eaten in the Palace had ever been the same—but today the tastes and textures, the very appearance of the food revolted him.

"My spraymask will pass," Michelle said.

"Now that I've seen it, I'm sure it will," Lozan agreed. "The computers can modify it for the holos."

"I hate it."

"You really don't want to go, do you? It's not just having to appear in public looking a way you don't want to look."

"Of course I don't want to go. The whole thing's disgusting. Barbaric. But you, you're looking forward to it, aren't you?"

—*Prepare her,* Janesha advised. *You may not be able to conceal your reactions completely.*

"I've always hated the priests. I don't think you'll ever understand what it's like to hate people the way I've always hated them," he said, finding that far more of his ingrained hatred for the priests had survived in him than he would have suspected. He was looking forward to the coming execution with a savage expectation he dared not admit to Michelle, and which shamed him in his own eyes: The priests had only been the instruments of the Lha's will.

Our will. I'm still too human, too irrational.

Yet there were always the surveillance devices recording his every word, every gesture, for computer analysis. "You forget that I've been forced to watch hangings all my life, only before it was the priests who were hanging people like me. I've seen them tear men apart on the blasphemer's rack. At one time," he admitted, "I would have liked nothing better than to put the noose around a priest's neck with my own hands, maybe tighten it just enough so he had a foretaste of what was coming"—he had her shocked attention now—"then kick him free, let him hang and watch him gasping and turning blue on the rope. But

226

now"—the lie came easily—"I wouldn't even go if I didn't have to."

"You shouldn't talk like that, about your feelings. About that kind of feelings. You should keep them to yourself."

"I'm talking about the past, Michelle, about the ways things were before. Not about what things are like now."

"You still shouldn't talk about feeling like that."

"Everybody you'll see there is going to be feeling the same way. Maybe a lot worse. I thought you'd be better off prepared."

After they finished eating they joined the Governor and the others below. Michelle left with Margaret and Umber in one hovercar. Lozan and the Governor took another.

"Remember," Lavelle told him as the hovercar approached the square where the hangings were to occur, "place the knot just under the left ear when you tighten the noose. That way, when your man falls through the trap the knot will be jerked around so it's just under his chin when he reaches the end of his rope. His head'll be thrown back violently enough to break his neck and he'll die almost instantaneously. I wish we could use a more humane method of execution, but the technicians tell me the people wouldn't understand it if we did. Anyway, it won't be like the hangings you're used to, where the priests used to let the victims dangle ten or twenty minutes before they suffocated."

You'd do the same, if your technicians told you it would help get the right effect, Lozan thought.

A platform of synthetic pearl had been erected in one corner of the square. It was morning and the square was still in the Temple's shadow, but intense white light from a sphere hovering overhead flooded the scene. As the packed crowd reluctantly parted for the hovercar, Lozan was buffeted by the hatred and rage the Governor's psychotechnicians had aroused in the crowd's members.

Lozan and the Governor stepped out onto the platform. The crowd below was held back by low-intensity neural stimulators. Lozan looked down into the dark waiting faces, feeling the frustration and tension building toward its carefully choreographed release.

In the center of the platform, about five meters above Lozan's head, stood the scaffold. There was a single noose hanging from the crossbar, a looped rope of the same pearly white as the beam from which it hung.

Clustered around the base of the scaffold stood the other executioners, an uneasy knot of humanity picked as the representatives of Jambu-lin's victimized populace. An orphan in his brown tunic, a civil administrator with the name of a distant village emblazoned on his breast, an old man in a ragged gray robe—.

The old man was Sren.

Startled, Lozan stared at him an instant before taking his place at the head of the line of executioners. Sren was about two-thirds of the way back.

Sren was bent, gaunt, his deeply lined face furtive and fear-ridden. His left ear was cropped. A long number tattooed in faded purple marked him as a beggar.

Lavelle had begun to talk to the crowd. From a newly constructed balcony on one of the buildings overlooking the square his family watched, invisible among the minor officials in their gaudy uniforms.

Sren could not follow the speech, though he tried. His mind was full of senile confusion, choked with half-thoughts through most of which ran the scarlet thread of his hatred of the priests. Agad was a dim memory; he no longer remembered the crime for which he had been condemned to spend the rest of his life as a beggar; he only knew that his life had once been good and that the priests had taken his happiness from him. Obviously not trusting in his ability to remember instructions, the technicians had conditioned him for his part in the execution, and as the vivid pictures passed again and again through his mind he licked old dry lips.

Lozan could no longer hate him. He could only pity him.

The Governor finished his speech. Guards in somber blue pushed the people back, clearing a path through the crowd for a line of bewildered priests, their arms bound to their sides beneath their cloaks. The priests made their slow way forward; in their dusty cloaks and rigid Nightmasks they resembled sorry black birds, as isolated from one another as from the crowd that watched them with avid, hating eyes and struggled to get at them through the protective cordon of guards.

Lozan felt his hatred dissipating. Like Sren, the priests were objects of pity.

Lozan ascended the scaffold by the left staircase and waited as the priests were led up the steps leading to the lower platform. The guards selected the first priest to be hanged. The other priests huddled together as they watched the first victim hesitantly climbing the final set of stairs, their masks turned to Lozan as he adjusted the pearly rope around the priest's neck.

The Governor's amplified voice said, "He dies as he lived, not as a man but as a priest of Night."

The priest said nothing, stood without moving. Lozan pulled the lever to release the trap—.

As the priest fell, Janesha absorbed his mind. Some of her ecstasy leaked through to Lozan and he smiled as the priest's dead body caught fire and burned, leaving only gray ash to fall from the gleaming noose.

Still smiling, Lozan descended his proper staircase. The village administrator was waiting at the bottom, and when Lozan stepped out onto the platform the administrator began to climb the staircase. A second priest was chosen. The executions continued.

As each body dropped, Janesha absorbed the priest's mind, so that what jerked and spasmed at the end of the rope was in every case a man already dead. Then—.

—I'm ready.

—Do you need help?

—No. And she was gone from his mind. Now it was Lozan who absorbed the minds of the dying priests and felt the full flood of a Lha's ecstasy. He was still linked with Janesha, he still shared her thoughts and feelings as she lay curled in Michelle's womb, but he sensed a sudden change in their relationship, some difference beyond that caused by their physical separation.

He would think about it later. Steeling his features to impassivity, he gloried in the sun-blaze of absorption.

Sren's turn as an executioner came and the old man haltingly mounted the stairs. His hands were clumsy as he placed the noose around his priest's neck; then it was all he could do to step back and pull the lever releasing the trap. The priest fell, jerked twice, and was still. Sren frowned. It had all been over so quickly.

Descending, the onetime orphanmaster found himself forced to take the stairs at the speed prescribed by the conditioning he'd undergone. The memory of the dead priests, disappointing though the actual sight had been, was unnaturally vivid to him, still charged with the force of the conditioning that was making him take the steps too rapidly. He missed a step and fell, frail bones snapping as he tumbled down the stairs to the foot of the platform, driving a splintered rib through one wasted lung. He was dying. Lozan absorbed his mind and he was dead. The guards took his body away.

Maybe they'll erect a statue to him as they did to Dorjii.

During sex with Michelle that night, Lozan was still gripped by the day's ecstasy. Though he could still sense Janesha's thoughts and feelings, she seemed far away from him in some way he could not quite define. It was as though he were alone with Michelle for the first time. On previous nights he'd been the detached puppeteer, using his perfect control over his body's

230

physiology and his ability to stimulate the pleasure centers of the girl's brain to give her the experiences he desired, but he had never gained more than a trivial pleasure for himself. His reactions had been feigned, his feelings more often than not dictated by the sexual mudras Janesha had had him practice during the act. He had made himself the embodiment of Michelle's fantasies—fantasies which, in many cases, he had planted in her mind to facilitate a particular mudra— but he had never abandoned himself to the sensuality of sex.

Floating above the bed, Michelle's legs locked tightly around him, Lozan surrendered for the first time to his own sexuality. This time he was a participant, not a puppeteer; this time the touch and taste and feel of her was as exciting to him as he had always made sure he was to her. Their lovemaking was violent in a way it had never been before, and when they finally floated together, spent, he felt a new kind of release, a quiet surrender that melted into his Lha ecstasies and left him fluid, warm, floating.

Later, feigning sleep beside her, he felt his consciousness expanding into those portions of his brain which had been occupied before by Janesha. Before the Refuge, alone in his brain, he had not known how to use more than a minute fraction of its true cognitive capacity, but now, with his Rilg and Lha knowledge to draw upon, he could utilize its totality. His perceptions became more acute, his intelligence more discriminating. New relationships were suddenly apparent in everything to which he turned his attention. He was thinking as never before, and he realized he was in danger.

Janesha. As a prisoner in his brain she could not have retained all the intelligence that had been hers when she'd had her whole brain's cognitive capacity. And now, trapped in the undeveloped brain of a fetus, she would have even less free intelligence at her disposal.

As when I was in the fish. From now on, Lozan

231

would have to be the one to plan and direct, Janesha the one to follow.

All their plans had been made while neither of them possessed a fraction of the intellectual capacity which was now Lozan's—while neither had been intelligent enough to integrate all the data flooding in from the thousands of minds surrounding them.

He began frantically reviewing their past actions, looking for unsuspected possibilities, overlooked errors.

And found the fatal flaw in all their planning.

The Lha know who we are. And the Terrans knew how to tap Rilg memories; it was only a question of time before their captured Lha betrayed Lozan and Janesha's identity to the Terrans.

They'd hunt him down as they'd hunted Yag Chan down, spend three thousand years chasing him if they had to. And when they caught him—if he was lucky they'd kill him. Otherwise he'd end up in one of those octagonal green crystals. An organic machine, but still conscious, still aware of what it had been reduced to.

How much longer did he have? The adepts were due in another week. Even if he found a way to keep them from learning his identity from the Lha they'd be studying, there were still those other Lha the Terrans had already taken back to Mig Mar for study. They'd be arriving there about the time the adept team reached Jambu-lin.

Once the MigMartians succeeded in tapping into the Lhas' memories, his discovery was a computational certainty.

He had a week . . . perhaps a few more days if they didn't think to ask the right questions at first.

Even if he managed somehow to cut communications between Jambu-lin and the rest of the Hegemony, he'd have eight weeks at the most before they could send a force like the one with which they'd defeated the Lha.

Can I free the others, hope they'll devise a better plan than I can?

He remembered the way the Rilg they'd absorbed had disintegrated. And Janesha had been unable to find a way to free the Lha and Rilg from the Terrans' modified suspension.

And even if they could find a way to free them, what then? They were still only a fraction of the number that Terra had already defeated, a far tinier fraction of the numbers Terra could bring against them. There were thousands of Rilg enslaved on Mig Mar, millions more in shaefi suspension in the vaults on Rildan—.

Free the Rilg and bring them here. There was a teleportation matrix attuned to Rildan in the Refuge. They could use it to make the jump there, free the Rilg, bring them back to Jambu-lin in overwelming force—.

—Unless the Votrassandra stop us. (The pain crawling from mind to mind, accelerating and decelerating, shifting and contracting as time altered and fragmented; meaning was lost in anticipation and resonance, and each mind found itself experiencing its existence at a shifting rate shared with no other mind. . . .)

—Their threats have gone unfulfilled for three million years, Lozan reminded her. *Yag Chan, Chordeyean and Dawa Tsong were able to come and go from Rildan without interference; the enslaved Rilg were taken to other planets by their human masters. The barrier may not even exist anymore. The Votrassandra themselves may even have died out, or lost all interest in the Rilg.*

—(Assent.)

Lozan's senses reached out, encompassed the teleportation matrix's sixty-four linked slavebrains. They were still alive, still functional, but human scientists had discovered them and were studying them.

Lozan activated the matrix. It was still attuned to Rildan. But how much longer did he have before the humans did something to destroy the link, either from this end or the Rildan end?

Days. Another computational certainty.

He reached out to the scientists studying the matrix,

impressed the need for caution on their minds. Convinced them that they'd been proceeding too hastily and carelessly, that they might well destroy the object of their study unless they adopted a slower, more cautious approach.

Perhaps another day gained. But there was too much he didn't know, too many possibilities he couldn't calculate. Only one course of action offered any hope, and he didn't have enough information to know just how real that hope was.

Janesha had followed his reasoning, agreed with his conclusions. It was up to him. He felt cold, detached, driven. Without choices.

He left without awakening Michelle and took a hovercar to the Temple. His route took him past one of the food-distribution centers where the Terrans were trading nourishment for conditioned allegiance.

The guards at the Temple recognized him and conducted him through the Temple and the Refuge below it to the arena, where the captured Lha were being kept. As they made their way deeper and deeper, through the ruined halls where the technicians and scientists were studying the surabhas and other artifacts the Lha had left behind, past the guard spheres with their dead-alive Rilg and human operators, Lozan could feel the time pressing on him, the inevitable march of events toward his discovery.

The Rilg were arranged in long rows. Three guard spheres hovered overhead; the space between the octagonal green crystals was full of scurrying technicians, gleaming machines, operators in their jeweled helmets. Lozan dipped into their minds, was relieved to find that none of them had yet discovered anything that could be dangerous to him.

Yag ta Mishraunal was not among them; he must have been taken back to Mig Mar for study. As soon as the Terrans made contact with his mind they'd know Lozan for what he was.

Lozan finally selected an elder Lha with whom he was familiar from Janesha's memories. He convinced

234

the soldiers in charge of the captives that he had the Governor's authority to have the Lha delivered to his rooms in the Palace, arranged to have it done.

On his way back Lozan reached out to his foster father's mind and planted a memory there of having authorized Lozan to take a vampire from the Temple for study. His tampering was clumsy, obvious, sure to be discovered by the first adept to examine the Governor's mind.

He made sure that Michelle would remain asleep, then accepted delivery of the octagonal green crystal containing the Lha he'd chosen.

Unlike most of the other Lha, Yaws had retained an almost human form. But his mind was a frozen thing, as crystalline as the murky green stuff in which he was encased. He was aware after a fashion, but he was unaffected by his awareness; his senses still functioned, but there was no one present to interpret the information they conveyed.

All the knowledge he'd amassed in his millennia-long lifetime remained, but there was no animating entity left to make sense of it.

He's dead, Lozan was finally forced to admit after having bent all his new cognitive capacity to the study of Yaws' condition for close to twelve hours. *An organic computer with psychic powers. A thing.*

All the other Lha were dead. Only Lozan and Janesha survived to create a new greater self, a new Goddess Night.

Another half day gone. That much less time until they were discovered and the hunt began.

Lozan commanded the dead-alive thing in the crystal to absorb him. Yaws tried to absorb him and was himself absorbed, his memories and life-force melting into Lozan, becoming part of him.

He fought against the ecstasy that tried to sweep him away, managed to contain it.

Michelle stirred in her sleep. He calmed her automatically.

—*Lozan, I can't function like this,* Janesha told him.

We don't have the time to wait for this fetus to develop. I need Michelle's brain, her body. I need them now.

Lozan felt a pang of regret, banished it.

Still too human, too irrational. Janesha was right.

He gave her his assent. Michelle would lose her identity in a blaze of ecstasy; her death would be more to her liking than her life had ever been.

We'll need all of them. All the humans of Jambu-lin, for the life-starved Rilg. Lozan had lived life as a human, had absorbed humans and experienced their memories as his own. There would be nothing to regret.

It would be safer if they left none of the dead-alive Lha or Rilg to be used against them. Fighting his ecstasies, he reached out to Janesha, gave her precise instructions, then took a hovercar to the Temple, where he made sure no technician or scientist would harm the teleportation matrix while he and Janesha were on Rildan.

Michelle arrived at the Temple, Janesha looking out of her eyes. Together they made their way down to the arena, Janesha's steps still slightly unsure as they followed their guide.

The arena was unchanged: the ranks of octagonal crystals, each with its dead-alive Lha, the three spheres floating overhead, the frantic, futile activity of the men and machines.

The operators first. They reached out, commanded the Rilg in the spheres floating overhead to try to absorb them, absorbed the operators' minds with the Rilg's, followed the operators' linkages back to the other operators and Rilg on Jambu-lin, absorbed them all.

Memories swirled and blazed, confusing them, far more vivid than the reality around them.

They began absorbing their dead-alive brethren. When the Terrans discovered Lozan gone with their Governor's daughter, and all their vampires and vampire operators dead, the resulting confusion would be more than sufficient to ensure they left the teleportation matrix alone long enough to give Lozan and Janesha the time they'd need to free the Rilg and return from Rildan with them.

It would take the Hegemony eight weeks to send a new force of Rilg from Mig Mar, somewhat longer to send one from Rildan. Lozan and Janesha would have to return with the Rilg before the Terran reinforcements could arrive.

Some of the operators and technicians on the floor of the arena were beginning to notice that they'd lost contact with the Lha they were studying. The uproar spread as they realized that the spheres floating overhead contained only dead men and Rilg.

In the panic no one paid any attention to Lozan and the Governor's daughter standing leaning against each other for support with their eyes closed as they absorbed the remaining Lha.

But there were too many crystal-encased Lha, too much life-force; there was no way the two of them alone could absorb it all. Yet they dared not leave any of the dead-alive Lha for the humans of Jambu-lin to use against them.

At last they let the dead-alive absorb the dead-alive, precious wisdom, memories, experience lost forever.

When there were only two dead-alive Lha left, Lozan and Janesha commanded them, absorbed them. The chaotic fragments of myriads of identities flared brighter than their thoughts.

There was no way they could contain all the lives they'd absorbed. To the humans around them they suddenly seemed to blaze with chaotic energies, hallucinatory fires through which half-glimpsed shapes of flaming nightmare stalked their prey.

Lozan and Janesha could barely distinguish between past and present, their acquired selves and their true personalities, their own thoughts and those of the dead-alive whom they'd absorbed when they activated the teleportion matrix and stepped through to Rildan.

Chapter Twenty

FALLING FOREVER, NEVER HITTING BOTtom.

No. A sense of something around them. Floating in darkness.

Cold.

A spherical space, around it metal. In the center, themselves.

So cold. They clung to each other, lost in the multiplicity of new selves coalescing within them, the blazing memories, the myriads of eyes that were not eyes through which they had to look to try to discover who they were, who they might be.

A velvet needle *piercing* the confusion, driving relentlessly to the core, the center, the essence. A voice so soft, yet so chill, so much itself that there was no mistaking it, no chaos when it spoke.

—*You have it within you to become Votrassandra. You need only open yourself to the change and we will take you for our own.*

Then it was gone and in their resurgent ecstasy all coherence was again lost.

Fragments of identity drifting, colliding, clinging to each other. A new center forming, desperately walling out the clamoring confusion. Lozan. Himself.

He tried to reach out to Janesha, could not tell if the chaos he encountered was in his mind or hers.

He retreated. It was easiest to think in simple terms, in human terms. He built walls in his mind, walls without doors or windows. He fitted the memories together, assembling a self. A self with gaps where parts of him had been, with memories and ideas that had never been his. He fitted them together and made himself a new Lozan.

Slowly, Lozan brought more of himself, more of his multiplicity of selves, into the protected enclosure within which he clung to his identity, assimilated the memories, grew. He tried again to pierce through to Janesha but could not make it through the confusion and chaos to her.

But he still had his body, where his mind would not serve. "Janesha?" he asked. "Janesha, can you hear me when I speak to you?"

She continued to cling to him without replying. *She'll recover her identity,* he thought. *Sort herself out from the others' memories. It'll just take her longer. Because of Michelle and the pseudofetus.*

But he couldn't wait for her to recover; he didn't know how long it had taken him to recover his identity, how much time he had left before the humans on Jambu-lin destroyed the teleportation matrix there.

It took him an interval to get his location and mission clear once again in his mind. It was a temptation to wait, assimilate more subsidiary selves, find out what advice and help they could offer.

No, I don't have the time.

The teleportation matrix was hidden below the deepest tier of the smallest vault. The vault contained eighty-one tiers, each of which housed about twenty thousand Rilg in shaefi suspension.

Using as much of his mind as he could and still maintain coherence, Lozan reached out for the bottom tier, trying to orient himself. It was a slow, fumbling process, but when he finally began to sense the configurations of the space around him he realized that what seemed to be to his right was actually above him. There, about forty meters away, he could sense a vast cavity containing row upon parallel row of what he knew must be shaefi-suspended Rilg.

He refined his concentration, shutting out everything but a single capsule chosen at random. The capsule was about four meters tall and a meter in diameter, rounded at the top and banded with rings of jewels. Inside, floating in a thick cloud of orange, was a pale, sinuous being with articulated fins and a ring of manipulatory tentacles around the base of its triangular neck.

Exultant, Lozan reached out for its mind, only to encounter void. The Rilg was dead.

Could he have been mistaken, confused? He reached out again. . . .

No. The Rilg was dead. He focused his attention on the inhabitant of another capsule. This Rilg, too, had been too long in suspension, was dead.

He tried a third Rilg. Dead. A fourth. Dead. A fifth. Dead.

In a moment of despair, he relaxed the rigid control he was holding on his mind, felt his coherence begin to go down before a tide of ecstasy and unassimilated identities. But he maintained his compartmentalization, managed to assimilate the identities and regain the coherence he needed to reach beyond himself.

Finally he found a Rilg in whom a trace of life still lingered, but it was so weak, so attenuated that it was almost nonexistent. He could not make the Rilg aware of him.

He found more living Rilg, but very few, and none in better condition than the first.

A memory he had gained one of the times his control had slipped told him there was a way to transfer some of the excess life-force with which he was charged to a Rilg. But the method required actual physical contact, or more subtle control of teleportation than he'd ever achieved, and he did not yet feel sufficiently in control of his faculties to even risk teleporting himself up to the vault.

But there might be very little time left. How long had he spent floating chaotic, how long each time he'd lost control? How long did he have before the Terrans rendered his return to Jambu-lin impossible by destroying the only means of escape from Rildan?

No, he thought, *I am Lha, not Rilg. I can escape, create a new matrix.*

If the Votrassandra didn't prevent him. But that chill velvet needle that had pierced to his essence with its message did not frighten him as his Rilg memories told him it should.

It could have been some sort of recording. It must have been; it wasn't the same, not as I remember it. And they did nothing to keep the humans from taking the Rilg they enslaved offplanet. Maybe they're dead, gone.

Something intruded on his awareness. A black machine was gliding up and down the corridors between the parallel lines of Rilg capsules. The thing's conical body was covered with lenses, diaphragms, orifices and electronic sensors of all kinds, and it moved in a welter of sonic and electromagnetic fields. At random-seeming intervals, it would perform chemical tests on the floor of the chamber with a jointed appendage it extruded from the base of the cone.

A human patrol robot, here to make sure no Rilg awakened spontaneously or was revived by an intruder. And if there was a patrol robot here, on the deepest level of the smallest vault, there would be one on every other level. Lozan didn't know enough to attempt to subvert the machine and it looked too alert to ignore. He would have to destroy it.

The memories he had gained from one of the human operators on Jambu-lin told him that machines of this sort were unarmed and that their primary function would be to report back to some central agency. And since the vault, like the Temple, was built of material impervious to electromagnetic radiation, that agency had to be somewhere inside the vault. Lozan would have recognized the Rilg-derived equipment necessary to control the machine by thought alone.

So there were humans inside the vault. They were still beyond the present range of Lozan's perceptive sense and he did not dare risk any sort of telepathic contact; in his present state he would be sure to give himself away to an adept.

With a minimum of attention concentrated on the robot, Lozan strove to increase the percentage of his potential mental capacity available to him. It was a slow process; anything that would have speeded it up would have resulted in at least a temporary loss of coherence and control, and he dared not take the risk; if there was an adept in the vault he could easily betray himself. But he was making slow progress.

There! An electronic bleep and one, moreover, which Lozan could easily counterfeit. If the next one was identical—.

It was. *Wait,* one of his human memories cautioned him. *Make sure the interval's constant. You've got to get that right, too.*

All eighty-one levels of the vault were becoming perceptible. The top nine were empty and there was a single man on the uppermost level overseeing the work of some hundreds of machines busy ten levels below him. Lozan was not yet sure he had regained the delicacy of touch he'd need to tap a human adept's thoughts in safety, so he studied the machines the man was controlling while slowly assimilating more of the fragmentary selves he'd absorbed.

Machines were attacking the Rilg capsules, piercing their walls and injecting a complex sequence of chemicals into them while bathing them in various sorts of electromagnetic radiations. Sometimes the jewels banding the capsule would flare for an instant with a weak, already dying fire; when that happened, the orange gas inside the capsule turned green and crystallized. More often, nothing happened, and the machines went on to try the next capsule.

A third bleep identical with the first two, with an identical interval between bleeps! Lozan could reproduce it easily. He visualized the wires he needed to sever in order to disconnect the machine's power source, then hesitated.

He still didn't know enough to risk putting it out of action, and his mind was almost clear enough for him to risk invading the mind of the man at the console. Better to wait, despite the overwhelming urgency hammering at him.

Finally he felt he could risk contact. He reached out, insinuated himself into the man's mind—.

Jomo Parsons sat at his console, nine levels above the nearest vampires, and even so he was afraid. They said the vampires could suck the life out of a man, just floating there in their tubes. A man spent only four hours a day in the vaults and only fifteen days a tour here on Nosferatu, but new though he was, Jomo had seen the difference in the eyes of the men returning from duty in the big vaults, seen the deadened luster of their eyes, heard their slightly slurred speech. He was glad he'd drawn duty in the smallest vault, where there were fewer vampires.

This was his first shift below, and he fingered the telltales in his clothing that would warn the men above if he died. His eyes traced the shielded cables leading from his console to the breach in the wall—his frail, useless connection to the outside. If a vampire got loose, he was a dead man; they all knew that, even if the official story was that there hadn't been an escape in over a thousand years.

He didn't believe them.

A light glowed on his monitor board and he slipped the telepath band sullenly over his forehead. There was no sensation, but he could imagine the adept at the surface—safely far away, where the vampires couldn't get at him—pawing through his mind with greasy mental fingers. The light winked out and he removed his headband.

What was he doing here alone? It was small consolation to know that a force of vampire operators was waiting on the surface. If a vampire got loose, he'd be dead before help arrived. Why didn't they keep themselves down here where they'd be able to help him if he needed help?

I'm bait, he realized. *That's all I am, vampire bait.*

Lozan was elated, grateful to Jomo Parsons for his insight. The man was bait, all right, but the Terran adept's attempts at monitoring his mind had been so unbelievably clumsy and easily evaded that Lozan need not worry about them. He searched Jomo Parsons's memories for more information.

There were very few humans on Rildan, and only a small number of them were MigMartian. Only the handful of men necessary to supervise the collection and removal of the vampires, and a small force of vampire operators and adepts ready to handle any escaping vampires or—to put a name to the Terrans' real fear—to fight off any non-Terran trying to collect a few vampires of his own.

At any one time, the greater part of the Terran occupying force was on Warg, as the Terrans had named the next planet sunward, where they lived sealed away from the poisonous atmosphere in domes and underground cities. There also they kept most of their crystal-encased vampires and the alien and human prisoners with which they were fed.

It was an open secret that there were seven phoenix bombs buried in Nosferatu's crust. The bombs were the least of Jomo's worries; he figured that if anything happened he'd probably be dead long before they turned the planet into a short-lived star.

If enough Rilg could be freed, the bombs could be located and disarmed easily enough, but Lozan was worried by the small size of the human garrison. He and Janesha had between them enough life-force for perhaps thirty Rilg, and the humans and crystal-imprisoned Rilg on Rildan would provide the life-force for perhaps twenty more; but fifty Rilg and two Lha could do little against the forces massed on Warg, especially since the Rilg were unable to leave the planet.

If, that is, the barrier still existed, as the presence of the Votrassandra's message (recorded message?) seemed to imply.

He'd hoped to bring hundreds of Rilg through to Jambu-lin, enough to overwhelm all resistance instantly, but he would have to hope that those few Rilg he could revive would be able to defeat the Terrans and maintain the matrix from their end.

How much longer until someone interferes with the matrix on Jambu-lin? He dared not test the linkage and give the Terran scientists studying it any further indication of its nature until the time came to bring the Rilg through.

Jomo was due to make a random spot check on one of the levels he guarded. Lozan guided his hand to the correct button and the vision screen lit up, revealing that all was as it should be on the deepest level. Lozan made sure Jomo would not check that level again this shift, then withdrew from his mind.

—*Lozan?*

—*Janesha.* She gained enough control of her secondary identities to complete her physical transformation and regain her former cognitive capacity. Though she'd made no effort to alter Michelle's appearance, she in no way resembled the Governor's daughter. She was vibrant, alive, her every aspect expressing the full force of her inner self.

Lozan gave her all he'd sensed and learned, deferring to her greater experience again, now that she had her full capabilities back.

—*I'll put the robot out of action while you revive the Rilg,* she told him. *Ready?*

Lozan reached back into Mishraunal's memories for the technique of teleporting himself without use of a matrix. He found himself confronting a host of incompletely assimilated memories of the act, each carrying with it a different personality trace and set of implicit attitudes. For an instant he almost lost himself in the confusion, almost found himself trying to teleport to a dozen impossible destinations simultaneously; but then he regained control and plucked the knowledge he needed from the chaos.

It made him realize how little of his true self he'd

regained. But he had enough control to do what was necessary.

—*Ready,* he told Janesha. While she reached out with her mind and severed the wires leading from the patrol robot's power source, Lozan teleported himself to a spot on the floor of the bottom level intermediate between the sphere in which he'd been floating and the Rilg. A second jump, and he was standing directly in front of the Rilg's shaefi tube, staring in at what looked like a long, slender, silver-scaled humanoid sea creature floating in the orange gas. A blind, eyeless merman.

He pressed his face to the clear tube to give himself the closest possible physical proximity, tentatively opened a channel between the unassimilated lives he carried and the dormant Rilg. At first nothing seemed to happen; there was only the life-force draining from him; then he felt the Rilg mind stir, begin actively reaching out for the life-force he was giving it.

Sluggishly at first, and then with amazing rapidity, the Rilg regained its mind and strength, and as it did, Lozan felt some of the confusion leaving him. Though he was in intimate telepathic rapport with the emerging mind, though he could feel its long-dormant intelligence and purpose reviving, yet there was no sense of the sharing, the warmth and the fusion he'd felt in his rapports with Yag ta Mishraunal and Janesha—not even the superficial closeness and sympathy he'd felt for Michelle. The Rilg was alien, alien to him in a way that the Rilg memories he'd gleaned from Mishraunal and the Rilg he'd absorbed had left him totally unprepared for. And as the Rilg regained full consciousness, Lozan recognized that its augmented mental capacity was beyond his comprehension.

The Rilg took from him all his knowledge, assimilated it and began to make use of it in the same instant.

—*Good. The plan succeeded. But you have concentrated too much on your manipulations and sensations, too little on the increased intelligence they make possible. Like all sexually motivated species, yours is essentially juvenile.*

My intelligence is far greater than yours; give me control of your mind so we can accomplish our purposes.

Lozan was too deeply committed to hesitate; he gave the Rilg control. Myriads of images flashed through his mind—an incredibly complex perceptual mosaic that was gone before he could even begin trying to interpret it. Suddenly he was elsewhere, facing a capsule in which floated a rubbery-looking toroidal creature and opening a new channel between his unassimilated selves and it. Then he was in front of another capsule, facing an amorphous, jellylike mass, repeating the process.

Each time he received a Rilg he felt less confused, less chaotic, more capable of functioning as himself. But his increased ability to function brought him no closer to the Rilg.

When a Rilg regained consciousness it merged instantly with those of its kind whom Lozan and Janesha had already revived, to create a composite being in whose formation Lozan did not, could not, participate. The Rilg composite mind was not a separate Self with an identity of its own, as Night had been; nor did the Rilg retain their individual identities while merged with one another, as the Lha had done. Each individual Rilg seemed a mere component, a mere appendage, of the greater mind, yet that mind seemed to have no individuality of its own. Lozan found himself unable to comprehend it.

—*We evolved mentally during our millions of years in suspension,* the composite mind told him. *Without bodies to distract us, without separate experiences and lives to keep us apart, we merged. Until at last lack of enough life-force to maintain our group mind reduced us to our individual selves again.*

All the Rilg it had been possible to revive with the excess life-force with which Lozan and Janesha were charged had been revived.

—Will you consent to relive your encounter with the Votrassandra? the Rilg composite asked Lozan.

—Yes. And the velvet needle pierced him again, drove through to his essence and proclaimed its unique identity.

The Rilg mind took the message, examined it from a thousand points of view, compared it with the Rilg's racial experience of the Votrassandra. This time Lozan managed to comprehend some fraction of the composite mind's thought processes.

—The message is exactly the same as the one we received, though for us it was (rotting, treacherous softness/mockery). Your racial perceptions are perhaps closer to the Votrassandra's than ours are; despite the fact that they, too, were once Rilg. But though the Lha and the Rilg are different, too different to ever truly fuse, yet we share a common way of life, a common interest in survival. We can complement each other.

—What about the Votrassandra? Lozan demanded.

—We have too little knowledge to answer you. We can only hope.

A new man was sitting down at the control console, relieving Jomo Parsons. The Rilg composite plunged into his mind, gleaned from him all his knowledge, correlated it with what it had learned from Jomo Parsons and Lozan.

Lozan followed the composite mind's thoughts, found himself confronting the new man's memory of a heavy-browed bald man with large, mobile ears like Lozan's own who could only be a MigMartian adept. The adept was sitting alone in a porcelain tower on the planet's surface. . . . Then the image was gone, lost as the strands of the composite mind's thoughts and perception seemed to shift, forming patterns that broke apart and recombined again before Lozan could make sense of them.

—The trap was more complex than you realized, and we have been discovered. Link with us!

Janesha and Lozan relinquished control of their

minds to the Rilg. Embedded in the composite mind—contained and linked like components in an electronic circuit as the Rilg drew on their perceptions and powers, using them yet never fully integrating them into its mosaic consciousness—their fragmented awarenesses reached out to accompany the thirty-seven Rilg as they teleported out of their shaefi tubes. Some flickered back into existence in the teleportation matrices in the other vaults, overpowering and absorbing the humans guarding the vaults before they'd had a chance to realize they were being attacked; the others, those teleporting themselves to destinations where there were no matrices to receive them, progressed by projective jumps, flickering in and out of existence thousands of times in the seconds it took them to reach their targets.

They appeared in the communications center in the starport the humans had established on the site of the original colony, absorbed the men and women responsible for maintaining contact with Warg and Terra before a warning could be given.

They flickered into existence in the MigMartian adepts' porcelain towers before the adepts had had the time to realize what was happening to the men in the vaults, absorbed the adepts and integrated their memories, then counterfeited the adepts' mental linkage with their offplanet counterparts before the momentary break in rapport had had a chance to be noticed.

They found the locations of the seven phoenix bombs Jomo Parsons had known about in the minds of the humans charged with detonating them, deduced the existence of two others whose existence had been kept hidden from everyone stationed on the planet, and which were set to explode automatically if anything happened to the other bombs, or if they received a triggering signal from offplanet. The Rilg teleported the bombs to the planet's surface, disarmed them and scattered their component parts too widely for anyone lacking equivalent powers to ever reassemble them.

All the humans and programmed aliens were absorbed, and with them the crystal-encased dead-alive Rilg, their lives going to revive more of the suspended Rilg.

The barrier was tested with a slavebrain created for the purpose. It was still in existence; the Rilg would have to use the link to Jambu-lin.

They gave Lozan and Janesha control of their minds back. The conquest of the planet had taken them less than three minutes.

—*You will precede us through the matrix; your human forms should serve to allay suspicion long enough for us to orient ourselves and secure the matrix from the other end.*

Lozan and Janesha found themselves floating in the dark sphere beneath the vault.

—*Mishraunal was (not like that/warmer/more like us)*, Lozan projected.

—*We never knew Mishraunal. Only Yag ta Mishraunal—only Mishraunal's memories as Yag Chan experienced them, modified and distorted by his human brain and psyche.*

—*Prepare yourselves.*

They felt the matrix's sixty-four linked slavebrains reach out for them, encompass them as they reached out for the linked slavebrains in the matrix on Jambulin—.

Then Rildan and the matrix were gone. But in their place, not the Refuge, not Jambu-lin, nor the Terrans.

In their place, nothing. Nowhere. A limitless void.

They were cut off from everything but each other. Had the matrix on Jambu-lin been destroyed, were they caught in some sort of limbo between the two matrices, outside of space and time without any way back to the material world?

—*Like the void I thought I escaped to when I was in the shaefi tubes*, Lozan realized.

But that had been subjective, not objective. A distorted perception of the real world around him.

Could he have fallen into some kind of Terran trap, be lying helpless and totally cut off from the world around him in the matrix on Jambu-lin while the Terrans decided what to do with him?

Panic-stricken, Lozan reached out with his perceptive sense, with all his senses, trying to pierce through to the reality underlying the void.

But there was nothing he could grasp with any of his senses, no taste, odor, color, no minds he could touch, nothing supporting him or pulling on him or pushing against him——.

Only Janesha. He tried to cling to her reality, to the identity he shared with her, but it fled him; they were bodiless, limitless, without needs or characteristics or qualities he could grasp; they were as empty as the void around him——.

But the void wasn't empty. It was full.

It was alive, as they were alive.

They felt a whisper—not of ecstasy, for ecstasy would have been thick and cloying in comparison, but of something so subtle that no amount of it would be too much, no amount of it would warp the judgment. The whisper that was the stillness at the heart of the living universe was breathing through them, but they were not being swept away from it; becoming one with it, they were becoming more fully the selves they had always been.

Returning to the stillness, the fullness, the life. The freedom. That which always had been and always would be.

A question became apparent: —*Do you desire to merge with us?*

The Votrassandra. But if this was the reality of their existence, this stillness and life, this freedom from all needs and limitations, from the necessity of preying on other beings and stealing their life-force to maintain one's own life——.

Lozan remembered the Rilg, cold and hating, remembered the horror and revulsion with which they'd greeted the merest intimation of this living fullness. He knew what his decision was, what Janesha's must be.

—*Through you we will bring redemption to the Rilg.*

A chill, sweet breeze was blowing in Lozan's mind and as it blew Janesha—not the Janesha with whom he had entered the teleportation matrix, but the partial entity he had absorbed from her in and after the Ritual despite her struggles to maintain her identity—wrenched herself free of him and rejoined the true Janesha.

Janesha?

—Yes. The two merged, melded, fused into a single identity as much Lozan as Janesha, as much Janesha as Lozan. Within that entity, every being whom either of them had ever absorbed began to take on shape and individuality. They were all there: Ugyen Dochen and his wife Tara, Lozan's parents, the hundreds of orphans Lozan had drained in the shaefi tubes, the priest and sister who had been Janesha's host-parents, the orphans she had drained of their life-force before encountering Lozan in the Ritual, the Rilg the two of them had absorbed with its human operator and the life-force it had taken from the other orphans, the executed priests, Sren, the crystal-prisoned Lha and Rilg, all reviving, all taking on new life. As each being separated itself from the entity they had become, Lozan/Janesha felt itself coming closer to an elemental state of purity.

Lozan/Janesha and the entities that Lozan and Janesha had once absorbed now existed in a state outside space and time. There was no need for communication or examination between them; each was apparent to all the others. Without ceasing to be themselves, with no loss of freedom or individuality, they fused, and created from their totality a new entity.

To the new entity they had become, another entity became apparent, a passive, balanced, static being existing in an atemporal instant that encompassed all time: the being that the Deviant Rilg had given birth to when the other Rilg had attempted to remake them in their own flawed image.

—Merge. Create me.

252

The two entities merged, became a being without need for life-force, one with the basic energy of creation, with the living stillness that always had been and always would be.

The past and the future were opening unto the new being and it knew what it was to do. There was no compulsion, no necessity; rather, it was as though those actions which it saw that it would take were the body which it animated, as though the future it foresaw was the substance of its being.

Lozan's body rematerialized in the darkness of the Rildan matrix. The Rilg sensed the change in him.

—*Janesha is with the Votrassandra,* he told them in answer to their demand for explanation.

—*And you?*

—*I have returned to you with the truth about their nature. What I know you can know, and knowing it you will never need fear them again.*

The Rilg sensed the truth in the new entity, knew it for Lozan, knew that the change they could sense in him had not made him their enemy.

—*Open yourselves to me and you can experience what I have learned and make it your own.*

The Rilg mind had no other hope. It opened itself to him.

—*I am a bridge,* the new entity told the Rilg as it invaded their composite mind. *Through union with me, you shall become Votrassandra.*

The new entity reached out, plucked the Rilg from the composite mind. Each individual Rilg found itself isolated, totally cut off from communion with its fellows, and yet no Rilg was alone, for the new entity was with each as it was wrenched from its place in space/time. In the chill, sweet fullness that was to the Rilg only sucking void, every being that each Rilg had absorbed regained its stolen individuality and was reborn to freedom, and with every birth each Rilg felt that which it had taken for its very self ripped from it.

In burning agony, the Rilg gave up their stolen selves and died, and in the moment of their dying, in the still purity of that instant between life and nonexistence, the Rilg were given a choice and chose to be reborn Votrassandra.

The new entity merged with the Rilg and the Rilg's reborn victims to become the Votrassandra. It abandoned Lozan's body, reached out to the Rilg still in shaefi suspension, and forced choice and union upon them. It reached out with the cleansing fires at its command to the crystal-prisoned Lha on Earth and Mig Mar and in space, brought them death and choice, liberation and completion. It reached out to the Rilg crystal-prisoned on Terra and Mig Mar and in the underground cities on Warg and brought them cleansing death, resurrection and union. It reached back in time to the Lha who had died on Jambu-lin in the Terran attack, back to the Rilg who had died in their shaefi tubes of life-force starvation; and to each, in the moment of its dying, the Votrassandra brought liberation and union.

The Votrassandra reached back to the time of the Rilg empire and brought cleansing death and resurrection to the offplanet Rilg. It placed the barrier around Rildan, planted its message in the minds of the surviving Rilg.

It reached back to the Rilg who had experimented with the Choskt sense of precognition and through him to the entire race as it then existed, and brought about the Change to which it owed its existence.

United, one being and many, the Votrassandra plucked Dorjii from the death of his body and showed him the future and the part he could play in its creation, then gave him Lozan's body for his own.

Dorjii stared down at his new body, up at the duplicate Lozan facing him. Behind Lozan, the ruins of the Temple, glistening black in the bright morning sunlight.

"Everything you showed me—," Dorjii said. "All of it. It's really going to happen like that?"

"Yes."

"Even the part about me? My future?"

"If you accept it and let it happen." The duplicate Lozan was watching him calmly, not trying to force his decision in any way. "The choice is yours."

Dorjii hesitated an instant longer, then nodded. "I accept." The duplicate Lozan smiled warmly at him and was gone, back to the stillness, the living fullness, back to await the end of time.

Dorjii turned his back on the ruined Temple and began to walk toward the Governor's Palace, the future burning within him.

He would tell Lavelle what he had witnessed at the end of time, when in the last moment of the universe that which humanity would have become would join the Votrassandra and the evolved descendants of a billion other races in the creation and animation of the universe to come. He would tell Lavelle, and at first Lavelle would not believe him. It would take years of imprisonment and interrogation and skepticism, years of fighting the Governor's conditioning and fears, but at last Lavelle would believe, would help him carry his message to all humanity so that in the end the human race could carry the truth Dorjii proclaimed to all the other sentient races of the universe.

He walked quickly but without haste, the course of his life-to-come as clear to him as the destiny of the universe. Somewhere to his left he could hear a bird and its mate calling to each other; in the thick grass of the Palace, lawn hoppers sang. He smiled.